KW-552-453

Ebook ISBN 978-1-80549-212-2

Kindle ISBN 978-1-80549-213-9

Audio CD ISBN 978-1-80549-204-7

MP3 CD ISBN 978-1-80549-205-4

Digital audio download ISBN 978-1-80549-206-1

Boldwood Books Ltd
23 Bowerdean Street
London SW6 3TN
www.boldwoodbooks.com

THE STRANGER

J A BAKER

C161069008

First published in 2019. This edition published in Great Britain in 2023 by Boldwood Books Ltd.

Copyright © J. A. Baker, 2023

Cover Design by Head Design Ltd.

Cover Illustration: Shutterstock

The moral right of J. A. Baker to be identified as the author of t
work has been asserted in accordance with the Copyright, Des
and Patents Act 1988.

All rights reserved. No part of this book may be reproduced in
form or by any electronic or mechanical means, including
information storage and retrieval systems, without written
permission from the author, except for the use of brief quotatio
in a book review.

This book is a work of fiction and, except in the case of historic
fact, any resemblance to actual persons, living or dead, is purel
coincidental.

Every effort has been made to obtain the necessary permissions
with reference to copyright material, both illustrative and quote
We apologise for any omissions in this respect and will be please
to make the appropriate acknowledgements in any future edition.

A CIP catalogue record for this book is available from the British Library.

Paperback ISBN 978-1-80549-209-2

Large Print ISBN 978-1-80549-211-5

Hardback ISBN 978-1-80549-210-8

KENT
ARTS & LIBRARIES

All concerns of men go wrong when they wish to cure evil with evil.

— SOPHOCLES

Never open the door to a lesser evil, for other and greater ones invariably slink in after it.

— BALTASAR GRACIÁN

To Theo, for your company on our writing days together, and our brisk walks even on the wintriest of days.

1

ME

I'm different. Very different. Not that you would know to look at me. To the people I meet, I am simply an average person. They have no idea. They don't know the real me, the other me. That's because the differences I possess are tucked away in the darkest depths of my soul. I keep them hidden, concealed deep inside the recesses of my mind. Only I know they're there. I sense them as they scratch away at me, forever reminding me that I will never be normal or neurotypical. Just like the scars some people have on their skin – marks and blemishes caused by birth defects or disorders, imperfections that set them apart from the rest of society – I too have scars, invisible flaws, indiscernible to the untrained eye. I don't think like you do. And I'm not sure I ever will.

I go over my thought processes again and again in my head. Perhaps I'm just a freak of nature, or maybe my brain is simply wired up wrong. Is it the old nature versus nurture debate we need to explore here to establish why I don't think, or act, like other people? Perhaps the two are so inextricably linked, it would be impossible to tease them apart, to work out which of them is the stronger driving force behind my primal urges and behaviour, to decide which of them is responsible for my dysfunctional conduct.

I do things, you see. Bad things. Unspeakable things. I'm a truly damaged being.

Am I a psychopath, I hear you ask? Perhaps. Would it matter if I was? Would being labelled stop me or put an end to my actions? Probably not. We are what we are. We all have our own little behavioural and emotional nuances, the subtle traits that set us apart from others. And I'm not all bad. In fact, I'm a first-rate actor. I can be whoever you want me to be: good, kind. Devious, murderous.

So, am I a narcissist if not a psychopath? Maybe I am. I guess it would take a qualified psychologist to make such a diagnosis, somebody who is willing to take the time to step inside my head and study its contents. I'm not the person that you should be asking such a question. I do have insight into my own conduct but it's extraordinarily difficult to judge one's own characteristics, isn't it? To take an existential look at ourselves and pass judgement without impartiality. I doubt many people have the ability to delve into their own minds to work out where they stand in the straitjacketed order of societal expectations. We're all too busy simply being us, going about our daily business and living our own sad little lives.

Growing up, I knew I wasn't the same as other people. I lacked emotion. I had to. It was the key to my survival. My parents were thought of as morally upstanding people, pillars of the community, and everyone expected me to be the same. A person to be trusted, somebody with identical ethics whose behaviour would be in keeping with their impossibly high standards. Somebody who would stand up straight, do exactly as they were told and never answer back.

How little they knew.

How little they still know. Because I'm a perfect liar. I've mastered the art of disguising my inner voice and replacing it with what is expected. I go about my daily life like any other law-abiding citizen. I have a nice house, make small talk with neighbours and associates, smile at small children and help elderly people cross the road. I am a model citizen. Nobody knows the thoughts that roam freely in my brain, the murderous dreams that see me through the day. I hide it all, tuck it safely away and be the person you all want me to be. I am your friend, your neighbour, your family. I walk amongst you, courteous, pleasant and friendly, and all the while I am thinking how beautiful it would be to hurt you or maim you in some way. It thrills me, sending a dart of electricity pulsing through my veins, the adrenaline elevating me to a higher plane.

And you know the biggest thrill of all, the thing that makes me superior to you? You have no idea about these thoughts. You think you know me. You're wrong. You don't know me at all. Not the real me, the true me. Nobody knows me. Absolutely nobody knows who I am...

2

There was a strange ambience to the place. I detected it as soon as I parked up and stepped out of the car. It wasn't an overt sensation, more of an underlying feeling: tiny ripples of unease that nipped at my subconscious. I ignored them. I was here now. No going back. I couldn't let sentimentality or unexplained hunches muddy my thinking. I had made my move and had to go with it. I was just tired, that's all it was. Exhaustion was allowing doubt and regret to creep in.

My skin tightened with tension as I dragged my bags out of the boot and slammed it shut. The drive from Birmingham had been pretty arduous with roadworks on the A1 causing tailbacks that went on for miles and miles. I had had to take many diversions that were unavoidable and it all helped to compound the stress that had been slowly building up in my gut. Only when the signs for Durham came into view did I feel myself begin to relax. What should have been a journey of three hours or so turned into one that took over six and I was feeling fatigued and fractious.

I rubbed at my face wearily and looked around. It was almost silent save for the whispering of the wind through the nearby trees. The eerie, metallic rustle of soft leaves shivering above me echoed in my head, sending a spike of unease down my spine. Telling myself everybody was at work and the village would spring to life after 5 p.m., I shook off the inexplicable feelings of dread that continued to niggle at me and headed over to my new home, pulling my overstuffed suitcase behind me and tucking some of my smaller luggage under my arm.

The privet will have to go, I thought to myself as I surveyed the small front garden then turned and pushed the key into the lock, leaning heavily against the door to open it. Ragged-looking and unkempt, the foliage and snarled branches gave the tiny patio and even smaller lawn a distinct air of neglect. I hadn't had time to view the property before moving in and had relied on photographs to give me an indication of how habitable it was. I just hoped the inside would pass muster.

Samantha's face flitted into my thoughts as I dropped my cases at the foot of the stairs and narrowed my eyes, slowly taking in every aspect of the hallway. It wasn't too bad. I'd seen worse. She would hate it, but then, it seemed that Samantha hated everything, especially things that exuded age and didn't smack of money. And this place definitely didn't smack of anything remotely resembling top dollar. It was very dated and smelt slightly of damp but it certainly didn't repulse me. It was, however, a far cry from our modern home that up until a few days ago, we had shared in Birmingham city centre. I'd left behind a plush loft apartment, the sort of property you see in magazines, the sort most people only ever dream about living in. I'd left it all: my partner, my home, my entire life. And now I was here, in a tiny village on the outskirts of Durham, living in an old cottage that needed modernising and smelt of old dishcloths. And I was fine with it. I really was. Because being here was far more appealing than being with her.

I wandered from room to room, sizing the place up, getting a feel for it, studying it and trying to work out what it could look like once I had unpacked, put my things in place and settled in properly.

But first I needed to eat. The services on the A1 had been crammed full of desolate, exhausted-looking people wandering aimlessly, bumping into each other with no apologies or regard for anybody but themselves, and the restaurants served an array of unappetising, greasy food that made my guts churn. I had bought a coffee and drank it as I drove and now my stomach howled at me for some sustenance and a drink, preferably something that contained alcohol. The coffee had helped me stay focused as I drove but I had to admit that a beer would hit the spot nicely.

Running my fingers through my hair and straightening my crumpled clothes, I headed back out of the house and closed the door behind me. With any luck, the village pub would be serving food. This was something I was going to have to get used to now I was living in the sticks: not having everything on my doorstep. City centres offered food and beverages at any hour. No request, no bizarre midnight craving, was too unusual or too difficult to obtain. However, I had grown up in a village and knew that life here would be very different to the one I'd become accustomed to over recent years. I would have to adapt, get used to it, understand how different everything would be from here on in. This was a seismic change to my life, the polar opposite to how I had been living for most of my adult life. I was determined to embrace it. I had no other option. I was here now. I had made my decision and would go with it. Ending the relationship with Samantha was never going to be easy but moving far away was a wise move. I could sense it, feel it in my bones. Living here would make my life complete.

I stepped outside and inhaled deeply, the tang of manure from the farmer's field close by taking my breath away. I stopped, looked around and smiled contemplatively. Welcome to the countryside. No more pollution from cars and buses, no more sirens piercing the air at all hours of the day and night. Just me and the birds and the pungent stink of cow shit.

* * *

To say the pub fell quiet as I walked in was an understatement. The silence was all-pervading as I strolled up to the bar and studied the beers on offer. I felt at least a dozen sets of eyes boring into my back as I glanced at the board behind the bar for a menu and scanned it for something that would fill my aching belly. I decided I would have a pint of weaker beer. I wanted to keep my wits about me. I had a feeling I was being closely scrutinised and felt a need to remain alert.

'A pint of John Smith's and a menu please.' My voice was brisk. I tried to inject some lightness into it but I was tired and the strained atmosphere was beginning to make me feel uncomfortable.

The young barmaid smiled and glanced beyond me to the array of faces seated at the table in the corner. Her eyes twinkled as she pulled the beer and then nodded at the board next to me. 'The specials are up there and the menus are on the table. I'd recommend the soup of the day. Potato and leek. Comes with warm crusty bread.'

I felt immediately drawn to her, grateful for her natural warmth. It was a far cry from the frosty atmosphere that had descended upon the place when I arrived.

'You've persuaded me,' I said to her. 'I'll have the soup. It sounds like a winner. Just what I need.'

I spun around and looked for a vacant table. The sea of staring eyes took on a look of embarrassment and shock as I glanced their way. They mumbled inaudibly and rapidly returned to their conversations, murmuring into their beers about the state of the economy and complaining about the warm weather.

They were right on that score. It was uncharacteristically hot – unlike the usual unpredictable British summers we were accustomed to – and as time passed with no sign of rain, it was apparent we were slowly but surely edging into drought conditions. A few areas had already implemented hosepipe bans and the newspaper headlines screamed that it had been the hottest and driest summer on record so far, even beating the long dry spell from 1976 into a cocked hat.

'Am I okay sitting outside in the courtyard?' I nodded towards the window and pointed to a small table in the shade that looked particularly inviting.

'Course you are. I'd be out there myself if I wasn't working in here till nine o'clock tonight.' The barmaid smiled at me again, revealing a row of perfectly straight and impossibly white teeth. 'I'll bring your food out as soon as it's ready.'

I thanked her, paid and ambled past the other customers who surreptitiously glanced at me as I shuffled past. In those fleeting seconds, I tried to take in their faces, to put to memory the eclectic mix of people who were sitting together, huddled in the corner in a small, tight throng, complaining about anything and everything while putting the world to rights.

A ruddy-faced individual wearing a checked shirt

moved his leg to let me through. Another guy in his mid-thirties was wearing tailored trousers and a white shirt. He pulled out his phone as I passed and punched at the screen, a grimace on his face. His tie was dragged to one side and he wore the look of a sharp-minded businessman, weary after a long day at the office. Though I tried my best to take in the dynamics of the group, they were simply a blur of faces as I slipped past them and out into the late-afternoon sunshine. I did notice one other person: a woman, incongruous amid the male-dominated gathering. She was sitting amongst them, trading stories about how torturous the heat was and how we needed another election. I listened to her voice as it trailed after me, her words eventually disappearing as I edged around the corner into the small beer garden, clutching my drink as if somebody was about to whip it away from me.

The table was clean and cool and I drained almost half the pint in one go. My belly was empty and my eyes dry and gritty with exhaustion. I would have to slow down or I could end up drunk before my food turned up. After such an arduous day, even the less powerful beers could blur my thinking.

I looked around the place. It was a small concrete courtyard and despite needing a sweep and a damn good clean, it was peaceful and exuded an air of calm. A trail of wisteria gave a flash of pale lilac to a crumbling old wall. The large, pendulous flowers hung from the red bricks, their fat, purple fingers drooping and sad-looking, like heads dipped in prayer. Seating was limited but the garden was cool and silent and gave me the peace and quiet I needed after leaving my life behind to start a new one here.

Yet again, Samantha stabbed at my thoughts. Her face filled my mind, her pleas, her fake tears that turned into threats when I told her exactly what I thought of her. I swallowed another swig of cold beer and pushed the image aside. I was here now. There was no turning back the clock. Not that I wanted to. That was my other life. I now had a new one. A better one.

My soup arrived smelling divine. I hadn't realised how ravenous I was until I started eating. It was hot and creamy and cooked to perfection. I was in the middle of shoving a bread bun in my mouth when a shadow suddenly appeared behind me, blocking out the light. I looked up and tried to swallow the doughy matter that clung to the insides of my mouth like putty.

A man in his thirties leaned down towards me, his voice gruff, his face looming close to mine as he spoke. 'Saw you pull up in your car earlier and unload your stuff. You're new to the village, I take it?'

I nodded, feeling a small swell of anger build in my stomach. I didn't care for his tone or the expression on his face. He had also disturbed my lunch. Something about him put me on edge and I wasn't in the mood to put up with any shit. I'd already left an abusive relationship behind and made myself a promise not to be subjected to any more. This village was now my home and all I wanted was to be left alone to eat in peace.

'Just watch yourself,' the figure said quietly, his tone softening slightly as he stared at me. 'This is a funny old neighbourhood. They don't take kindly to change. And they don't take kindly to anybody moving in and poking their nose into other people's business.' He nodded at me and smiled. 'Just so you know.' And with that he turned and left before I even had time to question him.

My mouth was glued together and my shoulders bunched into a tight knot as I fought to make sense of what had just taken place. I was unsure how to react, whether I should have perceived his words as some sort of threat or put it down to small-mindedness. The act of somebody who saw themselves as a spokesperson for his community and monitored every new face with the impenetrable fastidiousness of a rookie policeman keen to make a good impression with his superiors.

I continued eating my lunch, trying to remember his face. He was plain-featured: a dark-haired, middle-aged man wearing a navy-blue jacket and trousers. He had no outstanding attributes and I had no doubt that if I were to bump into him again in another location, I wouldn't recognise him. I couldn't even remember if he had been sitting with the group who fell silent and watched me closely as I stood at the bar. He was completely forgettable. And out of order. Who the hell did he think he was, disturbing my lunch with his thinly disguised threats and pathetic words of wisdom, designed solely to unnerve me? It would take more than some faceless, forgettable individual to scare me and spoil my day. I'd dealt with far worse than him in the past and was more than prepared to stand up to the likes of him again should I need to.

It didn't take me long to finish eating, by which time I had decided I would sit in the bar and have another pint. I wasn't about to shrink away from the gawping faces and prying eyes. If they were trying to intimidate me, they had chosen the wrong man. Whether they liked it or not, I was here to stay. This village was now my home as much as it was theirs. Making friends wasn't high on my agenda but neither was making a whole load of new enemies either. Thinking I would do my utmost to be courteous and genteel, I stood up, scooped up my empty glass and marched back inside.

3

The group had all but parted by the time I got back in there. A couple of stragglers were seated apart from each other, reading newspapers or staring out of the window, their drinks almost gone, their faces set into expressions of deep gloom. I was tempted to go over and introduce myself but thought better of it as one of the younger men caught my eye and gave me a steely glare. He then turned his gaze back to the barmaid who shuffled her way past me and into the courtyard, where she collected my empty dishes. I cursed myself for forgetting to bring them in. As well as being the new kid in town, I now also looked like a lazy, selfish bastard. Not a good start.

The silence was oppressive as I waited for her to

come back. I could almost taste the suspicion and anger bubbling up behind me. The air was thick with it. The burn of their eyes into my back heated up my entire body. I didn't take kindly to being scrutinised and made to feel like an exhibit at some sort of Victorian freak show. I wondered if this was how they treated all visitors and newcomers. They lacked manners and social graces if that was the case.

'Sorry,' I murmured as the young barmaid danced her way back through, her hands holding my soup bowl and plate tightly. 'I should have brought them back in with me.'

'No need to apologise,' she said brightly. 'It's nice to get out into the sunshine away from the dim light in here.'

Her words and wide grin seemed genuine and I found myself wondering how she could stand working in such a stifling and unappealing environment where banter from punters seemed to be thin on the ground and smiles non-existent. And she was absolutely right about the lack of natural light. The place was in dire need of a new lighting system. Either that or it needed more windows. I guessed the pub was a listed building and had been built in the early 1800s. The roof was low with overhead beams and the windows poky, covered with yellowing net curtains and surrounded by an array of paraphernalia. On the sill of one of the tiny windows sat a porcelain dog, so ugly it was breathtaking. It had its teeth bared in anger and was painted a dull black colour, serving only to enhance its look of pure menace.

'Horrible, isn't it?' the barmaid said, her voice catching me by surprise, her eyes following mine to the deeply unattractive ornament that appeared so angry-looking and lifelike, it gave the impression it could pounce at any given moment.

'The worst,' I replied and smiled, thinking how much she reminded me of my sister. She had a permanent smile and an air of wisdom about her beyond her years, this young-looking barmaid. Bumps of regret rose on my skin at the thought of Cassandra. I wished I could see her again. Just one last time so she could say, 'Good for you' as she squeezed my hand and smiled at me. Her eyes would twinkle and glisten as she watched me intently from under her dark lashes. She would be glad I'd moved here. She'd be delirious at my decision to leave Samantha far behind. She knew me and understood me better than I knew myself.

'Another pint?' the barmaid said, nodding at the empty glass in my hand that I suddenly realised I was clutching with so much force, my knuckles had turned paper white.

'Please,' I said, holding it out to her, watching as she refilled it to the brim with her expert touch. 'I'm Ray.' My voice was croaky. I rubbed at my eyes. The tiredness was getting to me. I let out a trembling sigh and straightened my posture. I had to get a grip. This wasn't the sort of environment where I could relax and let my guard down. Not with the many faces behind me, observing me and scrutinising me. One wrong word or move and I had the distinct feeling they would tear me to shreds.

'Pleased to meet you, Ray. I'm Lily. New to the village, are you?' She continued to busy herself behind the bar, sorting glasses into neat rows and straightening up the bottles despite the place being almost empty. 'Or just passing through?'

'New,' I replied. 'Just moved in today,' I added, although I suspected she'd already known the answer to that question before she even asked. Something in her manner told me she was the eyes and ears of the village. She had a quiet, knowing look that belied her youth. She was also privy to every bit of scandal and gossip – a confidante of the tongues that wagged in this place. It was that sort of pub and already my presence had been noted and was possibly being discussed as I stood and sipped at my pint.

'So, how about you then, Lily? Do you live locally or should I just shut up and stop acting like a nosy parker?' I asked quietly, hoping she picked up on the subtle humour in my words. It was like walking on eggshells in this place. I was doing my best to be affable and polite but the mass of serious faces behind me was making me nervous, making me question everything I said and did.

She rubbed at a glass with a soft, small cloth and spoke to me, her voice honeyed and carrying no trace of distrust or annoyance at my question. 'I'm home from university for the summer, which is why I'm working here. I live just down the road.'

She didn't make it clear what part of the village she lived in and I wasn't about to ask. Lily was a good fifteen years younger than me, perhaps even more. The last thing I wanted was to come across as a lecherous old man, so instead I nodded knowingly and waited silently, watching her surreptitiously as I drank my pint of beer, the bitter froth coating my top lip. I licked it away and drank some more. It was hot in here and I savoured the cool liquid as it hit my stomach with an icy punch.

I felt a sudden rush of air and turned to see a

burly-looking gentleman standing next to me at the bar. I smiled and nodded at him and was more than a little surprised when he returned the gesture. I watched as Lily served him and made small talk about the weather and other such banal trivialities. He then took his glass of red wine and sat at a table in the middle of the pub where he stared up at the TV screen.

'Nice to see a friendly face,' I said and raised my eyebrows haughtily.

'Ah, don't worry so much about the people around here,' Lily said with a meaningful smile. 'They're all just a bit uptight after everything that's gone on. They size everybody up before making friends with them. It's just how it is now, I'm afraid.' Lily dragged an old, chequered cloth across an already gleaming surface before stuffing it in a bucket under the counter and wiping her hands down the front of her starched cotton apron.

I held my hands up in mock surrender and widened my eyes dramatically. 'Okay, I've fallen into the trap. What went on to make them all so suspicious and shifty looking?' I knew I could be wading into unfamiliar and possibly dangerous territory here but she was the one who had paved the way for my question. I knew that I still had to be careful, add a degree of caution to whatever I said. For all I knew, these people could be her close friends and family. In a place as small as Whitchurch, the chances of that were pretty high, but I was intrigued by what she had to say. They hadn't been rude to me as such, but they hadn't gone out on a limb to be friendly either. I wanted to hear what she had to say about whatever it was that had made them all so distant and on edge, so stupidly suspicious of any new faces.

'Surprised you didn't see it on the local news,' she said and turned away. I wasn't sure whether or not I detected a note of wariness in her tone so decided to step in before she clammed up and moved away from me to the other end of the bar without telling me anything else.

'I'm not from Durham,' I said as casually as I could. 'I'm not even from the North East so I wouldn't have seen it. I've just moved here from Birmingham. It was a long drive and your soup made it worth my while, I can tell you. Hit the spot perfectly.'

She seemed to soften, if indeed she had become guarded at all. Perhaps my imagination was playing tricks on me but regardless, she gave me one of her toothy grins and reached up to drag a pint glass down from above her head before continuing, her voice tinged with an air of sadness. 'There was a body found here at the end of last year. A young woman in her late twenties. They never caught anybody and people are still a bit twitchy about it, really nervous and wary of anybody new. Shortly after the body was found, a few of the local girls said that they had been followed home from the youth club. They heard footsteps and saw somebody running off over the field when they turned to see who it was. And then just a few weeks ago, old Mrs Batton's cat was found dead. Somebody poisoned it. Poor woman was devastated. According to Sarah over there, who lives next door to her, its tongue was so swollen and distended, it probably choked to death before the poison did its thing.' She nodded over to the woman sitting with the group in the corner, who looked like they wished me gone.

I wasn't sure how to respond and sat for a short while shaking my head sadly and trying to work out how best to reply, but before I could say anything, Lily spoke again, her voice thin and scratchy in the thick pungent air between us. 'There's been other things too. Scary things that didn't used to go on here. This village was once a great place to live but now everybody's on edge, waiting for the next terrible thing to happen.'

'Awful,' I said in no more than a whisper. 'Just awful. What were the other things? If you don't mind me asking, that is?'

'I don't mind you asking but some of the locals might.' She pursed her lips and surreptitiously pointed behind me to the now dwindling group of drinkers who were watching us intently.

I smiled and nodded sagely, even though I didn't understand their thought processes one iota. It wouldn't do to upset people before I had had time to settle in properly, so I didn't say anything else.

Lily decided to fill in the blanks for me. 'Apparently, some of the parents reported an unknown vehicle hanging around outside the school gates. One of them tried to walk over to speak to the driver but they drove off.' She let out a deep sigh and I watched as her bottom lip trembled slightly. 'And then one of the kids in the village went missing.'

I found myself holding my breath as I waited for her to continue. I wasn't about to harangue her into telling me more. I had a feeling she would open up when she was ready.

All colour seemed to leach out of her skin as she ran her hand over her face wearily before readjusting her expression, the one she wore every single day for customers in The Pot and Glass. Not that they noticed or seemed to care. They were a strange lot for sure.

But then, who was I to judge? I didn't know their story, just as they didn't know mine.

'They found him wandering out of the woods a few hours later, dazed and frightened. To this day, he still has no idea what happened. No amount of questioning has worked. The police drew a complete blank.' Lily dipped her eyes and moved away from me.

I didn't speak immediately. What was there to say? My words wouldn't solve what had taken place and I ran the risk of saying something that could be misinterpreted, something that could be twisted and deemed offensive, so I chose silence instead. Lily seemed happy with this and started to hum as she went about rearranging beermats and menus that sat idly at the other end of the bar. I suddenly didn't feel like drinking any more and made the decision to leave once I'd finished my pint. I had plenty to keep me occupied back at the house anyway: suitcases to unpack, beds to make, cupboards to fill.

Draining the remainder of my beer, I slipped off the barstool and bid my goodbyes to Lily, who flashed me one of her warm, genuine smiles. 'I guess we'll see a lot more of you in here now you're living in the village?'

'I guess you will,' I said in return and for a brief

moment, considered sitting back down and ordering another pint. The sensible voice in my head told me to get up and go and for once, I took notice of it.

'Just remember to take things slowly around here and you'll be fine.' Her hips swayed slightly as she adjusted her apron and tugged at her sleeves, an act that for some incomprehensible reason irritated me. Perhaps it was what she had said that rankled me. Here I was, being sociable, trying to fit in with the local community, and here she was, telling me how to behave; a young woman barely out her teens, giving me lessons on etiquette and social graces.

'I'm not sure what you mean,' I said through slightly gritted teeth. Now wasn't the time to get angry or irritated. I took a deep breath and placed my hands on the bar. I was being ridiculous. I'd had a long drive here and whether I liked it or not, Samantha continued to drift into my thoughts. Lily seemed like a lovely girl and I should at least listen to what it was she had to say. She knew these people better than I did.

'It's just with all the goings on, everyone is still a bit tetchy. They worry when strangers come into the area. It makes them suspicious.' She raised her perfectly arched eyebrows at me before looking away and staring out at the crumbling courtyard and wilting wisteria.

'Suspicious? Why would they be suspicious of newcomers? Surely they don't think that each and every visitor or new villager had something to do with those events?' I tried to keep my voice low for fear of anybody overhearing me but was feeling marginally angry at her logic.

'It's not that,' she said, moving towards me, her eyes half closed as she rubbed at them with her small, clenched fists. 'It's just that we've had people here who come to gawp and get the inside gossip on events, especially the unsolved murder.'

Suddenly, I understood. I realised why I had been given such a cold welcome, why my every move had been watched and inspected. Why I had been warned by a perfect stranger while eating my lunch that I should be careful.

'You've had people coming in here pretending to be friendly and they turned out to be reporters?' I said quietly, everything abruptly slotting into place.

Lily nodded, her demeanour changing, sadness seeming to sweep over her as she watched me intently.

'Well, I can assure you I'm not a reporter. I have no desire to unearth any seedy pieces of gossip and get it into print. Whitchurch is my new home and I would sooner gouge my own eyeballs out than work as a journalist.'

'So, what do you do then?' she asked, her tone suddenly brighter. 'As your job, I mean?'

I smiled at her. I couldn't blame them for treating me with disdain, for glaring at me with undisguised contempt and wishing me gone. Not now I knew.

'I've just been given a position in a nearby village,' I said with a wry smile. 'I'm a teacher. Definitely not a reporter or some kind of spy here to question people and then spill the details on the goings on in the village. I'm just an ordinary guy, an everyday run-of-the-mill teacher, making the most of the summer holidays and dreading September.'

Before Lily had a chance to respond, I slid the empty glass across the bar and gave her a wave, thanking her for her hospitality, then made my way out of the pub and back to my new home.

4

I worked like a demon, cleaning and tidying the house, trying to eliminate the musty odour that permeated every available space and clung to the carpets and curtains, filling the place with a sense of loneliness. Samantha would have insisted we put flowers in every room to rid the house of the stale smell. She would have taken over the entire process, barking out orders and ignoring any of my input, insisting I was wrong and shrieking at me that I was lazy and useless. But then that was Samantha all over: thoughtless and insular. Completely unaware of the damage her words caused and utterly oblivious to anybody's needs but her own. Still, at least now I could please myself. I could do whatever I wanted, whenever I wanted, which included not having bunches of fucking geraniums and carnations and vintage roses in every room in the house. I closed my eyes, shut her out of my thoughts and ploughed on with my tasks until eventually darkness fell, causing shadows to lean in through the windows at peculiar angles, like elongated spectres desperate to enter and shroud every room with their sinister grey forms.

By the time darkness had completed its slow and sluggish descent, I had unpacked and felt surprisingly at ease in my new environment. I placed the portable radio on the kitchen table and switched it on to fill the silence that had begun to grate on me. The lilt of the music and easy crooning voices stilled my pulsing veins after all the effort of cleaning. I turned it up so high, the vibrations bounced through the wooden table, causing it to shudder. I then walked from room to room, acquainting myself with my new home, taking a mental snapshot, getting to know its nooks and crannies and trying to adjust to its uniqueness and hidden charm. The television wouldn't be connected to the cable services for the next day or so and the small radio was the only medium I had to keep me company. I couldn't help but smile. This whole environment was so starkly different from the one I had left behind, it surprised even me. But then sometimes, isn't that what we need to get over a cataclysmic change that may have occurred in our lives? I pictured the glossy, hi-tech apartment I had left behind and felt not a shred of regret. I should have done it years ago. This was now the new me, the real me.

Time sped by and exhaustion grappled with my aching bones until eventually, I succumbed and dropped onto the mattress in a heap. It was strange having the whole bed to myself; it was like a weekend away in a quaint boutique hotel except I was on my own and not part of a couple. It felt good.

I smiled contentedly and slipped into an effortless sleep, weightless and worry free. A whole new life ahead beckoned me and I needed every ounce of strength to face it. I slept soundly and awoke the next morning refreshed and lighter than air.

Breakfast was scrambled eggs on toast washed down with coffee. I had already made my mind up to go for a long walk before the predicted rain clouds came scudding in from the west, saturating the land and making discovering local areas a highly unappealing pastime.

I scrolled through the list of unanswered emails on my phone and decided against opening any of them. There was nothing there that couldn't wait, no pressing urgent matters that needed to be dealt with immediately. Instead, I made another coffee and took my time drinking it, savouring the slightly nicotine flavour of the caffeine as it hit the back of my throat with a bitter kick.

I finished my coffee, showered and got dressed, pulled on an old pair of boots and was ready to go. On impulse, I grabbed a jacket even though the forecast was already changing its mind, claiming the bubbling clouds would now make their way down the west coast before heading out into the English Channel. We needed the rain. The gardens were parched, the grass tinder dry. According to the local newspaper I picked up on the way into the village yesterday, fires were already beginning to take hold in the nearby hills, set off by the meddling hands of bored children who had taken to walking the area with matches and a need to be entertained and stimulated; a deadly mix when we were experiencing one of the hottest, driest summers on record. Still, despite the more recent forecast of no rain, I erred on the side of caution and hoisted my thin summer jacket over my shoulder and set off.

I had barely made my way out of the village and was heading towards a farm that sat on the outskirts when I passed an elderly gentleman, his back hunched, his countenance one of simmering anger.

Something deep in my gut told me to move out of his way, to give him and his fury a wide berth.

I tried to step around him, thinking it best to avoid any difficulties or confrontation, but as I made to do so, he grabbed my arm roughly, pulling me closer until our faces were almost touching. I stared at his skin, lined and flaking, and watched his rheumy eyes as he leaned in close to me. Flecks of spittle gathered at the corners of his mouth with each word spoken. 'Watch your back, boy. You just watch your back!' His voice was croaky, his accent suggestive of a life spent locally, having never ventured out into a world beyond the North East of England.

I shook my arm free and sucked in a breath as he pushed past me and kept on walking, his gait lumbering, his frame twisted and bent with age. His head rocked from side to side and I wasn't sure if the movement was a deliberate act or an unintentional, age-related tremor. I had a good mind to holler after him, to tell him to mind his own fucking business, but something deep inside me held me back. Shouting in the street wasn't my thing. I was better than that. There could have been any number of reasons why he did what he did – a case of mistaken identity, dementia perhaps, or maybe he was just the local idiot. Every village had one. People who roam around aimlessly, making stupid uncalled for comments to anybody stupid enough to listen.

I shrugged and kept on walking. I wasn't interested in any of his motives. I had my own plans for the day, and brawling and arguing with strangers didn't figure in them.

Determined not to let this strange scenario get the better of me, I lengthened my stride and pushed my shoulders back, my face pointed towards the heat of the sun. Had I not encountered Lily's warmth and friendliness yesterday, I would be questioning my decision to move here. I blotted out those thoughts, convincing myself that Whitchurch's locals were permanently on edge, suspicious of new faces and fearful of strangers frequenting the place. They were on red alert, perceiving everyone as a threat and expecting a barrage of questions from hard-nosed reporters desperate for any scrap of information, any morsel or piece of vicious gossip – whether true or completely unfounded – just so they could get a quick story and sell papers. This was just how Whitchurch was and I simply had to adapt to their quirky, peculiar ways and get used to it. I couldn't change these people. It would be me that would have to modify my ways and develop a tolerance to their distrust and borderline madness. I had infiltrated their world and they saw me as a threat. I would have to work hard to dispel that idea.

I tied my jacket around my waist, realising it was definitely superfluous on such a hot and muggy day, and tried to clear my head. Skylarks danced in and out of a field to my right, their irrepressible, sweet song filling the already near-scorching air. It was only 10 a.m. and I guessed the temperature to be somewhere in the late twenties. I thought again about how television broadcasters would be talking about it being the hottest day of the year so far and newspaper headlines would scream at us that the entire country was in meltdown. I laughed to myself. We were so easily roused to anger or hysteria in the UK, so easily led by the media and their emotive, controversial stories.

I stood still to take in the scent of nearby wild flowers and appreciate the beauty of my surroundings. I loved the cosmopolitan feel of city life with its immediacy and vibrancy, but rural locations always got me in my solar plexus, sending my stomach into a pleasurable lurch and stopping me in my tracks, making me take stock of my life. I inhaled deeply and closed my eyes, enjoying the sensation of the slight breeze as it tickled my warm skin, causing the hairs on my arms to stand to attention. It would work for me, living here in Whitchurch. I would make it work.

Walking on, I felt the vibration of my ringing phone as it rattled against my leg, where it nestled deep in the pocket of my cargo trousers. I stopped and lifted it out, squinting against the glare of the sun as I looked at the screen. Samantha's mother. I clicked the decline button. I would sooner stick hot pins in my eyes than speak to her. It was all behind me now. It was time to move on. Durham was my new home. Birmingham was a part of my other life – a life I was only too keen to leave behind.

Dropping the phone back in the side pocket of my trousers, I surged ahead, adrenaline racing around my system. I felt supercharged, as if I could take on the world, empowered by my newfound freedom.

I kept on for a good few miles, forging ahead, a sense of purpose driving me. Any anger or resentment I felt soon dissipated, escaping out of my body and disappearing into the ether. My breath pumped out in ragged gasps. Perspiration gathered around my hairline and on the back of my neck, trickling down my back, causing my shirt to stick to my skin. I stopped and rubbed at my face with an old handkerchief and unfastened a few buttons on my short-sleeved shirt, wishing I'd worn shorts rather than trousers. As I turned around, I could see Whitchurch on the brow of the hill behind me, a mere speck in the distance. It occurred to me that I hadn't brought any water with me. The temperature was growing by the minute – a relentless wall of heat that nipped at my skin and scratched at my dry throat. I would need a drink pretty soon.

I brought my hand up to shield my eyes against the glare of the sun and looked into the distance. Ahead lay a picturesque landscape of endless rolling fields. No other dwellings in sight. If I had wanted to buy a bottle of juice, I should have headed in the opposite direction, where I would have stumbled into the next village, but as it was, there seemed to be nothing in sight for miles and miles, nowhere I could purchase a few provisions. I knew then what I had to do. Reluctantly, I turned around and made my way back, irritated at my short-sightedness and lack of preparedness.

The walk back took longer, my legs heavy with fatigue, my body crying out for liquid sustenance. By the time I rounded the bend into Whitchurch, the cloying sensation in my gullet had developed into a raging thirst and I felt as if I had swallowed a sheet of coarse sandpaper. There was nobody around as I unlocked my front door and practically flung myself in, my body angled towards the kitchen where I held my head under the tap and glugged back as much water as my stomach could hold.

I dropped into one of the kitchen chairs, sweat blinding me and dehydration making my head thump. I closed my eyes and waited for the ice-cold water to do its thing, to replenish the stores of liquid in my body. Once again, I felt the vibration of my phone as it hummed against my leg. Lifting it out, I glanced at the name on the screen and declined the call. As soon as I got my breath back, I would block her from any future calls. Speaking to Delores, Samantha's mother, was something I could well do without. She had been a nuisance when Samantha and I we were together and had proven to be an even bigger one since we'd parted. I'd received three missed calls from her on the drive to Whitchurch and even now, she refused to stop calling me despite me not answering her. I wondered when she would begin to take the hint and leave me alone.

I let the phone slip from my hand onto the table where it see-sawed and rattled around on the knotted pine veneer before coming to a halt. I leaned over and turned it off, gladdened by the sudden blank screen. At least she didn't know where I had moved to. Knowing how tenacious she was, I had no doubt that she would try to follow me, desperate for me to speak to her about my relationship with her precious daughter. I wasn't about to let that happen. I had had a gutful of that family. It was all behind me. Time to move on.

I gulped down more water, unable to quench my raging thirst, then showered and changed into clean clothes. I would take a walk to the corner shop, buy a newspaper, perhaps even make small talk with some of the locals on the way there. I would establish myself as a proper villager because whether they liked it or not, I was here to stay.

5

ME

I have a memory. I am a child playing in the back garden. My parents are milling about, pruning roses, making tea, doing all the normal, sensible things that adults do on a clear spring day when the sunshine is warm enough for people to venture outside after a long hard winter. They aren't paying attention to what I'm doing. They know where I am, they know I'm safe and somewhere close by, but I am not in their direct line of vision. I am on the periphery of their activities.

They are keen to get the garden in order, to clean the patio area, to sweep away the rust-coloured dead leaves left behind by the harsh winter we have just endured. My mother shouts to my father that she is making him a sandwich. I see him nod and smile, then raise his hand to wave at her through the kitchen window. To all intents and purposes, they are an ordinary couple; their behaviour is typical of thousands of other married people throughout the nation, throughout the world even. Except they are not normal, and they are anything but ordinary. But we'll come to that later.

They're enjoying the onset of spring, looking forward to spending time in their garden, looking forward to being a family all together in the blissful warmth of the sunlight. The promise of summer is close by. They appear to be happy.

That's because they don't know about me.

They have no idea about the things that rampage through my brain, although they will soon find out. It will shatter their lives, smash everything they thought they knew about their small offspring into tiny little fragments, never to be repaired again. But then, maybe they helped play a part in my mental downfall. Perhaps they damaged their precious progeny with their unpredictable reactions and punitive sanctions. Or perhaps we will never know what caused me to be the way I am.

I glance at my father who is bending over, his shoulders shifting up and down as he digs, his tiny shovel pressing deep into the wet soil in a rhythmic fashion. Other children would sidle up next to him, ask to help, dig alongside him in a clumsy fashion, mimicking his actions. But not me. I see it as a chance to set my demons free, to unleash all the hurt and hatred that has built up inside me. While his back is turned and my mother is busying herself in the kitchen, I pick up a small rock and begin bashing it against my leg.

At first, I don't feel the pain, just a grazing scratching sensation against my bare skin. I watch as blood begins to trickle down my shin: two thin lines gliding downwards in perfect symmetry. I am fascinated by them, my eyes fixed on the trickles of scarlet, incongruous and garish against my pale flesh. I bash some more, small flaps of rapidly bruising skin beginning to shift, splitting like fruit flesh under the force of a sharp blade. More blood oozes out, the crimson rush of liquid bright and starkly different to the pink epidermis of my small limb.

I feel a flash of excitement and give my leg one final hard crack with the stone. The cry alerts my parents who come rushing over to me, their faces creased with concern. I shed no tears. The cry is reflexive. I am too young to stifle it. My parents are horrified, my mother in floods of tears. They have no idea what to do, how to react. What should parents do when they discover their only child has tried to smash their own leg and lies there, battered and bleeding? I am more in control than they are. Endorphins protect me, whistling through my system, giving me a sense of euphoria.

There is a lot of shouting and confusion, wet towels applied to the wound, which even I can see is pointless. Further medical treatment is required for my injury.

I am lifted into the house, into the aroma of fresh bread and coffee. Warm blood continues to pulse out, dripping over our clothes and smearing the furniture, staining the wooden table on which I am placed. A deep scarlet tinge bleeds into the grain, turning it a muddy-brown colour. It reminds me of coffins and dead bodies. I blink and look away.

In the end, I am taken to hospital, where the wound is cleaned and stitched. I don't cry. Doctors are astounded at my bravery. Children my age usually thrash about and scream when the stitches are administered. They cry for their parents and squirm for the love of their mother. But not me. I am different. But then, you already know that.

The medical staff talk to me softly, their words precise and gentle, asking me in measured tones why I did it, why I took a large rock and battered my own body with it, ripping at my own skin, bruising my soft young flesh. I have no answers. I remain silent and they take this as me being in a state of shock. They give me medicine to numb the pain that I don't feel. My mother holds my hand, her skin cold against mine, and my father places his hand against my cheek, his fingers rough and stained with blood. He speaks softly, his voice stilted and wary. He does his best to appear loving, ruffling my hair and trying to reassure me with carefully chosen expressions and phrases. None of these things soothe me. I felt a greater sense of calm when the sharp edges of the stone hit my soft flesh. I felt at peace at the sight of the blood.

After much talking and deliberation, I am taken home, the car ride back a hurried journey of sneaked glances when they think I'm not looking, and low whispers that have an air of menace about them. They utter to each other hushed words full of angst and fear. Words about me.

We have a rapid supper and then I am tucked up in bed. The exhausted eyes of my parents peer down at me. Their pallid faces are riddled with concern, confusion at my unexplained actions etched into their expressions.

I close my eyes and sleep soundly as if nothing

has taken place. I feel no pain, only a deep, gnawing ache to do it all again, such was the thrill I experienced from it. When I awake the next morning, the world is shiny and new. Nothing bad happened to me. I am cleansed and pure.

You might ask why I am telling you this tale. What does it have to do with anything? It is apropos to nothing, I hear you say. The answer is simple. I am telling you this so you know what sort of person I am, so you know exactly what you are dealing with. Because if you think this act of mindless violence is repulsive and way off balance then you need to brace yourselves. This, my friends, is nothing compared to what you are about to find out. This sad little story, dear unassuming people, is just the beginning.

6

'You're a reader then?' I watched as the man behind the counter scanned my magazines and newspapers with a certain amount of trepidation, as if I was about to turn and run without paying. His voice was brittle and gravelly.

I nodded, unsure how to answer such a strange question. His white hair glimmered under the glare of the overhead light, and his mouth hung open, concentration creasing his eyes as he leafed through all my reading material. I stared at his face, at his jaw slack with age.

'We don't sell many of these types of papers around here,' he said, pointing at the copies of *The Telegraph* and *The Guardian* that sat amongst the newspapers and magazines I had grabbed off the shelf out of sheer boredom. The *National Geographic*, a photography magazine and another glossy periodical about cars sat in a bulky pile on the counter next to them.

'The broadsheets?' I replied as I counted out the correct money and handed it over.

'Eh?' His jowls wobbled as he looked up at me, uncertainty evident in his face.

'The larger newspapers. That's what they're called – broadsheets,' I said, aware I sounded condescending. I tried to soften my words with a smile.

'Aye, well, there's only a handful of other people round here who read 'em. Other folk tend to go for the quick reads.' He looked up and surveyed my face, searching my eyes for some clue as to who I was.

'And what about you?' I asked, thinking I already knew the answer to this one. I had him down as a *Daily Express* sort of man. I was wrong.

'Don't do any of them, son. I don't read newspapers and I don't watch the news.' He looked away from me and I hesitated, unsure how I should react. 'Lost my daughter last year. Had a bellyful of bad news. My wife went shortly after her. I find it easier to just leave it all alone. Reading about it never changes anything, does it? Doesn't make any of it any better.'

I was about to ask how he managed it, working in a newsagent's, being confronted with the screaming headlines every day and never being tempted to pick one up and read it, when I felt a presence behind me. I turned to see an agitated-looking female standing close to me. She was in her mid-thirties and looked every inch the country lady. She wore a felt hat tipped at a jaunty angle and a shawl was wrapped casually around her shoulders. Despite the sweltering heat outside, she wore tight jeans and knee-high, black leather boots. Confidence oozed from her every pore and I felt sure she had never been in any situation in her entire life that had fazed or frightened her.

'Morning, Walt,' she said loudly as she moved forward, her body edging ahead of mine, surreptitiously moving me out of the way. I smelt her perfume as our bodies almost touched and I took a sharp intake of air, appreciating the scent that filled the shop around us. It was a deep, musky odour that probably cost as much as a small car. An expensive cologne from Italy or France. The kind Samantha used to talk about wanting to buy. I coughed and swatted all thoughts of her away.

'Thanks, Walt,' I said, my voice projecting over her head. I nodded at him and he gave me a cursory nod in return. I had a feeling it was going to take some time to become properly acquainted with the people in Whitchurch. Small steps.

* * *

I heard the crack of her heels on the pavement behind me before she called out. Her voice mirrored her expensive perfume: deep and powerful, commanding attention. 'Excuse me. You left these behind.'

I turned to see her holding my keys out on the palm of her hand. Her skin was pale, her nails painted a deep shade of pink. She cut a striking figure in the near emptiness of the village. I shook my head and let out a small laugh.

'Thank you,' I said. 'I don't know what I was thinking. So stupid of me.'

'Oh, we've all done such things. Most days, I don't know my arse from my elbow or what day it even is.' She smiled at me and tipped her head to one side. I got the feeling she was waiting for me to say something in return.

I took my keys, put them in my pocket and shook her hand. My palm felt hot and clammy against her cool dry skin. 'I'm Ray,' I said. 'I'm new to the place. Suffering from some sort of mind fog after the move here yesterday, I think.'

She grinned. 'Pleased to meet you, Ray. I'm Diane. And as for mind fog, welcome to the club. How are you settling in here at Whitchurch?' Her accent was sharp, determined. It suggested wealth and the sort of poise and self-assurance that a privileged upbringing instils in a person.

I was momentarily lost for words. How could I explain the tense atmosphere of the pub? Or the strange words of the man in the courtyard and then the elderly gentleman earlier this morning? Telling her these things would make me sound paranoid. So instead, I smiled and swept my hand around to the beautiful countryside not so far away from where we were standing and gave her a broad smile. 'Well, it's perfect here, isn't it? What's to not like?'

This seemed to please her. She continued smiling at me and as she nodded, her hair bounced up and down, featherlight and glimmering in the sunshine. I felt my eyes being drawn towards it and had to force myself to look away as an image of me curling my fingers through Samantha's hair jumped into my mind. I had to stop this. I needed to switch off whatever mechanism it was in my brain that kept implanting her there.

'I live over there,' Diane said as she pointed to a large property on the edge of the hill. I surmised it was probably a mile or so away as the crow flies. 'Whitchurch Farm. You must call over sometime. Do you ride?'

I shook my head and watched a small veil of disappointment fall over her face, her expression changing ever so slightly at my admission.

'Ah well. You're still welcome to call over. Always good to meet new people. Anyway, must dash. Terence and I are off out for lunch later and I need to get out of these scruffs and smarten myself up.'

She looked like she had just stepped off a catwalk. I wondered if she knew this and was simply fishing for compliments. Then again, I doubt she needed any affirmation of how glamorous and stylish she looked so instead I bid her goodbye, promising I would call over and see her sometime and meet her husband, knowing the chances of such an encounter were almost non-existent. We were different people living in vastly opposing worlds.

I made my way home, my reading material tucked under my arm. There was enough here to keep me busy for the entire week. I doubted I would even have time to read them all. They would keep. Living alone now meant I had plenty of time for flicking through magazines and newspapers, spending as long as I liked browsing through the classified section or reading the mundane minor stories and articles, or anything at all that took my eye. Nobody leaning over my shoulder, telling me I was wasting precious time when there were things that needed to be done in the apartment, nobody nagging at me to go places I didn't want to go to. Nobody repeatedly telling me what a useless waste of space I was.

I put the key in the lock and turned it, quietly delighted by the idea of seeing only my belongings inside, loving the thought of the silence that waited for me, even enjoying the sound the old door made as it swung open with a deep, rhythmic groan. I smiled as I stepped inside. I may not have had a state-of-the-art living space and now occupied a crumbling old cottage but at least I was free.

7

I spent the remainder of the day reading and napping, interspersed with a quick walk around the village, mainly to get a better look at Whitchurch Farm, the sprawling farmhouse Diane and her husband Terence called home. At least Diane seemed friendly and welcoming. I didn't mind admitting that after my meeting with the two other dubious characters both today and yesterday with their eccentric behaviour and veiled threats, speaking with Diane felt like a more auspicious start to my life here in Whitchurch. She was everything I'd hoped neighbours would be. And easy on the eye. And extraordinarily wealthy and married. Ah well.

A small, rectangular envelope with no markings

on it was sitting on the doormat as I walked through to the hallway with the intention of going back to The Pot and Glass for a pint and a bite to eat. There was nothing on the front – no name, no indication as to what was inside. Tucking my finger into the corner, I slid my nail along and ripped the envelope open. A small piece of folded paper fluttered out. I caught it before it hit the floor and opened it, my eyes scanning the typed words. I waited a few seconds before folding it back up and slipping it into my breast pocket.

The sun was dipping slightly as I headed out, draping a watery sepia blanket over the village and beyond. In the distance, beige fields deprived of water for too long stretched as far as the eye could see. Their usual glossy hue was absent, the verdant greens and squares of sage, olive and emerald-coloured landscapes we were so accustomed to seeing, now the colour of sand.

A smattering of people passed me as I strolled towards the pub. I didn't know whether or not my imagination was in overdrive, but they all seemed to avoid my gaze, their eyes darting everywhere: over at the churchyard, towards the Post Office, everywhere but at me. I shrugged. They didn't know me and I didn't know them. It was to be expected, I supposed. I just imagined village life to be rather more courteous than being in a city, for people to stop and chat. Villages are places where everybody knows each other, where everyone is well acquainted with one another's lives. That was most certainly my memory of them as a child, before my father's job took us far away from the rolling fields and lush countryside and into the city.

The Pot and Glass was crammed with bodies as I stepped inside. I was grateful for that. It made my entrance less conspicuous. No whispers or silent stares. No cliques of people huddled together in corners discussing my movements or thinking up wild and wonderful ways to warn me away from their precious little hamlet.

I could see Lily beyond the throng of bodies, bustling around behind the bar, her neat, peroxide-blonde hair bobbing about. There were two other people serving – a tall, middle-aged man and a rotund lady of approximately the same age. I guessed them to be the couple who ran the place, although I had no reason to make such an assumption other than the confident way in which they worked, quickly serving customers and making sure everyone was greeted with a ready smile.

The crowd thinned out and in no time at all, I was faced with the smiling expression of the tall man. 'A pint of John Smith's please,' I said through gritted teeth as the person next to me accidentally elbowed me while rummaging in their pocket for change. I decided against having any food. It was too full and too noisy to get any peace, and I would be lucky to get a table. All around me, families were eating, the tantalising smell of the carvery wafting under my nose.

'A busy one, eh?' I said to the tall man as he pulled my pint, his back half turned to me.

'You're not kidding,' he replied over the roar of voices. 'Always fairly busy on a Sunday, but to be honest, with the weather being so warm, we expected it to be dead today. People usually go off on picnics, preferring to eat outside in the sunshine. Just goes to show,' he said, as he handed my drink to me, 'you never can tell, can you? Folk are funny, unpredictable creatures.'

I nodded in agreement and gave him a handful of coins, then headed away from the bar over to a clear space near the doorway, where I hoped I would be hit by a slight breeze, giving me a modicum of respite from the blistering heat.

I was wrong. The door may well have been propped open but all that came through it was the occasional waft of hot air. Fortunately, the ale was cold enough to lower my body temperature and chill my belly, stopping the hunger from taking complete hold.

I drank over half of it in a couple of mouthfuls and found myself wishing I'd ordered two to save having to fight my way back through to the bar. Steeling myself, I set off and stopped at the sight of Lily walking towards me, her arm piled high with empty glasses.

'You ready for another?' she asked and I nodded enthusiastically, rummaging in my pocket for the cash. 'It's okay. I'll open a tab up for you.' She gave me another of her endearing smiles and I watched as she sashayed her way back to the bar.

I stood on my own and tuned into the nearby conversation of a group of people I assumed were local while I waited for my beer. Finishing my drink, I was fascinated to hear what they had to say and tried to piece it all together as their voices filtered over to me.

'...much more of this can we take?'

'...only spoken to Jim and Mary...'

'...them as well...'

'What does it say?'

'...put through the door this morning...'

I attempted to move closer but was thwarted by a stocky man who forced his way past me, a deep scowl etched onto his face. I watched, mildly curious as he ordered a pint and drank it nearly all in one go. The frown he had been sporting began to dissipate, smoothed out by cold beer.

The heat was getting to everyone, making them tetchy and unpredictable.

Next to me, the conversation continued. I listened in, keen to hear their words. In a strange way, I knew it involved me but had no idea how to broach the subject and attempt to join in with their discussion. I was a stranger to them and not involved in their dialogue but I was able to pick up what they were saying. Their irritation was palpable, crackling in the air like static. They wouldn't take kindly to interruptions from a passer-by, somebody unfamiliar, so I stood and pieced together the snippets of what they were saying, rapidly digesting each word.

'There you go, Ray.' Lily's voice shook me out of my trance-like state. I thanked her as she handed me my glass and returned my attention back to the huddle of people next to me.

'Seems like there's a few very unhappy folk around here today,' I half whispered over the noise as I looked back at Lily and shook my head in confusion.

She blinked hard and took a deep breath, obviously reticent to speak. Her arm touched mine as she pulled me closer to her. I picked up on the conflicting aroma of perfume and sweat as her face moved in nearer to me and she let her words trail softly into my ear. 'There's been some bother in the village again. A few of the locals have received threatening letters. Hand-posted through their letterboxes sometime today.'

I pulled away and widened my eyes, then reached into my pocket and presented the envelope that was on my doormat as I left the house not so long ago. 'Like this one?'

Lily looked at it and for a second, I thought she was going to either cry or walk away. But then she quickly snatched it out of my hand and half turned from me, tugging at my arm and indicating that I should follow her. We walked quickly to the far end of the room, pushing through the groups of people dotted around the place. Lily shook her head and ignored the pleas of the locals for her to replenish their drinks as we brushed past them, until eventually, we were alone under a small alcove, half hidden in the shadow of a low beam.

Only when we were tucked into the dark corner of the room did she speak to me. 'I can't believe you got one as well! You've only been here a few days. What does it say?'

I pointed at her hand and sighed glumly. 'Open it. You can read what is says for yourself.'

Her hands trembled slightly as she slipped her finger into the flap and pulled it roughly. She grabbed the piece of paper with her crimson nails and opened it, casting a quick glance around us to make sure nobody could see. I watched a line cut across her forehead as she read it. She tipped her head up to stare at me, her face pale in the gloomy shadow of an old oak beam.

'I'm assuming it was meant for the person who was in the house before me?' I said lightly. 'I'm guessing it was occupied by a female?' I smiled sardonically and looked down at the piece of paper. 'Very welcoming, the locals in this village, aren't they?' I read aloud the words clutched in Lily's hand. 'Die you fucking bitch.'

Lily didn't answer me. Her lip trembled as she stared once again at the small piece of paper in her hand. I reached out and took it from her, then carefully folded it back up and slipped it back into my pocket.

'It was an old lady,' she said eventually. 'God, I'm sorry about this. Why would anybody send an old lady a message like that? And if they lived locally, they would know she no longer lives there.'

I shook my head and waited for a short while before speaking. 'I'm assuming other people's messages were along the same lines as mine?'

'I'm not sure of them all, but Emily over there?'

Lily nodded towards the group of people we had moved away from, a gathering of elderly-looking individuals with worried expressions. 'Her letter was similar. Said something about her being a useless old hag. She was in tears earlier and that's not like her at all. She's usually made of sterner stuff.'

'Well, this is all new to me,' I said, exhaling loudly. 'I have no idea what to say.'

More people poured through the door, filling the place to the rafters. 'Oh God, sorry, I've got to get on,' Lily said apologetically and gave my arm a small pat before moving away from me and mouthing another apology.

I stood and watched the comings and goings of the pub while I finished my drink. The emptiness in my stomach was now filled with beer but I knew that I would have to eat at some point. Deciding against staying, I placed the glass on a table next to me and made to leave. I could cook a curry when I got home. I knew I would have to go grocery shopping pretty soon but had brought enough provisions with me to see me through the next few days.

It was while I was making my exit, my body angled towards the door as I wove my way through the crowds, that I felt it. A hand pulled at my right arm, dragging me back into the throng of bodies. I swung around to be confronted with a man who was roughly the same height as me. He was older – in his sixties – and his face was a complete blank, devoid of any emotion.

'Lily says you've had one as well?' His voice was weak but his grip was deceptively strong for a man twice my age. 'A letter?'

I pulled my arm free from his grasp. As if realising his error, he attempted to straighten out the creases on my shirt and then patted me affectionately. Standing with the man was a woman of roughly the same age. Her white hair was swept back with a black, satin band, and rested just below her shoulders. Her deep-set eyes watched me intently as she waited for my reply. I considered pleading ignorance and leaving. That would have been the easiest option, but I stayed and produced the note, opening it for them to see.

'Mary and me, we got one as well,' the man said croakily. His skin was ashen, his voice raspy. He looked as if he was about to break down right here in front of me. I watched as he read the typed words on the paper and I waited for him to speak. He blinked hard, glanced at his wife, then reread the note. He looked up at me, his eyes glassy and unfathomable. 'It's not right, is it? A small village like this being targeted. And you're new here as well. You don't deserve to receive anything like this.'

'It's actually lovely here in Whitchurch,' Mary said in a high-pitched voice. 'Well, it used to be...' Her voice trailed off and her eyes brimmed with unshed tears.

'I'm sure it's nothing more than some sort of childish prank by bored teenagers,' I said, and watched their faces for a response. I felt sure I saw a flicker of recognition in the man's eyes. 'Anyway, I'm sorry to have met you under these circumstances but I'm sure next time we'll have forgotten all about it. I'm Ray, by the way.'

'Jim and Mary,' he said, and held his hand out for me to shake. His skin was crisp like parchment. I suppressed a shiver. Mary remained still, her tiny face inscrutable, her eyes dark and dewy.

'Nice to meet you both. I'm guessing The Pot and Glass is the hub of the community, the place where everybody meets?'

Jim nodded. 'It is,' he said a little more enthusiastically. A lock of silver hair bounced up and down over his eye. He blinked and pushed it away.

'Well,' I said, tucking the letter away once again. 'I'll probably see a fair amount of you in here. Lily serves a damn good pint.'

I gave them both a polite nod and started to walk away. I could feel Mary's eyes boring into me and felt sure she and Jim were talking about me as I strode towards the exit. They were all apprehensive of outsiders and anybody different. I puffed out my cheeks. It was all so silly and pointless. Such behaviour was archaic, harking back to times when people lived by tribal rules and everyone was viewed with suspicion, as some sort of threat to their status quo. Nonetheless, I turned and gave them a polite wave, knowing I would bump into them again at some point in the near future. Jim smiled back and nudged his wife, who did nothing except keep her expression rigid and glare at me until I disappeared out of sight.

8

ME

I feel that since I have given you an insight into to what drives me – what kind of person I am – I should lead you through my life up to the present. That is the best way. You will get to walk in my shoes, to see everything through my eyes. Then you might understand.

Although I mentioned that I might be narcissistic or a psychopath, there are reasons why I do what I do. Of course, there are those times when things in life happen randomly. But not in my life. I won't allow it. I like order. I like to be in control and when things get out of control, then so do I. I work hard to put them back to how I want them, and if that means hurting people, then so be it.

I started school on a warm day in September. The memory of it is clear to me, the hurt of being left there sharp and raw. It had not been explained to me what was going to happen and so the resentment built in my brain, festering and growing until eventually, it all came pouring out. Isn't that what happens with all children, I hear you ask? Don't they all have to be left at school and simply get on with it? Indeed, that is undoubtedly the case. And I was surrounded by my peers, many of whom were as distressed as I was at being left for an entire day with complete strangers. But this is where my differences emerge. It's only when I recall memories such as this one that I know for certain – I am not like other people. One boy cried all day. Another girl wet herself. I watched, fascinated, as warm urine trickled down her legs and pooled in an amber puddle at her feet. Me? I found a drawing pin on the floor and jammed it into the teacher's leg as she leaned over to ask me why I looked so sad. Before she even had chance to do anything, to admonish me or cry out, I took my finger and jabbed it hard in her eye. It wasn't her fault that it happened, that I had been left in her company and was feeling furious because of it. But it wasn't mine either. I was unhappy and I wanted to lash out, so I did.

I remember the look of horror on my mother's face later that day as she spoke to another member of staff. I sat beside her, staring up at her contorted features, at her shiny eyes, wet from weeping. I listened to her words of sorrow and to her stream of apologies. I wasn't sorry. She had abandoned me, left me with a team of strangers. I was a child and needed protecting. She had done me wrong and I was angry. I felt justified in my actions. I was far too young to understand what was going on and had no means of escape. Lashing out was the only tool I had. And it wasn't the first time she had wronged me. I was simply paying her back for the previous hurt. It all made sense in my childish, undeveloped mind. My unsophisticated sense of reasoning told me what I had done was perfectly acceptable. I still think that to this day.

Once we got home, everything began to go terribly awry. My actions would have to be questioned, analysed. There would be consequences.

Which came first – the chicken or the egg? Did my parents begin to punish me because I was bad or am I bad because they punished me? It's a difficult one to work out, isn't it? Such a tricky conundrum. The old nature versus nurture debate. The punishments that I remember are unforgettable but for all I know, they may have started earlier than I recall. Perhaps I was a difficult baby and therefore reprimanded accordingly. Who knows what I was subjected to before my mind was able to comprehend what was happening to me? We'll never know, will we? I once read that a baby's brain is like putty, ready to be moulded into whatever you want it to be. Give it love and you get love back. Subject a child to hatred and guess what...?

But I digress. My parents, exasperated at my behaviour, tried to speak with me. I recall vividly their wide eyes and flaring nostrils as they tried to reason with me. They wanted answers. They would have a long wait. I was nothing if not tenacious.

We sat for what felt like an age, in complete silence, as they waited for me to talk. Their staring features didn't frighten me. I had reasons for doing what I did. Surely they could see that? People in their position should have known that deserting their only child was unacceptable. So rather than sit any longer and watch their simmering anger or listen to their endless probing questions, I got up and walked away. This seemed to set off a determined rage in my father, who grabbed my arm and dragged me back to my seat. I didn't shout out. I didn't do anything at all except sit and watch him. This obviously deepened his rage, unleashing something inside him, something monstrous that lay hidden deep inside his blackened soul. He brought his hand back and slapped me hard across my face. It stung. Of course it did. He was a grown man and I was a small child. But I didn't cry. Whether or not my lack of emotion made things worse, I will never know, but my dry eyes caused my mother to get involved, to be drawn into the whole sorry melee. Her expression crumpled and darkened, and she stood over me, her shadow formidable and menacing to my childlike eyes. She hauled me off my chair and took me up to my bedroom, throwing me on the bed, hollering at me that I wouldn't get any supper. Still, I didn't cry. Even my empty stomach wasn't enough to allow the tears to fall.

I wasn't normal. My reactions weren't normal. She told me so. Screamed it at me, telling me I had brought shame upon the family and that this would be the last time something like this would happen. They would make sure of it. They had a reputation to preserve. People looked up to them, thought of them as a good family, pillars of the community. They wouldn't allow my behaviour to drag them down into the gutter. They would change me, make sure I met all their expectations. They would do whatever it took to correct my behaviour.

And that's when things got a whole lot worse...

9

I awoke early with a sense of foreboding that I couldn't seem to shake. No matter how hard I tried to shrug it off, a heavy veil of gloom descended and stayed with me. There were lots of things I could be getting on with to help clear my mind: there was a garden to be tidied, boxes still waiting to be unpacked. I couldn't face doing any of them. Instead, I spent the day driving around Whitchurch and its surrounding areas, working out the best routes in and out of the village and finding out where I could go for supplies. Once I had done that and parked up, I pulled on my hiking boots and set off with a sense of purpose in my stride.

The weather was balmy as I ambled along, taking

in the scenery and thinking how quiet it was as I headed off through the main street of Whitchurch. And it was quiet, eerily so. No children about – just me and my thoughts.

I strode down Church Lane, a shiver running down my spine as I stared up at the spire of St Oswald's. In the distance, I heard the cries of excited children. They emanated from the field behind the old rectory. I guessed that must be where all the local kids played, away from the prying eyes of their families. Couldn't say I blamed them. Who'd want parents watching, breathing down their necks every time they fell over or kicked a ball too high or did anything that remotely resembled having fun?

The shadow of the church stretched over the graveyard, reaching the pavement where I stood. One day soon, I would take a walk around, have a look at some of the headstones, maybe even step inside the building itself. I wasn't a man given to religious tendencies but was interested in the history of the place, in the architectural beauty of it. But not today. Today, I would walk and try to shake off the niggling feelings of doubt that nipped at me. I silently chastised myself. This wasn't like me. I wasn't usually given to such sentiments. I must be going soft.

I continued walking, moving to the end of the lane

and past the field where the shrieks of playing children swam around me, carried along on the thermals like invisible strands of happiness billowing in the soft, summer air.

At the end of the gravel track, I climbed over a stile and found myself in a wide clearing with the sun beating down on my back. I decided I would follow the well-worn rut that dissected the field, and take the circular route that would lead me out of the village, along the foot of the hills and past the disused quarry, then past the golf club and back into Whitchurch. All in all, I figured it would take me just over an hour, possibly longer if the heat slowed me down. Not the longest of strolls but just long enough for me to free up my thinking and clear my head.

I stared up at the cloudless sky and ran the back of my hand across my forehead, beads of sweat trickling over my hot skin. I was out of shape, sweating before I had even begun the walk properly. It was a good time to get myself fit again. There was nobody at home to take into consideration, no one complaining when I visited the gym or went for a run. No whining and moaning. No Samantha. The perfect conditions for it.

Taking a swig of water, I set off at a good pace, promising myself I would keep it going but knowing deep down that I probably wouldn't.

The heat was relentless, stopping me every ten minutes or so, forcing me to slow my speed, the power of its rays biting at my exposed flesh. It didn't stop me completely, however. I wouldn't give up. This was a beginner's walk, not a long trek up the hills or over rough terrain. I turned and stared back in the direction I had come from. Whitchurch was far behind me like a distant memory. I thought of all the activity going on there, and everyone getting up and going about their business – people setting off for work, retirees tending to their gardens – while I stood out here watching them like some sort of voyeur. A small frisson of excitement bolted through me. It felt good to be away from the place, if only for a short while. Perhaps the gloom I felt was no more than a residual feeling of separation after leaving Birmingham so quickly, or maybe it was the cold reception I had received from the locals that was getting to me and dragging me down. Either way, I had to move on, shake it off and forget about it. I took a long drink and set off at a lick.

Only when I reached the quarry did I take a proper break. It had taken me over forty-five minutes to get there and I was feeling hot and weary. My back was wet with perspiration and I felt a raging thirst clawing at my dry throat. Lowering my backside onto a small rock, I gulped at my water and ate a cereal bar, my eyes travelling along the edge of the precipice just feet away from where I was perched. I sat there for a while, getting my breath back before standing up and moving forward. The drop was immense, much deeper than it appeared to be from a distance. I edged further forward, fascinated by its sheer magnificence. It looked like a huge claw had dragged the earth up, leaving a yawning wound where nothing would grow, just a gaping slab of dead, cavernous earth beneath my feet. The bottom of it was as dry as stone. During the cold months, it would likely fill up with rain, but the long, hot summer had left it barren and lifeless. On a whim, I shouted out, smiling at the echo of my own voice as it rang around the deserted area. I was willing to bet that very few people came this close to the edge. The ground was unstable, small stones slipping and moving underfoot as I stepped along the rim of the drop. Heights didn't scare me – never had. I was fortunate in that respect. I managed to keep any fears I had in check unlike many people who let theirs control their lives. Some people simply couldn't keep their demons at bay.

I walked around the perimeter of the quarry, peering down into its vast depths while finishing my snack. Only once did I experience a feeling of dizziness. Disappointed at my lack of self-control, I stepped back and dropped onto my haunches, dabbing at my face with an old handkerchief I had found scrunched up deep in my pocket. I looked up at the cobalt sky, squinting against the glare. The heat was unremitting and there was no shade. I stepped away from the edge and lowered myself onto the floor. I was hot and needed to rest for a little while longer before continuing my walk.

Giving myself a few more minutes to catch my breath and rehydrate, I waited, my eyes fixed on the distant horizon, on the ridge of hills that curved and sloped underneath the clear, burning sky. It was an awe-inspiring sight, good for the soul. Despite the gaping manmade hole beneath me, nature continued. It evolved and worked its way around our ruthless interventions, our ruinous attempts at utilising the minerals and natural resources we stand on, to make money and keep our society civilised.

I stood up and peered over the edge again. I supposed that even the quarry, a jagged, manmade hole in the earth, had its own unique beauty. Everything had a reason for being here – from the leaves on the trees to the tiniest insects. Even us. We all had reasons for our actions, whether they be conscious or subconscious. This quarry would serve a purpose for something. At some point, this unused, forgotten cavity would come into its own, nature melding into something that man had started and then abandoned, forgetting that it ever existed.

I stretched and set off again, my head clearer than earlier that morning, my thoughts more precise. I felt renewed, with a clear sense of purpose. My life in Birmingham was behind me. I had plenty to look forward to. Nobody else to think or worry about. Just me and my own needs. I could do this.

The building of the local golf club appeared like a mirage as I walked with the sun on my back. The putting green sat ahead of me, a sprawl of lush, emerald grass with curved edges and strategically placed trees. It was aesthetically pleasing, I could see that, but I preferred the rugged beauty of the landscape I had left behind, the organic quality that it offered. Even the quarry had its own particular dark appeal, an exquisiteness that had captivated me, punching a huge hole in my heart.

I took the route that ran around the edge of the green, preferring to fight my way through the unkempt path and dense undergrowth, and slowed my pace. I was close to the village now. No need to rush. No need to overexert myself. I could take my time, appreciate the rural surroundings. No blaring sirens, no traffic. No Samantha.

I smiled and closed my eyes briefly, inhaling the heady scent of the towering Himalayan balsam plant that covered every inch of ground, its pink flowers providing a carpet of pollen for the hovering bees.

The walk back into Whitchurch didn't take long. The path that ran alongside the golf course was overgrown but flatter and less craggy than the one I had navigated to get to the quarry. The church spire soon appeared above the canopy of trees, its lofty and austere appearance dampening my recently elevated spirits. The grey stone was an incompatible sight against the cool greens and wild splash of pinks and yellows from the spread of flowers and shrubbery around me.

I stepped into the shadows cast by the high building and felt the cold on my skin, a reptilian chill that wrapped itself around me in spite of the fact I had been walking for many miles. The sliver of ice that crept under my flesh was almost instant.

I broke into a slight run to move out of its dark presence, feeling as if somebody was watching me. It was ridiculous. There was nobody around – just me and my overactive imagination. In spite of my own reassurances, I began to walk faster, the sound of my footsteps echoing down the lane. This whole road was shrouded in darkness, the church and the wide spread of trees hemming it in, making it feel cold and claustrophobic.

I glanced over at the churchyard, at the rows of headstones, and shivered. The sooner I was back in the warmth of the sun and away from the darkness of the graveyard, the better.

10

The sound of the fractious chatter hit my ears as I rounded the corner onto the main road that ran through the village. Gathered by the roadside, on the grass verge, stood a small group of people. I moved closer and counted five of them, their arms raised in what appeared to be anger. As I neared the group, I was able to pick up their conversation and felt my skin prickle at their words.

'Enough is enough! I don't care what you say, we should call the police.'

'And tell them what? That some lowlife has smeared dog dirt on a few cars? Like they would ever come out for that.'

I stopped a few feet away from where they were

standing, my ears attuned to their every word. Before I could change my mind, I marched up to the angry-looking throng and cleared my throat. 'Sorry, I couldn't help but overhear what you were saying. I've just moved into the village. Over there at number twenty-six,' I said, pointing towards my humble abode. 'Is there something going on?'

An immediate silence descended. I watched as their eyes narrowed at my uninvited presence. One of the older ladies broke the awkward moment, her voice thin and reedy as she spoke to me, her words careful and precise. 'We've had a slight incident. Nothing to get too upset about. This is a lovely village, it really is.'

I knew then that something was wrong. Every time a resident insisted Whitchurch was a lovely place to live, the undercurrent in their meaning was patently obvious, so desperate were they to defend their little hamlet.

I nodded and tried to look concerned, thinking that would be it, an end to my involvement in the conversation. I made to walk away but a grey-haired man spoke just as I turned from them. 'Sorry, young fella. We're all a bit shook up about it. It's a nasty business, isn't it? I mean, who would do such a thing?'

I wanted to say bored teenagers would be the

most likely culprits for such a puerile pastime, which was what I'd suggested in the pub when the letters were received, but I remained silent. I was sure they wouldn't want my comments interfering with their already half-formed ideas. So instead, I asked questions, keen to appear thoughtful and empathetic, concerned by their current dilemma.

'How many cars have been affected?' I asked, choosing my words and tone carefully. I already knew from experience that Whitchurch residents were easily riled and given to taking offence at the slightest provocation. I needed to tread carefully, to pick my way around their sensitivities.

The grey-haired man looked to the others, as if he were asking for their permission to speak, before nodding and replying. 'As far as we can tell, it's four. One parked up by the Post Office, two in the back lane and one—' He stopped speaking and swallowed, the lump in his throat bobbing up and down as he did so. A flush crept up his face, covering his liver-spotted skin. 'Your car? It's not a blue—'

'Ford. Yes, it is,' I replied, following his gaze to the dark-blue Ford Focus that was parked up outside my house. I felt a flutter of something in my gut as I looked back at the small crowd of waiting people, an air of expectancy apparent in their pale faces and body language.

'I'm sorry about that,' he said, his face creased with sorrow and shame as if he himself had daubed my car with animal faeces. 'Not a nice thing to happen when you've just moved here.'

I shrugged and gave him a half smile. 'It's fine,' I said quietly. 'Just one of those things, I guess. I'll get myself home and give it a good clean. And if anybody needs a hand washing the other cars, I don't mind helping?' I phrased it as a question, my eyebrows hitched up as I waited for a response.

A murmur spread around the gathering of villagers who were nodding and whispering to one another as if I had just offered them the earth or volunteered to buy them a small island. I looked to each and every one of them, to their perplexed expressions, and almost laughed.

'That's very good of you...' the man said softly.

'Ray,' I added, filling the pause he left to identify myself.

'That's very good of you, Ray, but I think we've got it sorted. Jim, one of the owners, has already done his and the others are taking them to the car wash in town as we speak.'

'Okay, well if you get stuck, just give me a knock. I'll be only too glad to help.'

I started to walk away but was stopped by the voice of a small lady in her mid-fifties. 'The only assistance we need is from somebody who can help us catch this idiot. We've all had enough.' Her lips were tightened in anger. I caught her eye and waited for her to speak again. She said nothing else but her expression softened as she held my gaze.

'I gather none of you have any idea who did it?' I asked, aware I could open a can of worms. I prepared myself. These people didn't look particularly threatening or malicious. A handful of middle-aged locals wearing Crimplene trousers and worried expressions. What was the worst that could happen?

'I've got a fair idea!' a woman with black, wiry hair and a ruddy complexion shouted. Her voice was loud and on the verge of a screech as she continued unabated, despite the fact the grey-haired man had his arm on her shoulder to calm her down and was shaking his head. 'What?' she shrieked as she stared at him, wide-eyed with anger. 'Why shouldn't we talk about it? Over there,' she shouted, her finger wobbling about as she pointed to a house behind us, 'in that house, is a man who has been to prison for assault. He is abusive and rude and I have no doubt that it's him who sent the letters and killed the cat and spread the dog... *mess* over the cars and God knows what else.' She was breathing heavily, her mouth half open as she gasped for air. Her bottom lip wobbled theatrically; a perfectly formed pearl of saliva glistened on the edge of it, ready to drop off and run down her chin.

'Alice, that's quite enough,' an older lady said, her voice sharp enough to halt the conversation. She was tall and composed and her confident tone commanded respect. She had a quiet, reserved dignity about her, like a schoolmarm in her twilight years.

'I'm sorry,' I said as I shook my head. 'I shouldn't have asked. My fault completely.'

'No, it's okay,' the tall lady said gently. 'Everyone's under a lot of strain, worried that something worse is going to happen. We hoped this was all behind us, but now...' She shook her head wearily before giving me a thin, watery smile. 'And I'm really sorry about your car.'

'Nothing to apologise for,' I said. 'It's just a car. Nothing a bucket of soapy water won't sort out.'

'Emily!' she shouted out after me as I began walking away. I stopped and turned to face the group once more. Her eyes locked with mine, a fleeting moment of something unexplainable passing between us. 'I'm Emily,' she said, more softly this time, 'and this is Barry.' She pointed to the silver-haired man, who smiled at me. 'This is Alice,' she said as she lightly touched her arm, 'and Francis,' she said, gesturing to a slight man who had so far remained quiet throughout the whole episode. 'And this is Dominic, our village pastor. Reverend Dominic Baudin from St Oswald's.'

Dominic gave a slight bow, his face full of pity for his parishioners. He was young and wide-eyed and looked completely out of his depth. I felt a pang of pity for him, caught up in all of this.

'Pleased to meet you all,' I replied. 'As I said earlier, I'm Ray. I just wish we had met under more convivial circumstances.'

They all nodded and lowered their eyes, a murmur of agreement passing through them.

'Anyway. Best get on,' I added. 'Got things to do. A dinner to cook and a car to clean.' I let out a small laugh. Their faces remained inscrutable. These people looked as if they were on the edge of some sort of collective mental breakdown. I didn't say that it was only a bit of dog shit and nothing to get too worked up about. I knew they wouldn't see it like that. But in the grand scheme of things, it registered as a minor occurrence. The woman who had spoken earlier had been quite right – it was unlikely the police would want to get involved. Dog shit was hardly the crime of the century. They'd dealt with a murder in the past here in Whitchurch. These people were a hardier bunch than they liked to let on.

I gave them a wave with the promise I would see them in church next Sunday and then strolled away, thinking I had just sold my soul to God and all his believers just to have a few friends and to be accepted in this strange little village I now called home.

11

The smell of dog shit was rancid. I was unable to shake it off despite cleaning the car twice with hot, soapy water and polishing it until it gleamed. I worked solidly, trying to rinse away the pervasive odour of animal faeces, sure that the eyes of the neighbourhood were on me as I emptied the dregs of the dirty water down the drain on the roadside next to the kerb. Maybe it was just me being overly anxious but I could have sworn I saw a few curtains twitching when I turned around to look. Whitchurch was that sort of place. A village with secrets.

The road remained empty as I strode back into the house and slammed the door behind me. I stopped and stood for a moment, my ears attuned to the silence. I still enjoyed the quiet that an empty house exuded. I shut out all thoughts of Samantha and the apartment back in Birmingham. She had taken enough from me. Onward and upward.

Right on cue, my phone buzzed from the kitchen where it was sitting on the table. A sense of trepidation gripped me. I had blocked Delores. It couldn't be her. A fleeting wave of sadness shot through me as I realised how small my world had become. My sister and parents had passed away and my friends were few and far between – many of them had dropped off my radar once I met Samantha. It was both sad and laughable that the mother of my ex-partner was very possibly all I had left. And I didn't want her either.

I picked up my phone and checked my messages. No texts, but a list of emails. And all of them from Delores. I heaved an exasperated sigh and shook my head before throwing my phone back down onto the table. It appeared I would have to block her from sending me emails now as well, something I should have already done. I would check her missives later. Right now, I had better things to do, more pressing issues to attend to. Delores was nobody to me. She could wait.

I showered, ridding myself of the sweat and grime from my walk and the odious smell of dog shit that permeated everything, then dressed and sat with my laptop. In less than an hour, I managed to order most of my new furniture. I was sleeping in the bed of the previous owner and needed my own things. The bits of furniture I had in the house were either items I had had delivered here or things that had been left behind by request until I bought new. The family of the person who had lived here were only too glad to leave them for me when I asked. It saved them having to clear the place out, but I could only stick it for so long. I wanted to be surrounded by own things, my own belongings.

Deciding to bite the bullet, I braced myself and opened one of Delores' emails. I sucked in a deep breath and read it through, a small pulse tapping at my throat as her words sank in. I leaned back and exhaled, a pocket of heat circling in front of my face. She had no business sending this to me. Samantha was no longer anything to do with me. Why should I be concerned with her daughter's itinerary or whereabouts? Did Delores not realise that Samantha and I were no longer together?

I deleted each and every email, smiling as I

watched them all disappear from my screen. If she got in touch again, I'd tell her to leave me alone, concentrate on her own life and to stop interfering with mine.

After snapping my laptop closed, I wandered about the house aimlessly, my mind fractured, my anger simmering. I needed to do something, to push Delores and her threats out of my mind. I didn't want her inside my head. She had no right to be there.

A line of empty shelves caught my eye. I could do that – fill them with my things, make this place mine. Lifting my books out of the removal boxes, I gave them a quick wipe with my sleeve and began stacking them in order, largest to smallest.

I stared at the mound of boxes and containers sitting in the corner of the room. Still so much stuff to find a place for.

I began by sorting through my vinyl collection before moving onto a box of old photographs. A breath caught in my throat. I stopped, unsure of whether or not my mood was suited to carrying out such an emotional task. Rifling through old family photographs and stumbling across pictures of Cassandra wouldn't put me in the best of moods, and chances were, it would knock me off kilter for the rest of the day.

My hands trailed over the box and a slight pulse started up in my chest as I stared inside and thought about what lay in there, what memories it would stir up in me. I still missed her. My sister had been cut off in her prime, her life abruptly brought to a close by a tragic accident. I thought about her every single day.

I pushed my hand deep into the box and rummaged about, knowing which particular picture I was looking for. Pushing bits of paper and old photographs aside, I let out a sigh as I spotted it tucked between a pile of yellowed documents and plucked it out. Holding it up to the light, I couldn't help but smile. It was my favourite photo of us both and had been well-thumbed over the years.

We were teenagers when it was taken. My arm was draped over Cassandra's shoulder and we were dressed in the fashions of the time – me in a pair of low-slung, baggy jeans and a black hoodie, and Cassandra in a pink T-shirt with a long, denim skirt. My hair was long and straggly, greasy-looking actually, and Cassandra was wearing a wide-brimmed, black hat. I let out a small laugh and held the picture tight. If I wasn't mistaken, we were on holiday when this was taken. One of our last family holidays together.

A lump lodged itself in my throat. I placed the

photo down on the floor and let out an unsteady sigh. Running my fingers through my hair, I shook my head, incredulous at how such a small item could still get to me even after all these years. I would find a frame and put it up on a wall in the living room. She deserved that much. Nobody should be hidden away in a box, their face unseen simply because they are no longer with us. They never really leave. They're always here. Always.

The remainder of the day was spent sifting, sorting and generally unearthing items I either had forgotten existed or I no longer wanted. I found myself wondering why I had actually brought them with me at all when I could have left them behind or disposed of them before packing up and moving on. Like my old journal, for instance. I hadn't written in it for a long while and didn't intend to anytime in the near future. I used it at a point in my life when I was finding things difficult to manage. A relationship had broken down and my father was seriously ill. Writing helped me to work through those times, to put my thoughts down on paper and not carry them around in my head.

I stared down at it, at the pale-blue leather cover and yellowing pages inside, and considered throwing it out. This book held my darkest deepest thoughts.

Did I really want to discard them like a worn-out old rag?

Against my better judgement, I slotted the diary back in an empty box and placed it in a cupboard. I have mixed emotions about that book. It helped me through a tough part of my life but was also a reminder of times I would sooner forget.

I forged on, filing some things and discarding others. The more organised I became, the more settled I began to feel. It was a cathartic process and by the time I had finished, I felt renewed, like a different person.

I stood up and surveyed my work – pictures and photographs were in frames and hung on walls, books were dusted down and displayed on shelves and already the place looked more lived in. The house began to feel as if it actually belonged to me. Perhaps I would get settled in this village after all, and much sooner than I'd hoped.

I switched the radio on, poured myself a welcome glass of wine and dropped onto the sofa. I gazed around the living room, a smile spreading across my face. I was beginning to really love this old house and strangely enough, even Whitchurch itself. Despite the recent events and the fact that most of the people I had met acted as if I was the Devil incarnate, I was happy here. I laughed and took a deep glug of red wine, the rich flavour coating my tongue and blossoming in my mouth.

A strange sensation settled on me, shrouding me in its warmth. I was new to Whitchurch, yet it was as if I had actually lived here all my life.

12

The next week passed by in an uneventful blur. I took a few walks, unpacked and assembled furniture that was delivered, painted rooms and, bit by bit, felt myself becoming more and more relaxed. The tightness in my neck and shoulders, and the knot that had settled in my gut after receiving Delores' messages, began to unravel. She was still onto me, however. I received another email from her which I had yet to read. Her words could wait. I had a new life to be getting on with and reading her messages full of pity and woe didn't figure in it. She was so much like Samantha it scared me: controlling and permanently angry. Every message I got from her fuelled my belief that I had done the right thing and was well out of it. I would block her at some point, but in a warped sort of way, her pointless, desperate messages were starting to actually entertain me.

The summer holidays were still in full swing, the days long and hot, the few wispy trails of clouds that sometimes rolled in, empty. The promised rain had yet to show its face. Today was the hottest day so far and the air in the house was thick and muggy. It was too warm for walking. I decided to chance my arm in the pub. I hadn't ventured in lately and thought that I could order some food and sink a few pints, and if I got lucky, slowly ingratiate myself with the locals and not be the newcomer any more.

Lily was in her usual place behind the bar, her hair a more shocking shade of white than I remembered from last time. She had it styled in big, looping curls and her lips were painted scarlet to match her nails. She looked every inch the 1950s film star and was radiant behind the bar of a small village pub where locals scowled, supped and gossiped and barely noticed her presence. I heaved a sigh. She didn't really belong there. Nobody noticed her or seemed to care. All they wanted was beer and a corner in which to sit and moan about the government and the unfeasibly hot weather.

I strolled up to the bar, hoping my smile and easy

banter would brighten her day. She was her usual welcoming self as she took my order and handed me a menu.

'Not so busy today?' I said as I scanned the pub. There were a handful of people seated close by and a small group of locals who were sitting chatting in the corner.

'No, thank God,' she replied wearily. 'It's been really quiet, which is good as I've got the hangover from hell.'

I raised my eyebrows, feeling more like a father figure than a customer, and clicked my tongue at her. 'Oh dear. And here you are having to serve more of the stuff. Enough to turn your stomach I'll bet. Students, eh? Once you're properly grown up, you'll become more acclimatised to alcohol's devastating effects and how bloody rotten it makes you feel the day after.' I laughed and stared into her face, waiting for her response.

She gave me a withering glance and then softened and smiled. 'Yeah, but I'm a good few years younger than you so my recovery time is a lot faster than yours, Grandad.'

I laughed loudly. I liked this girl. She was clever and witty and was wasted in this place. 'Tell you what,' I said, suddenly feeling quite bold, 'I think I'm going to go and join those good folks over there.' I pointed to the crowd in the corner, some of whom I recognised from my first time in here, the very same group of people who stopped their conversation to watch me from afar. I was feeling more settled in Whitchurch, more able to withstand the contemptuous glances from the locals who thought me a spy or some sort of troublemaker. I was about to broaden their view of me, let them see who I really was.

'Good luck.' Lily laughed. 'Tough nuts to crack, that lot.' She nodded over to one of the men, who caught her eye and mouthed to her that he needed a fresh pint. 'I was just saying to Ray here that you're a right miserable bunch, aren't you?'

Her voice carried over to them and was met with a knowing smile. I loved Lily's humour and sardonic wit. She lit up a drab old building. The guy who ordered the pint looked to me and narrowed his eyes then unexpectedly pulled out a stool and nodded to me to join them. I took a deep breath and marched over, a pocket of air trapped in my chest as I sat down next to the group, who had fallen silent as I'd approached. I released a deep breath and pulled my stool in. Things were looking up.

I recognised a few of them from my first day in Whitchurch. I decided to start afresh, not hold their frosty demeanour previously shown towards me, against them. For the most part, I listened in on the conversation, inputting little apart from the odd snippet about football and rugby and steering well clear of politics. I was content enough sitting with them, chipping in when the need arose but being a bystander in the main. It gave me chance to observe my new neighbours, to work out their friendship groups and dynamics, to find out who the leaders were and figure out which of them were quite happy to be followers.

'I'm telling you, they need to confront him. He's a loose fucking cannon.' The man speaking looked at me briefly before continuing his tirade. I recognised him as the businessman who had been wearing the smart trousers and shirt a few weeks back when I first called in to the pub. His voice was clipped and determined and I pulled my chair just that bit closer so I could pick up on what he was saying.

'What proof have you got, Simon? He might have a previous record but for all we know, he could be trying to get himself on the straight and narrow again.' The man who offered me the seat spoke, his voice laced with reason and compassion. I caught his eye and he gave me a curt nod. 'They're talking about the guy up the road,' he said to me quietly. 'Gavin

Yuill. He lived here until his early twenties then moved away. Apparently, he went off the rails, got into drugs and ended up in prison for breaking and entering and battering the owner of the house half to death, after they caught him red-handed. The poor guy ended up on life support after suffering a fractured skull and numerous other injuries.'

'And now this Gavin Yuill is back living here again?' I presumed it was the same man that Alice had been shouting about last week after the carry-on with the dog shit on the cars.

'He is. His parents died and left him the house. Most of the locals hoped he would sell it but he actually decided to live in it.'

I nodded and thought about this for a second before speaking. 'Well, I guess everybody deserves a second chance. I'm Ray, by the way.' I held out my hand and caught his eye. He quickly looked away and clapped his palm against mine, shook briskly and nodded.

'I'm Davey. You'll get to know this lot in time, I'm sure.' He swept his hand over the heads of the rest of the group we were sitting with. They were talking animatedly, their voices raised as the conversation grew more and more heated.

I tuned into what they were saying, catching snippets and trying to piece it all together. Voices were raised, tempers beginning to flare, until Davey stepped in, his voice calm yet authoritative.

'Thing is, Simon, when you start talking like this, people get the wrong idea and before you know it, they're hammering at Gavin's door, demanding he move on. Or worse still, they start taking the law into their own hands and that's when things get really crazy.' Davey's words were as good as having cold water poured over the whole group. Silence fell and the ensuing air of simmering anger and resentment was so thick, you could practically grasp it with both hands.

'I take it you've been targeted as well?' Simon growled, his dark eyes cutting into me with such sharpness and intensity, I almost looked away.

'Well, I had dog dirt smeared on my car, but it soon washed off,' I replied, trying to appear unperturbed by it all.

'And a letter. You got a letter as well, didn't you?' A small, elderly man pointed at me with a bony, wizened finger.

I nodded. No point in denying it. Gossip obviously spread like wildfire in a village this size. Especially given past events. I looked at him, half expecting some sort of accusation. His features were hardened. I guessed his glum countenance came from years of working outdoors, peppered with a healthy dose of being permanently suspicious of outsiders and anybody who didn't think like he did.

'Well, we're all sorry about that. You're new here; you don't deserve to be dragged into it.' He cleared his throat as if embarrassed. I found myself admiring his honesty. Not as bitter as I initially thought.

'It's fine,' I said quietly. 'It's really not an issue.'

Nobody spoke for a few seconds until I decided to step in with my idea of who the culprit might be.

'It's the school holidays,' I ventured, clearing my throat before continuing. 'Could it be bored kids looking for something to do? They might not even live in this village. Could be teenagers from anywhere around the area.' I knew I was wading into dangerous territory with my suggestion of possible offenders. For all I knew, the people sitting next to me could have children of their own and as a teacher, I knew only too well how protective people were of their offspring, displaying animal-like tendencies when their kids were accused of any possible wrongdoing.

There was a short silence before Simon stepped in, his voice full of hostility as he spoke. 'My money's on Gavin Yuill, I'm afraid. He's got history. I knew him as a kid and he always was a nasty, selfish little shit.'

I didn't reply. Sometimes saying nothing tells you more about a person than their words ever can. Silence has its own unique power if used correctly.

The subject petered out and we spent the next hour chatting about football and a whole host of inane topics, keeping well clear of mentioning Gavin Yuill and his possible link to recent events. I ordered a meal of fish and chips which I ate heartily, leaving little room for any more drink.

Full and exhausted, I decided to leave and said my goodbyes, making sure to thank everyone for their company. Being accepted in this close-knit community was important to me. It would take time, I knew that, but every small step was a mighty achievement and I walked away feeling mildly euphoric.

'We're in here most days if you ever fancy joining us again,' Davey shouted after me. 'Especially Simon. He's a raging alcoholic. Mad as fuck as well.'

I watched Simon splutter into his beer as the rest of the crowd roared with laughter and patted Davey on the back.

I grinned and raised my hand to wave before continuing towards the door, leaving the sound of their cackling far behind me.

* * *

I napped and woke up relaxed. A feeling of deep contentment leeched into my bones, flooding my entire body with a surge of energy that soared through me in great waves. I needed to burn it off, to exert myself in some way.

I stood up, pulled on my boots and decided I would take a walk around the village and its outer reaches.

The heat rose steadily and sweat ran down my back as I walked the perimeter of Whitchurch. I wasn't going to go too far: just an amble around the nearby area. It was too hot for anything too strenuous.

I stopped by the village green and stared over at the isolated farmhouse, picturing Diane and Terence sprawled out on vast leather armchairs, a glass of brandy in hand and Schubert's 'Unfinished Symphony' playing in the background. I had no idea if that was how they lived their lives but I enjoyed letting my imagination take over, giving them a stereotypical grandiose lifestyle in my head.

Yet again, Whitchurch was disconcertingly quiet as I finished my walk and headed back home. The cries of children playing in the distance was all that could be heard as I strolled past St Oswald's then took a right turn towards the pub. I imagined the usual crowd would all still be inside, putting the world to rights and trying to fathom who the enemy was in the village – exactly who it was that seemed hell-bent on destruction.

The sun was making a slow descent by the time I got home, its rays still hot and powerful as it slid towards the horizon in a watery, amber hue. I unlocked the front door and pushed it open, the familiar ping of my phone inside indicating I had an email. My stomach tightened. A swell of tension grabbed at my insides. Delores. Again. A sixth sense had told me that was who it would be: my deluded ex-partner's mother sending me more futile messages. I slammed the door hard behind me and marched through to the kitchen where my mobile sat on the kitchen top. Tempted as I was to throw it to the ground in a fit of pique, I held it aloft, scrolling through the array of emails she had sent me. Three yesterday and another two today. As amusing as they were, I had had enough.

I slumped down into a nearby chair and opened the most recent one, my scalp prickling with indignation and fury as I read through it. I took a deep breath and read it again, letting each word slowly sink in, giving myself time to digest exactly what her message meant, to pick my way through the subliminal threats and white-hot fury that dripped from each and every sentence.

Dropping the phone back down on the kitchen top, I stared out of the window at the shadows cast by the last vestiges of the dying light outside. Tawny shadows stretched out over the lawn and crept over the red-brick wall, fingers of darkness that tugged at my emotions as I watched them closely. What Delores didn't realise was how strong I actually am. Stronger than I look, and although her daughter came across as self-assured and often feisty, I had already proved that I was the one who had the balls to walk away from it, to make the break and leave it all behind.

I clamped my teeth together and stood up, pushing my shoulders back in a deliberate act of defiance. I could handle this. Whatever Delores chose to throw at me, I could deal with it. I was a survivor with an inner core of steel. If it was a fight she was after, then she had picked on the wrong guy, because I was prepared for her and, although she may not have realised it, the one thing I never ever did was give in. I would battle on to the bitter end. So she had better be ready for me.

13

ME

They were dark times. I remember them well. Autumn had begun in earnest and the rift between me and parents grew wider by the day. They seemed to have forgotten I was just a child, that my brain was still growing, being shaped by its environment. They focused on my behaviour while entirely neglecting their own, believing themselves to be above any sort of rulebook. While attempting to mould and modify me, they forgot how to conduct themselves as decent human beings and allowed their own performances and decorum to slip, eventually becoming the very thing they saw and despised in me.

I am not qualified enough to decide whether or not their actions played a part in turning me into the monster that I am today but I am convinced of one thing – that they didn't do what it was they set out to do: to break me. If anything, I learned from them, greedily sucking up their hatred and propensity for violence. They were past masters at it, doing their best to drive the demons out of me when all the while, they were actually instilling them in me, letting evil burrow its way deep, deep into my soul.

I remember one time we had visitors – that was often the way with my father's job; our home was often a stopping point for anybody in need, a resting place for the weak and the weary. Anyway, this particular day, a local man had called in, wanting to speak to my father. I had been sent into the back room, away from the adults, away from their words which were private and not intended for my ears. I had been furious. I was sick of it – tired of being hidden away, fed up of being permanently restrained. Even at school, my mother made sure she met with the teacher almost every evening to make sure I was conforming to their needlessly rigid regime. So, this time, while my parents neglected me and chatted to their visitor, I decided to make my mark, to do something they wouldn't forget in a hurry. I snuck out of the room and took a pair of scissors from the kitchen while they spoke in hushed tones next door about matters I wasn't privy to, and returned to the dining room, a rage building inside me, towering over my sensibilities, obliterating any childish reasoning I had.

Now I know you're expecting some kind of ghoulish story next, some act of blind hatred involving wickedness and savagery after the self-harming incident and the attack on my teacher, but you must remember that I was only a small child, and you have to ask yourself, is evil born or made? I have no idea whether or not I was capable of doing anything too destructive or malicious at such a tender age. However, what I did was bad enough. This time it didn't involve injuring innocent bystanders or myself. I took my rage out on an inanimate object. I took the scissors and dug them into the sofa, enjoying the sensation of foam and fabric splitting and tearing under my touch. With limited dexterity – my hand-eye co-ordination not yet fully formed – I tore and slashed, pulling out lumps of sponge with my small fingers, spreading the interior of the cushions all over the floor. It was a sight to behold, a thing of beauty in my undeveloped mind. I didn't see it as damage, viewing it instead as a way to unleash my anger and frustrations, revelling in the carpet of white and yellow material spread at my feet.

I continued to pull and tear at the fabric until exhaustion overwhelmed me and I eventually slumped onto the floor, my small body alight with excitement and terror. Because I knew even then that what I had done was terribly wrong, but I didn't have enough willpower or self-restraint to stop myself. Or perhaps I just didn't care. I'm almost certain had another child been present, they would have tried to stop me rather than join in because other children had that cut-off point. That part of their brain that pulled them back from such acts of unadulterated destruction functioned properly in their minds, whereas mine was non-existent. But there were no other children around to stop me, just me and my anger and my utter lack of self-control.

I heard the adults making their goodbyes and listened the slamming of the front door, the thud of footsteps as my parents headed towards me, causing my skin to prickle with fear and excitement. Time seemed to stand still for those few seconds. The earth rocked precariously on its axis. I knew what was coming and experience had already taught me that it wouldn't be pretty.

The door to the dining room swung open. Oxygen swept out of my lungs. The air in the room thinned. Everything happened in slow motion, a dulling of time coupled with a sharpening of my senses. My mother's hand flew to her mouth and her shriek pierced the air, even drowning out the roar of my father's voice as he raced towards me and wrenched the scissors out of my hands, grazing my skin with his thick, sharp nails. It was all pointless really. I hadn't hurt anybody. Their reactions were disproportionate to my infantile misdemeanour.

A burning pain tunnelled through my body as my father dragged my arm upwards, lifting me up off the floor, leaving my legs dangling in mid-air. And still I didn't cry. Once again this aggravated him, sending him into a rage as he yanked me about, hollering at me that I wasn't normal, that I had ruined the furniture, that he wished I had never been born. Rather than feeling slighted or upset or rejected by his reaction, all I felt was anger and a deep sense of injustice and that was why I did what I did next. With my free hand, and despite the flames of agony that bit and burnt at my other arm, I used my small, paper-thin nails and scratched at my father's face, digging them in and trying to gouge at his eyes. The sound that emanated from his throat is one I will never forget. An animalistic visceral howl filled the room – again an overreaction, excessive and unnecessary. I was a small child. He could have easily have controlled me; instead, he chose to use the situation to display what a warped individual he really was. With the back of his hand, he slapped my face, the noise of skin hitting skin echoing throughout the room. It had the effect he had craved for so long and finally, after so many attempts to break me, he reduced me to tears. Great gulping sobs were jammed in my gullet as hysteria took hold. I thrashed about and wailed and screamed until I had no tears left in me, no energy left to cry or even care.

Now you would think, or at least hope, that my reaction would have brought him to his senses. I wish I could tell you that that was what happened. It didn't. But then, I guess you already know that, don't you? And you would also hope that my mother would have stepped in, taken me from him, saved her only child from further harm. That didn't happen either. She watched, blank-faced, as my father dragged me upstairs, cursing and swearing all the way up that I was evil, the spawn of the Devil and needed to be taught a lesson, to be purified and cleansed of the demons that lived in my soul. They fed on me, used me as their host. Allowed evil to leak out through my pores.

We got to the top and I held my breath, unable to guess at what was about to occur, unable to process the seriousness of the situation. We headed towards the small bedroom, the one that had always scared me. It was empty – no carpet, no bedroom furniture, just a bare light bulb that hung from the ceiling, casting an eerie, ominous glow throughout the room as he switched it on.

I felt myself being held at arm's length before he threw me to the floor with his big, strong arms. I hit the floorboards with a painful thud, my bones aching as I attempted to manoeuvre myself into a comfortable position, my tiny limbs grappling for purchase on the slippery lacquered floor.

I turned my face up to his and knew then that I was doomed, that all was lost. His eyes were fixed on me and all I saw in them was darkness and hatred. I had hoped for love, forgiveness, some sort of recognition that I was only a child and needed his tolerance and compassion, but instead he gave me a glowering stare, stepped back and slammed the door shut, the wood rattling in its frame. I heard the jangling scrape of metal as he turned the key, retrieved it from the lock and walked away, his footsteps fading until I could hear nothing but the thrashing of my own heartbeat as it pulsed against my ribs.

Time meant nothing to me and I had no idea whether it was midday or midnight. All I knew at that point was loneliness, fear and confusion. I curled up into a ball and closed my eyes, praying that when I awoke, I would be in my own bed, covered with blankets and no longer afraid.

The sad reality is that when I did wake up, I was still on the floor, sore and scared and lying in a puddle of my own urine. So when I talk about dark days, don't for one minute think it's hyperbole used for effect or to garner sympathy; I really do mean very dark days indeed. And believe me when I tell you that they didn't get any better. In fact, the horrors that lay ahead of me were worse than anything you could imagine. Rather than help me to become a better-behaved child, my parents did things to me that caused an ever-open wound in my mind, unleashing an inner darkness that could never be put back in its place. An inner darkness that is still present today.

14

I had got into the habit of going for early walks and was finding it both refreshing and enlightening. It was marginally cooler then, easier to tackle in the morning temperatures rather than in the ferocity of the midday heat. The woods were atmospheric and the echoing birdsong was magnificent. There were times during the day when the village was so quiet, it bordered on sinister, but there were also times, like early this morning, when Whitchurch had a completely different feel to it and you were likely to see things you wouldn't ordinarily see. And today I saw things. Not wildlife or flowers springing to life in the balminess of the gentle summer breeze. Other things. Questionable things.

I was making my way back from my walk down Church Lane when a shadow passed in front of me, the sight of it making me jump. I wasn't used to bumping into anybody and the sudden movement in my peripheral vision caught me off guard and set my heart thumping. I stepped back under the shade of the nearby hedge and watched as a figure moved out from the churchyard and through the lychgate, their shoulders hunched, a baseball cap pulled down over their face.

'Morning,' I said, my voice ringing out clearly in the calm still air. The shadow made to dart back under the lychgate but I stepped forward and blocked their way. Something about their posture and manner unnerved me, and I don't like feeling threatened or out of sorts so I made my presence known and took my chances with a lurking shadow wearing a baseball cap.

'Morning.' The reply was barely audible, a mumble from under the hat, the murmurings of somebody who didn't want to be seen.

'Nice time of day, isn't it?' I spoke briskly, determined to force them into a conversation with me. This was the first time I'd ever encountered anybody on one of my early morning walks. It was unusual. Mysterious. I was sure something was amiss with this person. Their body language screamed underhandedness and duplicitousness.

'Not too bad,' he grumbled, making to turn away from me.

Again, I moved, my body blocking the pavement. 'I'm Ray,' I said, and stuck my hand out while trying to catch his eye. The mysterious figure did his best to evade my gaze but eventually lifted his head and stared at me. I tried to not flinch at the sight of the scars that criss-crossed his face, the many red welts that covered his skin.

He glared at me then looked away, his eyes flitting everywhere but at me. I refused to give in. I stepped closer, my hand still outstretched towards him. I gave him no other option than to reciprocate.

'Now then. I'm Gavin,' he said begrudgingly. And that's when I knew. I tried to act nonchalant but the sound of his name scratched at my skin like needles repeatedly tearing at my epidermis. So, this was Gavin. At long last we had met each other. The infamous, unwanted Gavin.

'Nice to get out for an early morning stroll, isn't it? Sets me up for the day ahead.' I realised I was gabbling and repeating myself but I wanted him to hang around so I could hear his story, get to know him a little better. Everyone had a past, a tale to tell, and I wanted to hear Gavin's from him. Not the gossip that the locals peddled. I wanted the truth. I knew he wasn't about to divulge all his secrets to me here on the street after only knowing each other for a few minutes, but if I could break the ice and perhaps pave the way to become a casual acquaintance of this man, then he may well confide in me at some point in the near future. His scars also intrigued me. Nobody in the pub had mentioned his face or the scars, which was surprising considering their severity. This man had a past, and I wanted to hear it.

He shrugged and nodded, seemingly unsure of how to react. His shoulders remained hunched and every fibre of his being screamed that he wanted to get away. I wasn't about to let that happen.

'I've just moved into Whitchurch. I've not seen you in the pub at all. You don't frequent the place then?' I should have felt guilty for my words, knowing how his presence would be treated at The Pot and Glass, but I didn't. My curiosity was high. What exactly was his background and, more importantly, why was he skulking around the church so early in the morning?

There was a short silence as he gazed at the floor.

His voice was gruff with resentment when he spoke. 'I wouldn't be welcome in there. Not my sort of place anyway. I'd rather drink at home.'

'Well, I'd welcome you in there, Gavin. I've only recently moved here and new friends are always nice to have.' My voice was croaky. I tried to convey an element of sympathy in my tone, sympathy I didn't necessarily feel. My driving force was curiosity.

'Maybe,' he said quietly, and kicked a few stones around the floor with his scruffy-looking trainers.

'Okay, tell you what,' I replied a little too buoyantly. 'Why don't I give you my number and if you ever change your mind, just give me a call and we'll go for a pint.' I pulled out an old receipt and searched for a pen to scribble my number on the back of it. I tapped at my pockets, realising they were empty, and stared at Gavin. He looked at me blankly and shook his head, then made to walk away.

'Hang on!' I called after him as he took a few steps away from me. 'I'll drop it through your letter box. What number do you live at?'

He hesitated and for a brief moment, I thought he might be about to tell me to take my fake concern and attempts at being friendly and shove them where the sun don't shine. It wouldn't matter. I could easily find out which house he lived at by asking around the pub. We both knew he wouldn't want that. We stood for a second or two, and in that short space of time, we were able to read each other perfectly, to see inside one another's heads and navigate our way around each other's thoughts. It was an unnerving moment and one that I longed to end.

'Right, well, I live at number ten. But as I said, they're a funny lot in that pub and they don't like me. Too many bad memories and not enough forgiveness, so don't hold your breath about that drink.' He nodded at me and walked away.

This time I let him go, watching as shuffled along before disappearing around the corner out of sight. I was torn between feeling irritated by him and feeling a small amount of pity for his plight. We all had our issues and problems. Gavin would just have to come to terms with his. It had been his choice to move back here. I guessed he should have expected some kind of backlash from locals who had stupendously long memories and horribly short levels of clemency and compassion. Unless, of course, they were right and we all had every reason to be wary of him. Only time would tell on that score.

I shoved my hands in my pockets and walked towards home, knowing I would definitely contact him. Whether it was out of a sense of duty or loneliness, I felt obliged to befriend him. And I wanted to do it sooner rather than later.

15

The exterior of Gavin's house was much like any other. There were no defining features that screamed *a criminal lives here!* Nothing that made it stand out from any of the other houses in the village.

I strode up the gravel path, stopped in front of the door and pushed through a piece of paper with my number written on it. I listened to the slight whisper of noise as it gently fell on the doormat on the other side and wondered if Gavin was there, watching it, waiting to tear it up, or alternatively stuff it somewhere safe with the intention of looking at it later.

After our meeting, I had gone home and had some breakfast and thought about whether or not I should pass my details on to him. Gavin Yuill was a person whose reputation preceded him; I could have been making a huge mistake, although my gut instinct told me I was definitely doing the right thing. I'd only taken a short while to come to a decision. The friendship could be beneficial for both of us. Gavin was lonely and I was interested in his background. I don't mind admitting that everyone's hatred for him fascinated me. You could say I was drawn to his propensity for wickedness. So I marched down the road to his house and posted my number through his door. I always did like to court controversy. I also didn't like being told who I could and couldn't socialise with by people who barely knew me. I was a grown man. I would do as I damn well pleased.

I stood for a few seconds, wondering if he was inside. The curtains were open but I couldn't hear anything from within. I debated knocking but thought better of it. I didn't know the guy and certainly didn't want to come across as some sort of stalker after pestering him earlier. He'd only agreed to letting me do this because I'd badgered him into it, so instead I turned, ready to head back down the path, only to be met with the angry, puckered face of a woman I recognised. Her ruddy complexion was even redder than the last time I'd seen her and her hair bobbed about like a huge, black mane as she pushed her way towards me and attempted to barge past. I pulled my shoulders back and made myself bigger than I actually was.

'Alice, isn't it?' I tried to keep my voice as affable as possible, to try and defuse a situation that was obviously brewing. 'I recognise you from a few days back. Ray?' I said gently, and held my hand out, hoping it would soften her resolve.

I obviously caught her by surprise as she suddenly became deeply flustered and unsure of what to do next. I had stopped her and taken the wind out of her sails, which was good. It didn't take a genius to see that she was hell-bent on some sort of confrontation with Gavin. Meeting with somebody in that frame of mind was a bad idea. She lacked any clarity of thought and her logic was being fuelled by raw anger.

'Yes, I'm Alice,' she said through gritted teeth, the words spat out at me as she moved again to force her pay past. I was too fast for her. I dropped my outstretched arm then moved my body in front of her diminutive frame, disguising my step as an inadvertent lean to one side to listen to what it was she had to say.

'I thought so,' I replied with a smile. 'I've just been for a walk around the village and I have to say, I'm so pleased I made the decision to move here. I did have my doubts initially as it was so far away from where I lived, but I've discovered some fantastic walks and seen some gorgeous scenery. I suppose you know the area well, do you, Alice?' I was rambling – we both knew it – but she at least did me the courtesy of listening and looking if not interested then at least not wholly bored.

'Well enough,' she said. It was clear her anger was still bubbling, threatening to spill over at any second as her face grew hotter and hotter. 'Well enough to know when somebody has done something abhorrent, and that... bastard in there has done something terrible, so if you wouldn't mind moving aside so I can speak to him?'

I continued smiling, using my best rictus grin, and raised my eyebrows, only too aware that this could annoy the shit out of her, but I refused to step away to let her through. I had turned into an immovable object and wondered what her next move would be, whether she would elbow her way past or give up, turn around and leave.

'Can I ask what it is you think Gavin has actually done?' The words that came out of my mouth felt too big for my throat. She had stepped forward and was so close, I could feel the heat emanating from her rosacea-covered face and smell the stale odour that clung to her unwashed, wiry hair.

'Go to the churchyard and see for yourself.' Spittle flew out of her mouth, tiny flecks and bubbles of saliva popping and bursting in front of my face. I took a small step back and watched her as the anger almost consumed her, making her forget all about social niceties and graces when speaking to near strangers.

I stared at her, studying her face as she ranted and raged. She was verging on some kind of meltdown and I got the distinct feeling she was also angry at me, or perhaps she was simply so wound up and consumed by fury that anybody who got in her way was going to be a witness to an explosion of ferocity and rage of monolithic proportions.

'Perhaps another time,' I said, my head now beginning to ache. What had begun as an early stroll was fast turning into an irritating farce. I couldn't stop this irate woman from knocking on Gavin's door but I could cause a diversion. At least, I could try. 'Or maybe if you'd like, you could take me there and show me what this is all about? Perhaps I could help in some way?'

I didn't expect a positive response from her; she was too far gone, a long way down the path of blind fury, trampling everything and everyone who got in her way. But to my surprise, she stopped, took a long, shuddering breath and stared at me, blinking hard. The cloud of suspicion and doubt that filled her eyes rapidly cleared, a flicker of hope evident in her expression. 'Well, I suppose you could. It's awful, you know. And as for Dominic! That poor man is in there trying to clean it all off on his own and—'

'Come on,' I said, doing my utmost to appear calm and compassionate. 'Why don't we both go and see what we can do for Reverend Baudin?' Gently taking her elbow, I guided her out of Gavin's front garden and we walked down the road towards St Oswald's, chatting and smiling together like old friends.

16

Alice's demeanour and general mood had begun to soften, losing its sharp, jagged edges, becoming much smoother as we walked past The Pot and Glass and headed towards the church spire that beckoned us from a distance. I had kept my voice even and low and steered her in the direction of neutral subjects such as the extreme weather and the general history of the village in the hope it would have a calming effect on her raging disposition. It seemed to work. She delighted in telling me all about the Saxon settlements in the area and regaled me with tales of the summer of 1976 when people were banned from washing cars and told to limit toilet flushing to just a couple of times a day.

By the time we reached the lychgate, she wasn't exactly a pussycat, but she was a far cry from the demonic woman I had encountered outside Gavin's house just six or seven minutes earlier. She did, however, continue to moan about Gavin's past and criminal record as we walked and informed me she was sure he was responsible for all the damage that had been caused in the village, but on the plus side, she no longer appeared to want to tear Gavin or me from limb from limb.

'What about his scars?' I asked tentatively, my whole body braced for another onslaught of anger from this tiny lady with a towering temper. 'I saw him earlier this morning when I was out walking,' I added quickly as she stared up at me quizzically. I didn't add that he had been emerging from the churchyard when I bumped into him. That would undoubtedly send her into a frenzy.

'Fighting in prison from what I heard,' Alice replied, with more than a hint of smugness in her tone. 'He didn't have them when he lived here, that much I do know. Maybe he got what he deserved while he was inside.'

I nodded at her reply, not exactly satisfied with the vitriolic tone in which it was delivered, but aware that her answer made perfect sense. Prisons were hardly the friendliest of places and I was under no illusions that violence was rife in many of them.

We walked further into the churchyard, a cool breeze blanketing us as we dipped our heads to walk underneath the low-lying branch of an overhanging cherry tree.

'There,' she said, her stout finger outstretched towards a row of gravestones that I could see had been badly desecrated. Crouching next to the row of marble slabs was Dominic Baudin, his back to us, his head dipped as if he were conducting a serious sermon. I took a deep breath and watched his movements before looking back at Alice. She raised her eyebrows in consternation at the scene before us and pursed her lips tightly, nodding that we should go and help.

I walked towards the crouched vicar, hardly daring to breathe, watching as his body shuffled from side to side, his hands working furiously at something in front of him.

'Dominic,' I whispered.

He was deep in thought and was obviously alarmed by my unexpected presence. His head swung around and for a second, I could tell he had no memory of ever meeting me. Why should he? I was almost certain he saw lots of new faces in his line of work and I was simply another of them. But then something clicked and his expression changed from one of shock and moroseness to an openness that looked so welcoming and innocent, it made my insides flip.

'Ah, hello there...'

'Ray,' I said, quickly filling the gap to save his embarrassment.

'Ray,' he quickly chimed. 'Of course! Ray. We met on the village green.'

I thought of my promise to attend the service on Sunday and felt my face grow warm.

'We did indeed. Seems we always meet under upsetting circumstances, Dominic.' I shifted my eyes away from his and stared at the gravestones where he knelt. His body cast a small shadow over the bucket of soapy water sitting by his side. Droplets of white foam clung to the rim and spilled over the edge, running in slow, snaking lines down the side of the shiny orange plastic.

He stood up and wiped his big hands down the front of his jeans, then took a step forward. Alice acted like a buffer, appearing in front of me as if from nowhere, her voice turning into a shriek as she flung herself at Dominic, big fat tears bursting out of her eyes, her face once again an unearthly shade of scarlet as her words hit the air like a sonic boom.

'Oh my word, Dominic! I still can't believe this has happened. It's all so awful.' Her voice shattered the near silence of the graveyard, bouncing off huge, sturdy tree trunks and whistling through the leaves above us. I found myself wondering how badly she would react in a situation that was truly traumatic, and hid my smile. I sensed that Alice revelled in the histrionics and gaining comfort from Dominic's gentle words and soft, welcoming arms.

He nodded his head and reached out to placate her, resting his arm over her small, heaving shoulders that shook with every sob. 'Come on now, Alice. Let's not get upset all over again. What's done is done. We need to think about how best to move forward from all of this, don't we?'

Alice nodded, grabbed a tissue from the pocket of her cardigan and sniffed miserably. 'I've called the police. Enough is enough, Dominic. They said somebody should be out later to take a statement. Probably one of those PCSO people, but anybody is better than nobody, aren't they?'

I couldn't swear to it, but I thought I detected a small eye roll from the exhausted-looking vicar. He exhaled softly and extricated himself from the sobbing bundle beside him. He bent down again to examine the words daubed on the headstones with blood-red paint. An inappropriate mark: an incompatible scarlet smear next to the smooth paleness of the stones and surrounding foliage.

'From the snares of the Devil.' My voice was a hoarse whisper as I read the words sprayed on the stones; each utterance was thick in my throat, sticking to my gullet like flypaper. I swallowed and turned away.

Dominic coughed and picked up the brush from the bucket. He began to scrub again at the sandstone, his hand moving in a large circular motion as he tried to erase the words beneath the soap and water. Even from where I was standing, I could see that his efforts were futile: a small attempt at removing the immovable.

'We need CCTV around this place,' Alice wailed from behind her ragged, wet tissue. 'The whole village needs cameras so we can prove once and for all who's behind all these crimes.' She blew her nose hard, the noise she made from behind the tissue sounding like a distorted foghorn.

We all stood for a short while in the cool of the large churchyard. Leaves suddenly rustled, a gust of warm wind pulling at them. Birds hidden in high branches sang, but nobody spoke. Our eyes were drawn to those words, large and unmissable, loaded with malice in an area that exuded calm, hatred and spite in abundance in a secluded space that was supposed to be a place of peace. The silence stretched on and on until eventually, I spoke. I felt sure somebody had to inject something into the protracted, uncomfortable air of nothingness that was making me uneasy.

'When did this happen?' My voice rang across the top of the slabs of stone and ricocheted off the shadowy north wall of St Oswald's.

Dominic stopped scrubbing and wiped at his forehead with the back of his free hand. He turned to face me and closed his eyes for a second to think. 'I got here at nine o'clock and it was here then, so any time before that. Could have been sometime last night after I left, or early this morning.'

I nodded and bit at my lip, unsure of whether or not I should say anything. Deciding to leave things as they were, I remained silent about my encounter with Gavin Yuill earlier that morning. Hearing it would probably tip Alice over the edge and poor Dominic would have to calm her down once more. I also didn't think I could handle another of her screaming episodes. Saying nothing was definitely the most sensible option. For now.

'You might want to leave that for the police to see,' I half shouted, although from what I could tell, Dominic could scrub until the cows came home and he still wouldn't remove that paint. He was wasting his energy. It would take a shedload of chemicals to get rid of those ghastly words.

He didn't turn around and instead shook his head and carried on scouring the stone, his body shifting back and forth as he put his back into it, determined to blot out the hatred and harm that now permeated his holy ground, his place of work and worship. And the one thing that crossed my mind as I took Alice's arm and guided her out of that place was that if this could happen to the dead and the blessed and divine, then nothing was sacred and nobody was safe.

* * *

Alice Milburn was all bluff and bluster. Beneath the outrage and the tears and the near hysteria lay a woman who was quite simply exhausted, scared and in need of some guidance as to how she should deal with the turmoil currently unfolding in her village.

We spoke as we walked out of the church and

back towards home, Alice surprisingly candid and open about life in Whitchurch, giving me plenty of background information on its residents.

'The people in the pub, the regulars, they're all okay really,' she said as we spotted the squat building in the distance with its pale-green, antiquated sign proclaiming the pub's existence to passers-by.

'Davey and Simon?' I enquired. 'I've met them and they seem like good guys.'

Alice gave me a half smile and then shook her head as if to challenge my opinion. 'Davey's my neighbour and he's a good person to have around. Always reliable. He's a landscape gardener and sometimes I pay him to look after the trees at the bottom of my lawn. A hard worker and always on time.'

'And Simon?' I asked, suddenly spurred on by her face, by the lines of discontent that had settled around her mouth at the mention of his name.

'Simon is a childish individual,' she said sourly. 'He calls himself a financial advisor, telling everyone he's an expert in his field, but the only bit of advising he does is from the bar stool in the pub. His working day finishes shortly after lunchtime and he can be found propping up the bar by 2 p.m. As lazy and stupid as the day is long, if you ask me.'

I shrugged, unsure why Alice would be so offended by this. Weren't Simon's working hours his concern?

She spoke again, as if reading my thoughts. 'He advised me to move some of my savings and they're now worth less than they were two years ago. The man is a drunken idiot. The only thing he is an expert at is ruining his liver and spouting rubbish to anyone who'll listen.'

Suddenly, I understood her dislike of him. He had made a dent in her finances, which, judging by her appearance, weren't huge, and she was still furious with him. And Alice did have a point. From what I'd seen, Simon came across as immature and crass and spent an inordinate amount of time in the pub.

'And what about you?' I asked, keen to hear her story. She seemed unhealthily emotional, her moods oscillating at the slightest provocation, and although I didn't know her, she appeared to be overly attached to Dominic and his church.

'Me?' Alice half shrieked, shocked at my sudden interest in her private life.

'Yes, Alice, you. You seem to be an integral part of this community. I was just curious as to how you spend your days.' My voice rose in pitch as I spoke, a humorous urgency in my tone.

She looked up to me and grinned, the rose-coloured hue of her cheeks deepening even further. An almost infinitesimal twinkle took hold of her eyes as she let out a small sigh and spoke. 'Well, I live alone. My husband died some years ago and I spend most of my days at the church or with Dominic at the Rectory.'

I raised my eyebrows and gave her a knowing grin. 'Really? Do you indeed? Well, well, well.'

She reached out and gave me a playful slap on my arm. Her hands were small and puffy and lined with pale-green veins that bulged and snaked under her pink skin. 'Cheeky! I'm Dominic's housekeeper. I work for the church.'

'Right,' I said with a half laugh. 'Of course you do. I knew that.'

She smiled, then shook her head at me as we walked along together, past the village green and the pub until we reached a small lane that curved to the right of us. Alice stopped abruptly.

'Well, this is where I live,' she said as she pointed over to a small bungalow that was tucked behind a neatly clipped privet. A modest building with no outstanding or defining features, it was dwarfed by larger houses on either side of it and suited her perfectly.

I looked down at this strange lady beside me, with her dowdy, brown clothes and ruddy complexion, trying to work out what her age was. I guessed she was only in her early to mid-fifties and yet looked and acted so much older.

'Well, it's been lovely chatting to you Alice,' I said and held out my hand.

Another sudden fluster overcame her, her face turning an even deeper painful shade of pink as she grabbed my palm and shook it forcefully. Her flesh was cold and dry, unlike her face, which looked like a permanent furnace was raging just beneath her skin.

'Thank you, Ray. For being so kind, I mean. Pity there aren't more men like you in the village. Apart from Dominic, Davey and a tiny handful of others, this place wouldn't be worth living in.' She shook her head pitifully and took a deep and dramatic breath before marching up the path, turning to give me a final wave and closing the door behind her.

17

ME

School should have been my saving grace. Despite my rocky start, and my initial overwhelming feelings at being abandoned, I settled in, and although I didn't exactly make friends or have any special people I thought I was close to, I had peers I played with. Sadly, they were not enough to make my days any brighter. The teachers knew my parents and had already been informed of my difficult behaviour at home. They were told almost daily how unmanageable I was and as a result, began to believe it. My parents, you see, were austere people, folk who were taken seriously within the local community. People not to be messed with.

And so, my every move was closely observed and monitored. I was a lab rat, a being who could be controlled, manipulated and steered along a certain path. Or so they thought. Unwittingly, what they really succeeded in doing was turning me into the person I am today – someone who refuses to be ground down, a person who feels aggrieved and is driven to wreak havoc on the world that wronged them.

One particular day, I was kept back after class for an incident that shouldn't have been categorised as anything but ended up being everything. A child had taken something from me – I don't remember what, perhaps something as simple and unimportant as a piece of paper – and I had taken it back. A scuffle ensued: a harmless, childish scuffle that should have been handled properly by the adults present, but wasn't. The scuffle turned into something more ominous, something almighty and ghastly simply because they expected it to. My reputation preceded me.

The other child refused to let me have the object back even though I had had it first. I pushed them and they fell backwards, their head hitting the floor with a sharp crack. Perhaps my reputation was well-deserved because while all the other children cried and shrieked, I felt nothing. Just a hollowness where fear and shame should have been. I remember standing over the child, staring at them, fascinated by the bloom of blood that oozed from their head, being vaguely amused at the twitch of their fingers and the fluttering of their eyes as they lay on the ground before me.

Then mayhem ensued. Adults dragged children away, the noise level reached a shrieking crescendo, and I was violently hauled up off my feet by a furious teacher who, much like my father, felt it was perfectly acceptable to grasp me with force and scream in my face.

An ambulance was called. I was blamed. The other child was too injured for anybody to even consider getting their version of events. It emerged that they needed sutures for the wound on their head and had a seizure in the ambulance on the way to the hospital.

Nobody asked what happened or why I pushed them or what the starting point was for the incident. Nobody. After countless attempts by my parents to paint me as a misfit, a social pariah, everybody was only too happy to go with that narrative. It was easier than carrying out any basic investigative work and unearthing the truth. I was an easy target. And so, the vicious circle of my life finally completed itself that day. Everybody knew. They had all witnessed my capacity for evil, seen how damaged I was, what it was I was actually capable of. That was the day when it became perfectly acceptable for me to be treated like a second-class citizen, an outcast, for my parents to think it absolutely normal behaviour when they pinned me down and tried to drive the Devil out of me. And nobody told them it was unacceptable – none of their friends or people in positions of authority. In fact, some of them even assisted. I was a bad child, a deviant who had to be stopped.

So, when I tell you that I am a deeply damaged individual, you have to ask yourself, as I have for many, many years, who caused the damage? Was I born that way or was badness thrust upon me? Or is the answer to that question just too complex to analyse? There are so many elements to a person, layer upon layer that make up the very essence of our souls, and in between those layers and woven into those strands are our experiences and memories that become trapped, defining who we really are, or to be precise, who we will become. And it is what I have become that we need to focus on here – what I turned into after the horrors of my childhood.

And that is why I do the things I do. Because I

know no other way. It is all part of who I am. Does that make sense to you? No, I don't suppose it does, but then why should it? Looked at from a neutral perspective, none of my life makes any sense. I don't doubt for one minute that you are all good, caring people. Unlike me, because I am rotten to the core. We are oceans apart, you and I. Oceans apart.

Anyway, I just knew that seeing my parents that evening would be something I wouldn't forget in a hurry. And I was right. After my previous transgressions, they had insisted we all pray together every evening for hours at a time. Not in the usual sense, as in a gathering of people chanting their own silent wishes or giving praise to the Lord above for His goodness, but more of a forced mantra where I was held fast on a pew and told to repent for my sins.

However, this time my father took his religious tactics to a whole new level. His belief that I was evil obliterated any common sense that may have stopped him from doing what he did next. And I would have hoped that his job as a vicar, a senior member of the clergy, would have instilled in him some sort of responsibility, a sense of compassion that held him back from what was an act of cruelty, an occurrence that was so breathtakingly brutal and unethical, it bordered on madness. But it didn't. I had embarrassed him. Yet again, I had brought shame upon our family, and he couldn't live with that. He couldn't allow his good name to be tarnished, dragged into the gutter by his own child, so he set about stopping it by any means necessary. Any means, which even included exorcising his own child.

18

I didn't expect to see her. It was a warm morning, even hotter than the previous few days, and her being there was completely out of context. I had been for my usual early walk and was on my way home when I bumped into her. She wasn't wearing any make-up and her hair was scraped back into a severe bun. Her mind was clearly elsewhere and I think we were both caught unawares, our thoughts focused on other things, our minds locked onto more pressing matters.

I was behind the church, chilled in its dark shadow and on my way back into the village, and she was coming around the bend, her head dipped, her hands pushed into the pockets of her low-slung, tight-fitting jeans. I almost decided to leave her be, to let her pass me by, but something about her gait made me think she could possibly benefit from seeing a friendly face so instead I moved forward and made my presence known to her.

'Lily?' I said quietly.

A second or two passed with no response. It felt much longer than that brief period and I considered walking away before any awkwardness could settle in. I didn't want to run the risk of spoiling our recently formed friendship. Then she looked at me, her head snapping up, her eyes widening at being seen and I was taken aback to see she had been crying. Strong-minded, witty Lily standing here in front of me, weeping. Her eyes were glassy and swollen and her skin had an uncharacteristic rosy sheen about it. My immediate instinct was to cough politely and back away. That was what I should have done. Instead, I stepped closer to her, tilted my head to one side and spoke softly.

'What's wrong?' My words sounded hollow, laced with faux concern. I didn't know what else to do except ask and then wait for a response.

She blinked repeatedly and rubbed at her eyes with the back of her hand, shaking her head as if trying to erase the tears and misery from her face. 'Oh, honestly, it's nothing. Nothing at all.' She looked up and down the lane, her gaze sweeping over the road and into every nook and cranny. She surveyed every high hedge and gnarled tree stump as if searching for people who might be hiding, ready to creep out and catch her out, to see her at her weakest and publicly shame her.

'You're out early,' I said, knowing it was a useless platitude. I wasn't good at this sort of thing and was desperately clutching at the right thing to say.

She shrugged and let a small sob escape, her chest rumbling with the force it. Her eyes rested just above my shoulder. 'I had an argument with my parents and needed to get out of the house for a bit.'

'Ah,' I murmured as I nodded sagely. 'Families, eh?'

She didn't reply. I said nothing. We stood for a few seconds. Her perfectly white teeth tugged at a loose piece of skin on her lower lip. I was just about to give her another hopeless and utterly inept piece of advice to fill the awkward silence between us when she spoke. 'Mine isn't like any other family, I can assure you.'

I almost reached out and touched her arm but thought better of it. The age gap between us was too vast to allow such an aberration. I would lose her friendship, her trust, and I didn't want that. 'We all say that, Lily, but whether you like it or not, every family has its problems and they often feel unsurmountable, but generally speaking, they're not. We all find our ways to deal with them, to put right the wrongs and allow ourselves to live our lives without constantly worrying about the harm caused by family arguments.' I thought of Delores and shivered.

'And how would you know?' Her voice was clipped, her eyes suddenly full of fire. Her chin quivered and her mouth was pursed into a thin, determined line.

I sucked in a lungful of muggy air and shrugged my shoulders. 'I'm a bit older than you and have experience is what I'm saying, I suppose. My family, for instance—'

'Don't try to compete, or attempt to tell me your own pathetic stories about how fucked up your family is. And what the hell do you know about me and my family? Who the fuck are you to lecture me when we barely know each other?' A flush crept up her neck and her fingers twitched as her words came tumbling out, hot and raw and full of sharp edges, cutting into the calm, tranquil ambience of the early morning air. 'You know nothing about me and you know even less about my mum and dad. Especially my dad. He's nothing but a bully. A big fucking useless pathetic bully.'

I took a step back and raised my hands in mock surrender. She shook her head and moved forward, towards me. I remained silent. Then she lowered her head and let out a small moan of despair.

I watched slow, silent tears roll down her face and drip onto her top, and stood motionless, unsure of what to do next. Did she want me to speak? To comfort her? Or would she rather I backed away and left her to cry in peace?

We were held in a spell that I was loath to break. I couldn't simply walk away and leave her like this. So I stepped closer, a breath suspended in my chest, a slight flutter in my abdomen, and placed my arm around her shoulders. She initially froze, her body stiff with anxiety, then without warning she burst into tears. Her body was racked with huge sobs as she leant against me and cried over and over until she eventually burnt herself out, her warm tears wetting my shirt and smearing over my skin. Lily's chest rose and fell repeatedly as she gasped for breath and tried to compose herself. I said nothing. Silence seemed more fitting.

We stayed like that for at least a minute. It was an eternity. I felt the heat from her body, the warmth of her breath on my neck, soft and sweet as it filtered up to my face. She shifted to get closer. Her small breasts pushed against my chest. My arm trailed down her back and hung by her waist. I felt a stirring in my groin and closed my eyes before snapping them open then gently pushing her away from me.

'Come on,' I said, my voice sounding as if it was coming from somebody other than me. 'Let's wipe your eyes and get you sorted.'

I pulled an old cotton handkerchief out of my pocket and handed it to her. She ran it over her face and blew her nose.

'Keep it, 'I said as she tried to hand it back. 'Plenty more at home.'

'Sorry,' she muttered feebly. Her eyes bulged with sorrow. Even in the midst of a breakdown, she looked breathtakingly beautiful. Her radiance shone through her distress.

'For what?' I whispered.

'For swearing at you. No need. No need at all.' Her bottom lip quivered and I pictured myself licking it, pictured her lay next to me naked, our warm skin pressed together.

Jesus Ray, stop it!

'There's every need. For all I know, your dad may well be the biggest twat known to man.'

She laughed and more tears fell, rolling down her face, glassy orbs falling across silk. 'God, I feel like such a big baby, crying like this. I can't seem to stop. It's me who feels like a right twat.'

Even when she cried, Lily still had the ability to turn heads, to make grown men like me stop in the street and stare at her. I doubted she knew it. Women like her rarely did. Her skin was smooth and creamy like porcelain, her lashes dark and seductive. I sucked in a breath. What the fuck was I thinking? She was young. Too young for me. I guessed half my age. Too large a gap; a boundary that should never be crossed unless you're a celebrity or a politician and happy to have a young model hanging off your arm for photo shoots.

'Anyway,' she sniffed, 'I'd better be off. Got an early shift at the pub.' She looked at me, as if waiting for my reply.

I didn't speak. What I wanted to say was that she should move out away from her parents and move in with me. I wanted to tell her that I'd love to fuck her. Thankfully, the words didn't come. They lodged in my throat, almost choking me. I tried to think of other things – football, cars, rock music. Anything but Lily.

We continued to watch each other, assessing, scrutinising, wondering where to go from here.

'Right, well I'd better get moving as well,' I said at long last. 'Always loads to be getting on with in an old house.' That wasn't true. I had done all I intended to do for the time being.

'I might see you later in the pub, then?' She looked hopeful. My blood ran hot, spreading though my veins like lava.

I smiled and nodded. 'Why not? A cold pint in this heat could be just what I need.' A cold beer was exactly what I needed at that point to cool my raging ardour and lust.

'The usual crew will be in there,' she added with a smile, 'but don't let that put you off.'

I laughed. 'Ah, like you said, once you get used to them, they're not so bad. Not a bad bunch at all.'

She nodded and another silence descended. Our eyes were locked together.

She knows what you were thinking!

Desperate to appear gentleman-like, I shifted my gaze over to a row of trees in the distance, focused on their shape, studied the vibrancy of their colour. Anything to keep my mind off Lily and her hot breath on my bare flesh.

'Right,' I said finally, 'I'll let you go. Might see you later though.'

I watched her features. She seemed happy with

that. Not repulsed by the older man, not disgusted by our age gap. Happy.

'I'll keep an eye out for you and have a pint at the ready.' Her voice trailed over my skin, sensual, seductive. 'Oh, and Ray?'

I waited, feeling on edge if I'm being truthful, wondering what she was about to say, wondering if she had read my mind. I like to think I'm a closed book, but we all have our weak points, don't we? Chinks in our armour that let the light in and the secrets out.

'Yes?' My voice came out as a definite squeak. I cleared my throat and braced myself for what she was about to say.

She gave me a toothy grin, her large, wet eyes glistening in the sunlight that filtered in through the gaps in the trees above us. 'I still mean every word that I said about my dad. For a man of the cloth, he's a real nasty bastard. A horrible, horrible fucker.'

19

Lily's words should have shocked me. They didn't. If anything, they added to her appeal, gave her a bit of grit and heightened my attraction to her. She was a tough young thing, well rounded and ready to stand her ground. I admired that in her, saw it as a redeeming feature. She had charisma and whether I liked it or not, I was drawn to her.

All the way back, I tried to block her out of my thoughts. I would go home, eat, hang around the house, potter in the garden and go to the pub. I would sit with the people in there – Davey if he was in, and Simon – and I would make small talk and not think about the eighteen-year-old serving behind the bar. I was thirty-seven, more than twice her age. It was unthinkable. So rather than lust after the young barmaid, I would drink and talk and then drink some more, pushing all thoughts of Lily to the back of my mind.

I saw the figure as I drew closer to home; they were tall, and wearing a dark hat, a short-sleeved shirt and a high-vis jacket. And standing at my door. I stopped, my heartbeat a thick pulse that travelled up my throat, pushing at my skin, constricting my windpipe and stopping me from breathing properly. My scalp prickled as I neared the house. Why was he there? Why would a police officer be standing knocking at my door?

I could hear the rap of his knuckles as he hit the wood, a hard, dull thump that echoed around the village. In no time at all, curtains would twitch, people would saunter out to wash cars or clean windows and mow lawns. There was always a job to be done outside when there was gossip to be had, something out of the ordinary going on in the vicinity. I picked up my pace, eager to reach him, and was behind the tall figure before his knuckles hit the door for a second time.

'Can I help you?' For somebody whose job it was to carry out investigative work and have a keen eye, he seemed shocked by my appearance, jumping visibly as my voice came from behind him.

He swung around, eyes wide and face lined with shock as I strode up to him, pushed past and shoved my key in the lock.

It didn't take long for him to regain control, for his authoritative air to restore itself. He appeared to grow another three inches as he tugged at his hat and shoved his shoulders back. He smiled at me and spoke sharply. 'Yes. You live here, I take it?'

I was tempted to say no, to pretend my key didn't fit and smile at him helplessly. I didn't. Instead, I nodded amiably and opened the door, nodding for him to go inside. He held out his arm to indicate I should go first. I entered and he followed me, our shadows merging into one bulky mass as we headed though the hallway into the kitchen.

'You're Ray?' he said as he removed his hat and placed it on the table. Without asking, he dragged a chair out and sat down, the wooden legs scraping across the flagstone floor, the noise repellent to me, causing my skin to shrink and stick to my bones like clingfilm.

'Yes,' I replied. 'Can I ask what the problem is?'

He smiled and ran his hand through his hair. The day had barely begun and already drops of sweat lined his face and formed an arc around his hairline, tiny iridescent pearls of perspiration that glistened against his tanned skin. He was lean but his body was bulked out by his police vest. I was wearing thin clothes and the heat was unforgiving. I imagined a police uniform would push a body to its limits with so many thick layers, the fabric heavy and dark with starched edges and creases so sharp, you could cut through stone with them. Hardly the best outfit for a hot summer's day. An inferno raged on his reddened face as he took a handkerchief out of his pocket and dabbed at his brow.

Without asking, I poured us both a glass of water and watched as he thanked me and glugged it back gratefully. It was the least I could do.

He set the glass down and met my eyes. 'I spoke to a Mrs Alice Milburn earlier. We have a report of some damage and vandalism at St Oswald's. Gravestones defaced with spray paint?'

'Ah. Yes, sorry,' I said. My chest loosened and my pulse stopped its wild thrashing as I sat down next to him. 'I'd forgotten about that. She did say she'd called the police yesterday when I spoke to her.'

He took this as some sort of slight, bristling visibly at my words. 'Well, Ray, we take all calls seriously but with it being a low-level incident – no casualties as such – we sometimes take a bit longer to investigate. Anyway,' he went on, 'I was just wondering if you could tell me anything about it?'

I was curious as to why he had come to me and whether he'd already tried to speak to Gavin Yuill and got no response. I imagined the sight of a police officer at Gavin's door would be enough to send him scuttling behind the sofa where he would hide out, ignoring the hammering and knocking at his front door. Or maybe he had fled out the back door and was currently way out of reach, on a bus to somewhere else, cursing this village and wondering when everybody would stop dredging up his past and blaming him for every single minor crime and misdemeanour that happened around here.

'I spoke to Alice and accompanied her to the church,' I said. 'She was upset, obviously. I'm not sure what it is you want from me.' Flashes of Gavin skulking out of the churchyard that morning filled my mind – images of him trying to sneak past me. I could tell this police officer, spill the beans. With Gavin's track record, they would have him arrested in no time, hauled into the station and cautioned for criminal damage. The quiet life he worked hard to preserve would be in tatters.

'Mrs Milburn said you were at the door of a certain Mr Yuill when she met you. I was just interested as to why you were there?'

I eyed him cautiously, tried to work out what he was getting at. Did he think I was Gavin's accomplice? More to the point, did Alice see me as some sort of suspect? If she wanted to know why I was trying to see Gavin, why didn't she just ask?

'Well, PC...?' I stopped, my tone suggestive of an introduction. He was here, in my house, and I had no idea of his name or rank. I should have asked earlier. In fact, he should have told me. Without knowing who he was, I should not have let him in.

'PCSO Greening,' he said, and I watched with a certain degree of satisfaction as a web of crimson crept up his neck, stopping at the tips of his ears, which glowed bright red, his skin shiny and raw like dead meat. I didn't know whether to pity him or tell him to leave for being so inept.

'Okay, well, as I was saying, PCSO Greening, I was putting my number through Gavin's door when Alice saw me.' I didn't offer any more information. If he wanted to know, he would have to ask. I wasn't on trial here.

Greening slowly turned to look out of the window at the pale stretch of garden, the once lush grass now straw-coloured and dry, bleached and parched by the relentless heat and lack of rain. Blue tits and chaffinches fluttered around the bird feeder, their tiny, perpetually moving wings a distraction to the awkward atmosphere that had suddenly descended. His eyes remained on the feeding birds as he spoke. His deep, rumbling voice was like shifting gravel in the silence of the room. 'And can I ask why you were putting your number through Mr Yuill's door?'

I could so easily have replied that no, he couldn't ask, but of course knew all too well what sort of reaction such a reply would provoke. So instead, I did the right thing and gave him the answer I knew he wanted. 'Alice has probably already told you that I'm new to the village. I passed Gavin that morning. We chatted. I suggested we go out for a beer sometime and was putting my number through his door so he could contact me.'

'Couldn't he just knock?' Greening adjusted his jacket and idly drummed his fingers against the frame of the chair. The noise was insidious, growing in crescendo, like somebody hammering a small nail into my skull.

I sighed heavily. He was going to make me say it. Did we really have to go through the finite details? The minutiae of poor Gavin's life since his release from prison? 'PCSO Greening, I'm almost certain

Alice will have told you about Gavin's past, his criminal record and how all the villagers hate him. Do you really think he's going to walk around the place being sociable and knocking on people's doors?'

'But you were prepared to go out for a drink with him? Isn't that considered a social activity?' Greening looked inordinately pleased with himself. I wanted to reach over and slap his fingers away to stop the incessant noise he was making on the wedge of wood beneath his fingers.

'Like I said,' I said through gritted teeth, 'I'm new here. Maybe I feel sorry for him? He's paid for his crime, hasn't he? Don't we all deserve a second chance?'

Greening moved about in his chair, adjusting his posture and straightening his substantial layers of clothing. Any thoughts I had of telling him about Gavin's sneaky exit from the graveyard yesterday morning were immediately quashed. Clearly, Gavin was already a suspect. Nothing I said or did would change that. My words would have him banged up in no time. The locals would make his life a misery, possibly even drive him out of his home. I wasn't about to let that happen.

To my surprise, Greening nodded. The dark veil of suspicion that sat behind his eyes began to lift, revealing a human soul, somebody who appeared to care. A fleeting sense of something shot through me – hard to pin down and classify.

I stood up and shook it away. We were both grown men. We knew the rules, the boundaries. Some things are best left unsaid. Greening also stood up and shook my hand. As expected, he had a firm grasp, the grip of somebody who knew his place in society, the grip of somebody who always walked on the right side of the law. I thought of Gavin and what could lie ahead, how his life here in Whitchurch could eventually turn out. I had expected Greening to ask about the dog shit on the cars and the letters. I was ready for more questions from him. Had Alice even mentioned those things? She was so churned up about Dominic and the graffiti, maybe it had slipped her mind, wasn't on her radar as a priority. That didn't surprise me. I reckoned Alice's day began and ended with Dominic and the church. Everything else was on the periphery of her existence.

'Thanks for your help, Ray. And well done for being a good neighbour. All I will say is, just be careful who you socialise with. Not everybody is as friendly as you. Some people have another agenda behind their words and actions.'

I nodded and led him into the long hallway. For a

brief time, our shadows merged again as we walked together. I turned and stared at the silhouette our combined shapes made in the narrow vestibule. My flesh prickled as Greening turned to face me. Behind him, our nebulous form had suddenly morphed into something else, something more sinister. I couldn't say exactly what it was. My eyes stung. Heat rose in my belly. My skin grew cold and clammy. I moved. Or perhaps it was Greening who moved first. It was too quick to say but the image disappeared as rapidly as it had come. I let out a deep, shuddering breath.

'Everything okay?' Greening had leaned towards me, his hand outstretched. 'You've gone pale all of a sudden.'

I shook my head and made a deliberate attempt to push my shoulders back. I was still a good six inches shorter than this guy but the adjustment to my stance ruptured the moment and gave me a swift adrenaline rush. 'I'm fine, thanks. It's this heat, I think.'

'Try strolling the streets in this lot,' Greening replied with a smile. He patted his jacket and sighed. 'Weighs a bloody ton. I may as well be wearing chain-mail. It's absolute torture.'

He towered above me. His shock of dark hair was swept back and his features were softer than when I'd first let him in. I had gained his trust. I wasn't sure if that was a good thing or not. He placed his hat back on his head and stepped outside into the blazing sun, turning to say goodbye before striding over the step and onto the pavement.

I watched him saunter off down the street and get into a patrol car, then I turned away, slammed the door and slipped back into the shadows.

20

ME

The church was freezing. It was always freezing; even in the grip of a heatwave, the inside of my father's church was always cold. No matter what the season was, or what the weather like, ice settled in the pit of my stomach at the thought of going in there. And we went there a lot.

The pew was hard and cold, its solid frame digging into my backside, tiny splinters of wood scratching at my bare legs. We had been there for over an hour, just me and my parents. We had sat alone and prayed and prayed and prayed. I wasn't told as much but I got the feeling we were all praying for my soul, for my redemption and for me to be taken from the clutches of the Devil and placed in the arms of the

Christ Almighty. According to my father, every single one of my misdemeanours required the Lord's help. I was beyond any assistance my parents could ever possibly offer me. They had all but given up trying. Only Jesus had the power to save me.

Anyway, on this particular day I was bored and cold and tired. Every time I moved or tried to complain, my mother would hush me, tugging at my clothes and giving me her best stern face. My father was too locked into his holy rites to notice my fidgeting. His calling came before everything – my mother, me, our needs. They meant nothing to him compared to the pull of his parishioners and his life within the walls of his beloved church.

Eventually, the boredom became too much for me and while my mother's head was dipped and her thoughts deep in prayer, I slipped away. I was still small enough to be light on my feet and make my escape without causing any noise or vibration. By the time they noticed I was gone, I had made it to the altar, fascinated by the vivid colours of the flowers and the reflections from the stained-glass windows. A huge, wooden crucifix hung from the arched ceiling, casting a grey ominous-looking shadow across the pulpit below it. I stared at the face, at the lean body and the nails pressed into the palms of Jesus, and winced. I had been told all the stories about the crucifixion over and over and each time I heard them, my skin turned cold. The thought of the blood and the screams filled my mind; the sound of the cold, sharp metal being driven through fragile bones and soft flesh was all I could think about.

'For the love of God, child!' My father's voice roared over my head. Flecks of spittle landed on the back of my neck. I cowered. I knew what was coming next. I braced myself for the usual smack to the face, for being dragged up to his height where he could take full advantage and get a good aim, swinging his arm back ready to hit me with full force. I squeezed my eyes shut and stiffened myself, my bones rigid, my skin taut, ready for the explosion of violence that would inevitably ensue. Nothing happened. His tirade, however, continued.

'You've no right to be up here. You're not worthy. Do you hear me, child? You're not worthy!'

My entire body went into a spasm as I continued to wait for the hit. My muscles were locked in place, cramp threatening to convulse me. I felt a warmth spread over my groin, cooling rapidly as liquid trickled down my leg and dripped onto the perfectly polished floor. Horrified, I stared down at the tiny golden puddle forming at my feet, then up at his face, at the fire building in his eyes.

Before he could do or say anything, I was swept away by a set of arms. I turned to see my mother, smelt her musky perfume and was warmed by her embrace. For once she had intervened. I had been saved. Just the once.

'I'll sort it. You go back to your prayers. I'll clean this up.'

And that was it. Just like that, my father retreated and shuffled back to his pew where he no doubt prayed for me and asked for forgiveness for bringing me into the world.

I sat close by and watched as my mother mopped up the urine, then stood like a rag doll, floppy and malleable as she yanked my shorts down and cleaned me up with a handful of tissues from the bottom of her handbag.

Her eyes swept over me, as if assessing me, trying to work out what was going on inside my head. She didn't want to know; she really didn't.

After dressing me, she gave my hand a quick squeeze. Tears sprung into my eyes, bulbous and hot as they escaped and ran down my cheeks. Her sudden and unexpected show of affection had reduced me to tears. Violence, pain, continual abuse had never once moved me but her touch was enough to make me cry, to stir a well of emotions in me so deep, it felt like a bottomless pit of despair that, once cracked open, could never be sealed.

Her expression was unreadable: a combination of sorrow and fear perhaps. As quickly as she could, she used her sleeve to dab at my face, making barely audible soothing sounds, then grabbed at my hand and yanked me back to the pew in silence where my father knelt, his head so low I felt sure his chin could touch the floor.

I had evaded his wrath. Just that time. That one and only day when his thoughts were too immersed in prayer to be bothered with me. Next time, I wasn't so lucky.

Of course, I found out later the other reason I was spared from punishment and kept away from the sting of his hand. Even my father knew not to explode in front of my mother. Not when she was in such a delicate state. They told me later in the day about the baby. I wasn't sure how I felt about it all. It was a new experience for me and we weren't exactly the happiest of families. We didn't celebrate as other families would have done but instead sat quietly, discussing how amazing it was that another child was being brought into the world where Jesus could welcome them and cherish them. I don't ever remember feeling cherished but then I guess you already know that, don't you?

I recall staring at my mother's stomach in the following weeks, at the taut fabric, puckered and ribbed as it stretched over her belly. How had I not noticed it before? All of a sudden, she looked positively rotund, her previously slim frame now curved, her hips carrying an extra layer of flesh that wasn't there the last time I looked.

I became fascinated by her ever-growing abdomen, trying to picture what was inside, and more importantly, how it had got there.

The first time I asked, I was told to hush my mouth. The second time I asked, I received a slap. The third time I enquired how a baby could get inside another person, I was thrown into 'the room' and told to repent for my sins, that I was a true sinner and only God could judge me for what I had just said.

So I gave up asking. But the punishments didn't stop. It seemed that anything and everything I did warranted a beating. Eating with my elbows on the table, not wiping my feet on the doormat, using a handkerchief to wipe my nose, not using a handkerchief. There were no set rules I could live by and those that I thought I had sorted changed daily. It was hardly surprising my behaviour deteriorated faster than a slab of raw meat left out in the baking hot sun.

Like the time I decided to set a fire going. The matches had been accessible, sitting invitingly on the fireplace next to the old coal scuttle that was pitted with black ash. Despite having central heating, we still used the open fire, my father insisting we turn the radiators off to save on fuel bills. It was too tempting. I'd seen my parents do it and smelt the addictive scent of a freshly lit match, been attracted to the golden flicker of a naked flame. I had longed to get my hands on that box, to strike it and get that first whiff of sulphur and be so close to the tiny spark that changed from blue to orange and danced about magically. That tiny ochre spark of heat held such promise.

I knew that wood burnt better than most things. I'd seen my parents put logs in the grate and toss the match onto them. Then I would watch as the logs caught on and red and oranges flames bounced around, their forms casting eerie, pirouetting shapes on the adjacent wall. But we were out of logs and I needed something to burn.

The large crucifix my father kept hung on the wall in the living room went up a treat. I observed it, transfixed as the wooden cross turned black, its definite form slowly losing its shape and turning to charred splinters, ash floating off it as the flames licked at it ferociously and did their worst.

That's where I was when they found me – sitting by the fire, watching it burn. And smiling. According to their frenzied screams, I was smiling as Jesus shrivelled and turned to ash before my very eyes.

I'd like to say the following few hours were a blur of frenzied activity. But they weren't. I remember all of it. Every single second of those excruciating moments after that fire. To this day, they are still etched into my brain.

I had ruined everything, they said. Made their lives unbearable. Put the baby at risk by upsetting my mother. I was the Devil incarnate and needed to be stopped. And they tried. God knows they tried.

21

Lily was serving behind the bar as I strolled in and ordered a pint from a small, rotund lady who bustled about with a great deal of intent, huffing and puffing as if every movement required a gargantuan effort. Apart from the gathering of locals, the place was almost empty. My gaze swept along the bar, a streak of white causing me to stop and blink. Lily's bleached blonde hair was on the periphery of my vision, catching my eye every time she moved. If I edged along the bar, I felt sure I would be able to smell her perfume, the heady scent of bergamot and roses that clings to your clothes and sticks to your pores like honey. I diverted my gaze and picked up my pint.

The usual crew were seated in the corner, their

voices a buzz in the distance, like flies circling overhead. I made my way over and sat down on a stool. Davey gave me a curt nod and the elderly gentleman I spoke to last time I was in tipped his cap at me. Simon was gassing off about something or other and every now and again Davey looked at me and gave me a wry, knowing grin.

It was a pleasant enough afternoon and time slipped by without me giving Lily a second thought. I was onto my fourth pint – too many for me to consume in the daytime – when I felt a gentle tap on my shoulder. I set my glass down and looked up at Lily's fragile features. Her eyes still looked glassy and her mouth was set in a pout, like a small child admonished for something they are adamant they haven't done.

'This one's on the house.' She set another frothy pint down in front of me and stood with her hands on her hips. 'A thank you for earlier this morning.'

Before I had a chance to reply, she sashayed away, her tiny hips set in a seductive wiggle as she slipped behind the bar and smiled her toothy grin at a customer as she made small talk and took his order.

'Well, well, well!' Davey stared down at the pint of dark ale, at the creamy head and trail of taupe bubbles that edged over the rim and ran down the sides of the glass in slow motion, and then back at me, a knowing glint in his eye. 'I've been drinking here for almost half my life and never had one on the house. What did you do to get on her good side then?'

I shrugged and tried to suppress a grin. 'Ah, that would be telling, wouldn't it?'

He laughed, patted my back and sucked in his breath.

'No!' I half shouted. 'I was just being friendly. We're mates. I gave her a shoulder to cry on earlier, that's all.'

'Yeah? Is that a euphemism? Oldest one in the book that one, old chum.'

I laughed and finished my drink, keen to drink the next one, to smell the scent of Lily's fingers on the cool glass, to put my mouth where her skin had touched. 'I bumped into her this morning. She was upset after a family row and we chatted, that's all.'

I hoped I hadn't given too much away. Then again, if she had wanted to keep it secret, she shouldn't have shoved a pint down for me in front of everyone, should she? What was I supposed to say when they all asked?

Davey nodded sagely, a look of comprehension rapidly settling onto his weather-beaten features. 'Ah, that old bastard. Still at it is he, then?'

I raised my eyebrows and stared at him. It seemed Lily's dad was well-known in Whitchurch for the way he treated his family. And I thought she had confided in me and me only.

'You already know about it?' I said, a strange mixture of resentment and curiosity building up inside me.

Davey took a long glug of his beer and turned his stool sway from Simon and the others, then moved closer to me as he spoke. 'Lily's dad is a horrible old bastard. How he ended up with such a good kid and such a great family is beyond me. And how Lily remains so well-balanced is a sodding miracle if you ask me. He doesn't deserve any of them. Neither Lily or her sister. Poor buggers, having to put up with his shitty moods and behaviour for all these years.'

I shook my head, my vision blurring and my guts churning as I tried to make sense of Davey's words. How bad was this guy, for God's sake? I'd presumed it was a normal family argument, but by the sounds of things, Lily's family had a history and her father was known throughout the village for being a bit of a shit. I began to wonder what depth and strength of maelstrom I had inadvertently stumbled into.

'Like what?' I asked quietly. 'What sort of stuff does he do that's so bad?'

Davey kept his head low and stared off over my shoulder. I guessed he was watching Lily, his mind trying to dredge up the myriad misdemeanours her father had perpetrated over the years. But rather than speak, he simply shook his head and repeated how awful it was for them all. How awful. No more words. No more information. Just constant head shakes and a sad-eyed look as he cast his mind back and thought about it, but stayed infuriatingly silent.

I turned and stared over at Lily. She looked thinner. Or perhaps I was imagining things, attributing characteristics that weren't really there now I had more background knowledge on her now that I understood her plight. She was slight; her skin was pale. That was just how she was. There were no visible bruises. Maybe it was mental? Abuse takes many forms. I wondered what profile her family's story fitted, what sort of nightmares they had endured over the years. Was he a drinker? Suffering from some sort of mental disorder? There were so many possibilities. And he was a vicar too. I inhaled and closed my eyes for a second to let it sink in.

'They've lived here for years.' Davey's voice was low, a whisper in the commotion of the rush of people that had suddenly entered the bar. Their voices flew in all directions, killing the quiet that had been present just a few seconds earlier. A scurry of bodies pressed themselves around the bar, staring at menus, their eyes travelling around the tables, scrutinising the patrons, pointing to the ancient beams and murmuring their appreciation of the many antiques dotted around and the general patina of the place.

I swung back to look at him, to catch his eye and make him tell me more. We had bonded, Davey and I. He could trust me. I needed to find out about Lily's family and he had all the knowledge stored in his head. I wanted to know all about the man who had made her cry.

'Lily's family?' I said quietly, willing him to open up. 'I guess you know them pretty well then, eh?'

'Well enough,' he said under his breath. 'As well as anybody else who's lived here as long as we all have.'

My breath was ragged. I swallowed and took a gulp of the cool, creamy liquid. It was bitter and had an acrid aftertaste: just what I needed.

'And?' I asked lightly, keen to appear mildly interested, not desperate to know, even though I was. For some unfathomable reason, I saw Lily as an enigma. She fascinated me. I wanted to know more about her. I wanted to know everything.

Stop it, Ray!

'And like I said, her dad is a twat.' His voice was silk-like, soft as air in the ever-growing noise around us. I moved closer. Stupid tourists and hikers stopping me from hearing what I had to hear. I had no idea why Davey was suddenly being so evasive, clamming up and being so fucking obstinate about it all.

'Okay.' I sighed resignedly. 'You've told me that, but can you explain what he does that makes him such a twat and why is he so horrible to his family?'

Davey dipped his head then looked up at me. 'He knocked Lily about. Not so sure about her sister. Ciara is quieter, more submissive. Always does as she's told, whereas Lily has more about her. Refuses to put up with his crap and then gets the shit beat out of her for answering back. The old man is used to getting his way and being boss of the entire village. He's forgotten that he's retired and no longer has any clout around here.'

I squinted and pulled my head back in confusion. Who the hell was Lily's dad anyway? The way Davey was talking, anybody would have thought he was the squire of the place. I took another slurp of beer and swallowed, a lump sticking in my throat – a hard pellet of annoyance. 'Boss of the village?' I said and locked my eyes with Davey's. 'Who the hell is this guy anyway? You're talking about him as if he's royalty.'

Davey laughed, a spread of wrinkles gathering at the corner of each eye. 'Not quite, but he thought he was. And when you're a kid, somebody who wields authority is scary. He frightened the crap out of me whenever I saw him. Every bloody Sunday, listening to him barking out his sermon from the pulpit, wincing if he caught your eye, knowing you'd see him in school and he'd corner you with questions about the gospel.' He cleared his throat and the smile disappeared from his face as he spoke once more. 'So yeah, Lily's dad was the reverend here at St Oswald's for a long time before he retired a few years back, and believe me when I say, he was and still is a complete and utter bastard.'

22

I finished my pint and left, Davey's words ringing in my ears. I had no idea what I would do with this new piece of information, what I would say to Lily when I saw her next. Was I even supposed to say anything at all? It was hardly classified information, for God's sake, but did I really want her knowing I'd been talking about her to the people in the pub? I could picture her face, her scowl and narrowed eyes as she listened to me harping on about how I knew all about her past and her father. I visualised her swearing at me, telling me to mind my own fucking business. I smiled. I admired young Lily while also feeling sorry for her. Mixed emotions stirred deep within me, causing my skin to prickle. Lily was one of two things

– either extremely level-headed after having to endure a traumatic childhood, or deeply damaged, a bubbling cauldron ready to overflow at the slightest provocation. I had no idea which one she was.

I was still thinking about her as I stepped in the front door and heard my phone ring from inside. Its insistent shrill made my toes curl, its high-pitched whirring sound bouncing off every wall. Slamming the door behind me, I dropped my keys on the hall table and headed towards the source of the sound. Stepping into the dining room, I grabbed at the phone and stared at the screen. An unknown number. I took a chance and answered it, immediately wishing I hadn't.

'You've finally decided to answer me then?' the voice at the other end barked at me.

My legs turned to water. I thought about slamming the phone down, trying to escape from the sound of her nasally whining as she shrieked at me down the handset.

'I've been busy, Delores. I fully intended to get back to you but time ran away with me. What do you want?' I tried to be civil, to sound interested and be the caring, almost-son-in-law she'd never wanted me to be.

'Busy? You've never been busy in your life. What

have you had to do that's taken up so much of your fucking time, Ray – getting out of bed and going to work like everybody else? Making your own lunch and cleaning up your own shitty mess?' She was practically screaming at me. I could picture flecks of spittle flying out of her mouth, spraying into the air, noxious and venomous, poisoning the very oxygen that she breathed. Pity she didn't choke on her own hatred and sink into her own pit of loathing and misery and drown. 'And as for getting back to me, you bloody well blocked me! Did you honestly think that would stop me getting hold of you? Did you really think I'd give up that easily when this concerns my daughter? You're deluded, Ray. You really are one deluded, sad little man.'

Anger boiled up inside me. I should never have answered the phone. I should have cut her off, let her keep her vile opinions to herself. But I didn't. I made a mistake. I blocked her other number and she still managed to contact me. I let my guard down and she found a way to speak to me. More fool me. I wouldn't let it happen again.

Against my better judgement, I waited for her to finish ranting and venting her spleen and answered in a voice that belied my inner repugnance for a woman who thought herself superior to everyone else, a woman who spent every spare minute of her time finding faults with the lives of others, dragging them down and ripping at their self-esteem until they felt empty inside.

'So, what *do* you want, Delores?' I knew this would rile her all the more. Despite hating her and despite Delores utterly despising me, I enjoyed throwing bait her way and watching her bite. It was the only pleasure I got from my encounters with her. I had to salvage some mere morsel of positivity from this conversation. I refused to let her get the better of me and for once wanted to emerge from one of our encounters as the glorious victor.

I heard her splutter and gasp for breath as she listened to my voice, and I smiled. Already I was winning. I had made her lose her focus, caught her off guard.

'What do I want? *What do I want?*' Her pitch went up a full octave. I grimaced. It was like nails being dragged down a chalkboard. 'You know fine well why I'm ringing you, Ray! Jesus Christ, you know why!'

My chest contracted as I inhaled, enjoying the cooling effect of the ambient air on my scorched lungs. The day was another hot one – no breeze, no let-up from the intense heat. The only way to stay cool and half sane was to sit in the house in the shadows, away from the glare of the burning sun.

I suppressed a laugh. I had to be calm, to remain in control. So instead, I adopted a soft voice and a soothing tone. I was the better person here. I was the one acting like an adult and not screaming obscenities and throwing accusations around like a salivating banshee. I would make sure my responses were well thought out, measured and logical. I would make sure I gave as good as I got without raising my voice or breaking a sweat.

'Enlighten me,' I said softly. I was tempted to say more but stopped myself. Less is always more.

'I'll bloody well enlighten you all right! Samantha – that's what I want.'

'Samantha and I are no longer together, Delores, so we don't actually need to be having this conversation.' My voice was so low, I thought for a moment she hadn't heard me. I was not about to repeat myself. Not for Delores, not for anybody. Samantha and I were over. I was on my own and free of her constant demands and nagging. And it felt good. And listening to her mother shriek and scream at me, I knew I'd done the right thing. No regrets, no turning back the clock.

'I know you're no longer together, you ignorant arsehole. I'm not an idiot.'

I wanted to stop her there and then and remind her that she was indeed an idiot as well as lacking in any sort of decorum or dignity, but knew the repercussions of such a move. So I let her go on and listened to her mad accusations and half-baked theories about how I had ruined her daughter and torn their family apart, about how I was a worthless piece of shit and that I should watch my back because she was onto me. Her voice became a monotonous drone as she rattled on, throwing every insult she could think of my way until eventually I could take no more of her screeching and I cut her off, but not before I heard her utter her final menacing words, chilling and full of hostility.

'I'm coming for you, Ray. You'd better watch your back because this isn't over.'

I ended the call, sat back in the chair and closed my eyes. I didn't have to listen to this mad old bitch or endure her wailing and cursing. Outside, the distant chatter of birdsong reverberated through the trees. I took a deep breath and savoured the moment, giving my racing pulse time to slow down and restore itself to normality.

I opened my eyes and stared out into the garden. I tried with her, I really did, but as was usually the case, Delores only ever thought of her own immediate needs. Not once did it cross her mind that maybe, just maybe, I was happier now I wasn't living with Samantha. The apple didn't fall far from the tree with those two. Delores had passed on her toxic approach to relationships to her daughter. They both seemed to relish controlling people, making them miserable and then being totally and utterly bewildered when those same people turned around and rebelled against them. It was beyond Delores' comprehension that I no longer wanted to be with her poisonous offspring. Even blocking her calls didn't work. She still did her utmost to track me down and bully me into her way of thinking.

The birdsong outside ceased. The sudden silence was deafening. I could hear my own heartbeat, feel my blood as it roared through my ears and coursed through my veins. A breath shuddered in my chest, uneven and arrhythmic as it forced its way out of my throat in a stuttering gasp.

Swallowing down a sliver of fear that had begun to rise in the pit of my stomach, I stood up and walked over to the window. I had no need to be fearful. No need at all. I was a strong guy, a man who, after many years, was finally in control of his life. Everything I needed was right here in this village. Whitchurch and I were becoming well acquainted, like new friends slowly beginning to understand one other. We would be happy together. I could feel it in my bones, sense the air of acceptance as I strolled past the village green. I was one of them now, a true local. Somebody who could be trusted. A man of his word. My other life was behind me; Whitchurch was my new one. I had friends here, people who had begun to listen to me, to care about me. I had a sense of purpose and at long last, I felt happy. And nobody was going to take that away from me.

As far as I was concerned, Delores and her family could all go to hell.

23

ME

Being pinned down, held fast by strong adult hands, stayed with me. The memory of being trapped, unable to move, haunted my dreams for years afterwards. And then there was their voices – the dreadful menacing incantations that echoed around the place, the acoustics of the high ceiling accentuating each and every word.

We exorcize thee, O every unclean spirit, satanic power, infernal invader, wicked legion.

I was trapped. At their mercy. Their hands on me, holding me still, their wild eyes and pale faces looming over me. It was the whole fucking ritual. It terrified me. I had no idea what was going to happen, what they were going to do to me. I expected the worst. And that was exactly what I got.

I had hoped that my mother, in her advanced state of pregnancy, would have helped me, tried to stop it, done anything she could to protect her child, to stop me from being subjected to the horrors that were inflicted upon me that day. Or any of the days my father decided I was possessed by demons and needed to be cleansed. But she didn't. She may not have participated, but she stood by and watched, her face expressionless, her features a blur to me as she stood idly by and observed it all from a distance. Staring lifelessly, doing nothing. Absolutely nothing.

He was insane. I know that now. In hindsight, I'm pretty sure I knew it even then. In spite of the fact that I was only a child, I could see my father for what he really was – a psychopath. He wasn't a religious zealot or driven by his allegiance to God. He was quite simply a psychotic man. And they were just as bad, his friends and allies, helping him, urging him on, insisting he was doing the right thing by me when all the time, everybody knew that he was unhinged. They had the power to stop him, to persuade him that he had overstepped the mark, broken laws, risked losing his position within the church. But they didn't. They backed him up, told him I needed to be reprimanded, enabled him every fucking step of the way.

I screamed and spat and thrashed about, which in turn fuelled their belief that I was indeed some sort of demon. Two of the most faithful parishioners that my parents called friends aided and abetted my father throughout the entire procedure. Their large hands on me, pressing my head back, forcing my limbs into place while my father stood over me, his voice a boom in the emptiness of the church, his voice echoing across every pew, down every aisle and up into the rafters where Jesus Christ hung, watching it all from above, his compassionate expression of no use to me whatsoever. I had been abandoned in my hour of need. Nobody to help me, nobody to rescue me from the hands of the adults who inflicted all kinds of cruelty upon me. I was alone. Left to the mercy of a handful of callous, insane people who were convinced I was possessed.

Even at such a tender age, I knew it terribly wrong, illegal and horribly cruel, but I was powerless to stop them. The one person who could have helped me stood by meekly, her stomach distended, her hands hanging limply by her sides, as they held me fast and chanted those words.

Thus, cursed dragon, and you, diabolical legions, we

adjure you by the living God. From the snares of the Devil, deliver us O Lord.

They shouted the words they all believed would expel the demons that lived deep in my soul over and over – the same demons that controlled my behaviour and made me an outcast in my own family. An outcast. I had been on the periphery of everybody since I was born and by the time I was of school age, they fully believed that I was evil. Is it any wonder I turned out the way I did? What happened to talking and persuasion and compassion? Whatever happened to guidance and love? Would my life have turned out differently had I been exposed to those emotions rather than the back of my father's hand and my parents' uncontrolled religious beliefs? Who knows. Nature versus nurture. Love versus hate. I was shown little love, and now I am filled with revulsion and malice. It dwells within me, growing, expanding, ballooning day by day, consuming me from the inside out.

I have a burning desire for retribution, an overwhelming need to get even. These people will pay for what they did to me. I might well be a monster, but they are the ones who did it to me. I know that now. I've had plenty of time to think it through. I'm intelligent enough to reflect on past events and disturbed enough to do something about it. Soon they will know. Soon enough, it will become apparent that they were the demons, that they were the ones who needed to have their souls cleansed. The time will come when they will all pay for what they did to me. I'll make sure of it.

24

I decided to break with habit. The day after the call from Delores, I took an evening walk through Whitchurch rather than my usual early morning ramble. Her call had really got to me, niggled at me and wormed its way under my skin. As much as I'd convinced myself I wouldn't allow her to drag me down, her words really rankled with me and no matter how hard I tried, I couldn't shake the low-spirited feeling that trailed in my wake or the dark emotions that ravaged my mind. I did exactly what I swore I wouldn't let her do, and allowed her to climb inside my head and mess with my thoughts.

I simply couldn't face seeing anybody, having to make small talk when I was still focused on Samantha and her mother, so opted instead for strolling in the dark. When I say dark, I don't mean pitch black. Summer evenings never really close in fully, do they? There is always a distant veil of light present, a streak of amber that stops the blackness from completely enveloping everything.

I stared over towards the distant hills, at the silhouette they cast against the backdrop of a shimmering, burnt-orange sky. A watery, sepia-tinted light hung on the horizon, a thin stream of dusk that refused to descend and allow night-time to begin. As a child, I found evenings like this less oppressive, less threatening. The promise of daylight was always close by, always so near, ready to smother the darkness and quash my fears, to rip in two the nightmares I suffered from for so many years.

Exhaling loudly at the thought of those terrors that had robbed me of sleep for decades, I turned and headed down Church Lane, the sudden presence of unexpected shadows causing my skin to prickle. Tall trees and dense foliage blackened the lane and stopped what little light there was from filtering through. I shivered despite the warmth of the balmy evening and picked up my pace.

The shape of a figure hung about at the end of the road, a grey outline in the distance. I didn't stop. This was a safe place. Recent events, classified as minor crimes, didn't frighten me at all. I was getting used to this quirky little village, with its eccentric locals and their suspicions. I knew about its unhappy past and how everybody was trying to move on from it. An unidentified shadow wasn't going to scare me. People walked down this lane all the time. Every single day, folk strolled up and down this beautiful little patch of land, taking in the views and general ambience. Except the shadow in the distance wasn't walking. It was still, a dark, motionless silhouette, staring at something, or somebody. Maybe even staring at me.

My scalp prickled. I gritted my teeth, furious at my lack of self-control. This was ridiculous. I was a grown man, more than capable of taking care of myself. There could be any number of reasons why a perfect stranger was standing at the bottom of the lane watching me. Were they even focused on me anyway? I was letting my imagination run amok, allowing fear to overrule logic. I had nothing be anxious about. No need for fear. No need at all.

I continued past St Oswald's, moving closer to the shadow, past the rows of gravestones that were probably still daubed with paint despite Dominic's best efforts to remove it, and nearer to the figure that was still unmoving.

The sound of my footsteps echoed in my ears, crashing through my head and causing me to stop momentarily to adjust my collar. Anything to delay reaching that shadow. I just needed a couple of seconds to gather my thoughts before I got to whoever it was that was still there, standing at the end of the lane. Waiting for me.

I shook my head and laughed bitterly. Not everything was about me. All I had to do was keep walking and find out. I figured I was going soft. Either that or Delores' call had knocked me off-kilter more than I realised. The thought of that made me hate her even more, strengthening my slightly weakened resolve to ignore any more of her calls and threats. I would do whatever was required to protect myself from that mad old bitch.

Only a few more steps and the identity of the murky outline would be revealed. I just had to keep on walking. Narrowing my eyes, I tried to gauge whether it was male or female, but the answer soon presented itself.

'Evening,' a voice boomed out as I approached. His voice was powerful, confident. A self-assured individual standing in the shadows.

A wave of shock rippled through me. I stiffened my body and ignored the reflex action to reach out and punch the person who had caused my blood to race and my heart to pound on hearing their voice unexpectedly.

'Evening,' I replied, my throat constricted by a knot of anxiety as I spoke. The word hissed out of me, tight and hostile.

'Hope I didn't scare you. Just taking a few photos of the farmhouse. Been meaning to do it for a while now but the light hasn't been quite right. Tonight is perfect.' His tone was lighter now, less threatening. The figure moved and stepped closer to me.

On instinct, I stepped back. I nodded and cleared my throat.

'Nice sunset at the end of the lane,' I said, attempting to inject an air of friendliness into my tone. Despite doing my best to appear self-assured, unmoved by their presence, my voice was croaky. I coughed and pushed my shoulders back. Why would anybody stand here, nestled amongst the foliage in the darkness, when the sky was much lighter at the opposite end of the village?

'Can't see the house from there though I'm afraid. Damn old oak tree blocking the view.' The man lowered his camera and appeared to assess me for a moment before stretching his hand out for me to shake. 'Sorry if I alarmed you. I was trying to keep still. I spotted an owl up in the branches of that sycamore and thought it would add a bit of character to the picture. It might have been a long-eared one, which is pretty rare around these parts, but I couldn't be certain. Too dark to see properly. Anyway, I'm Terence. Apologies again for possibly scaring you.'

I leaned forward and shook his hand. It was strong and firm. No sign that he was feeling alarmed or worried by my presence. So, this was Terence. I presumed it was the same guy who was married to Diane. He had the same cut-glass accent, the same air of sureness brought about by money and the knowledge that the world would always dance to his tune.

'It's fine,' I said, pulling myself up to my full height. 'I walk down here regularly. I think I may have already met your wife.'

It was too dark to see his reaction properly, to see if his expression was one of shock or jealousy or any of those primeval responses that many men display when another male mentions that they have spoken to their other half without them being present. I figured Terence was above all that, too self-possessed for all that alpha male stuff, and imagined him being level-headed about it all.

'Diane? Yes, I'm sure you have. She likes to get out and about. I'm more of a stay-at-home guy but Diane likes to come over into Whitchurch as often as she can, catch up with everybody and have a chat. She likes nothing better than a good old gossip.'

I stared at the dim profile of their farmhouse, the large property set on a slight hill on the edge of the village. Far away enough to not be bothered by all the pointless chatter and tittle-tattle but close enough to visit whenever needed. A property that estate agents would refer to as being in a prime location – and probably worth a fortune.

I glanced down at the bulky camera hanging loosely in his hands. A thick strap hung around his neck. He smiled and tapped at it. 'I like to come out and take photographs of the house through the changing seasons. I plan on making a montage to put in the hallway. Get a half-decent frame. It's a hobby of mine, taking photographs of wildlife and such.'

'Good idea,' I replied, unsure what else to say. He seemed like an affable guy. Just a nice, normal man out for a stroll, doing what he enjoyed, but it was clear to me that socially, we were on different planets.

'You should call over to see us sometime,' he added. 'The farmhouse is bloody ancient. We've got mice that the cats can't seem to track down, woodworm and dry rot in the old beams and windows that are about as much use as a chocolate teapot. The place is freezing in the winter but at least we can get a good roaring fire going to combat the ice that's on the inside of the glass.' He let out a barking laugh and I found myself laughing along with him.

'I'll do that for sure,' I said, knowing it was unlikely. I had no idea if I had anything in common with Terence and his wife, and even less of an idea how I would introduce myself if I made an unannounced visit. This is what people do, isn't it? Extend invitations in the knowledge they will never be taken up by the intended recipient. It's a gesture we make to assure people we're harmless and friendly, that we are welcoming of neighbours, but most of all that we are trustworthy.

We chatted for a little while longer about photography and weather conditions until I eventually said goodbye, assuring him I would call over.

I continued with my walk, arcing around the village, clearing my head of all thoughts of Samantha and Delores until the light finally faded and it became too dark to go any further.

By the time I reached home, I guessed it was well after 11 p.m. A slight ache had set in the back of my calves and I was feeling pretty tired. A welcome vacuum had consumed my brain. Already Delores' threats and vitriol were fading. By tomorrow morning, they would have vanished completely.

I closed the door quietly and double locked it, savouring the solitude that lay ahead of me.

I ate a small supper of cheese on toast, cleared the plate away and turned the lights off. I headed upstairs, showered then slipped into bed where I slept soundly.

* * *

I was awoken the next morning by the sound of voices emanating from further down the village. Lots of them. Too many to ignore. Grabbing my clothes, I clambered out of bed and peeked through the curtains at the huddle of bodies that were gathered on the pavement a few metres down the road.The sight of an ambulance made my stomach lurch. A policeman appeared and parted the small crowd, beckoning for them to move back. His large hands waved the onlookers away. He was flapping his arms furiously for them to make some space as a medic appeared behind him, closely followed by two more carrying a stretcher.

Swallowing hard, I closed my eyes for a second and listened to the sound of my own breathing as the crowd outside grew silent. The sea of pale, solemn faces watched intently as the medics carried the patient to the back of the ambulance. They slid the stretcher into the vehicle seamlessly and closed the doors with a slight thud.

I turned away from the window and sat on the edge of the bed, my heart beginning to race. Another thing for the residents of Whitchurch to deal with. We had ourselves another incident.

25

The police were interviewing everybody in the village. It was hardly surprising and to be expected given the circumstances of the crime. An elderly man, beaten black and blue in his own garden as he stood on the back lawn looking through a telescope, admiring the clear evening sky.

Jim and Mary only lived five doors down from me and already the police were interviewing people, asking everybody what they had seen and heard last night, questioning them on where they were when Jim Speight, a retiree and long-time resident of Whitchurch, was viciously attacked.

Only an hour after watching the ambulance pull away, I heard the knock at my door and, without peering through the window, knew who it would be. The police. Again. This was becoming too regular an occurrence.

Taking a deep, ragged breath, I marched into the hallway and pulled the door open. Two police officers stood there, their expressions grim as they introduced themselves as PC Redmayne and DC Trewitt. I stepped aside to let them in, then followed them through to the living room where they stood, slowly looking around, their eyes scanning every book, every picture. Every single thing. I wondered what they were hoping to find – clues of some sort? The perpetrator hidden behind the sofa, ready to hand themselves in? I tried to hide my look of bemusement as I motioned for them to make themselves at home.

PC Redmayne waited for DC Trewitt to take a seat before sitting down himself, perching awkwardly on the small chair next to the living room window. Trewitt spread himself out on the couch, his legs wide open, taking up the space of two people. I sat opposite Redmayne in the other chair and waited for one of them to say something. They glanced at each other and remained silent. I cleared my throat and spoke first.

'I expect you're here about poor old Jim,' I cut in. Somebody had to say something. Their silence was too awkward, the air thick with tension and unspent energy.

They both nodded before Trewitt answered me. His voice belied his large frame. It was a thin beam of sound in a silent room and somehow felt out of place. 'I guess you've spoken to the other neighbours?'

I nodded and let out a deep sigh. After getting dressed, I'd rushed outside and was almost crushed in Alice's arms as she grabbed me and held me close, barking into my chest that the most dreadful thing had happened and that Jim had been killed. As it turned out, Jim wasn't dead but had in fact been brutally assaulted as he had stood gazing up at the stars in his back garden. According to reports, which hadn't been entirely verified but came instead from his wife, Mary, as she sat in the hospital with their daughter – who had travelled up from Manchester in the early hours – Jim had sustained broken ribs, a fractured cheekbone and multiple lacerations and bruises. Traumatic for any fit young person, let alone somebody of Jim's advancing years.

'Terrible thing to happen,' I said quietly as I sat with my knees tight together. I shook my head and waited for one of them to say something.

'It is indeed,' PC Redmayne replied. 'We were just wondering if you saw anything untoward last night or heard anything that could help us with our enquiries?'

I inhaled and nibbled at the corner of my mouth, tugging at a loose piece of skin and thinking back to last night. 'Not that I can think of,' I said as I looked over to the window and then back to Redmayne. 'It was a fairly quiet evening. I went for a walk, chatted to one of the locals, came back, had supper and went to bed. Pretty uneventful really.'

'Who was it you spoke to? Do you have a name?' he said sharply, his eye flicking over to his colleague, then back to me.

'I only know his first name, I'm afraid. I've not lived here for long.'

They both nodded and smiled as if I were about to say something deeply revealing. What did they think I was about to do – unveil the killer to them?

'Terence, he's called,' I said as I looked from one to the other. 'He's called Terence and lives at Whitchurch Farm, but he was at the other end of the village, down Church Lane. Nowhere near here.'

PC Redmayne wrote it all down. The reedy scratch of his pencil on the paper began to grate on me. 'What time was this?' he asked, never looking up from his notepad.

I tried to think back, drumming my fingers on the

edge of the chair while delving into my memory. The dull *thunk* of skin hitting fabric reverberated around the room as I tried to put the timeline together in my head. 'I think it was probably at about ten o'clock. I couldn't say for certain. I didn't keep a close eye on the time but I'd say it was later than nine. Sorry I can't be of more help.'

'It's fine,' Trewitt said with a heavy groan as he leaned forward and rested his hands on his knees.

'What time did… this happen?' I said, my words sounding clunky and contrived. 'The attack, I mean?'

I dipped my head and stared at the rug, counting the tassels as I waited for one of the police officers to speak, to answer the question I had thought long and hard about before asking. It felt as if I were probing, overstepping an invisible line and venturing into unknown territory.

I looked up again and saw Trewitt quickly glance at Redmayne before he answered me. 'We don't have an exact time as yet but we're possibly looking at somewhere between the hours of 10 p.m. and 5 a.m. Had it happened during the winter, I doubt he would have survived the night.'

I didn't know what else to say. My palms felt sticky and a hard stone was lodged in my windpipe. Behind me, the rhythmic whirr of the washing machine cut into the quiet, slicing through the intense atmosphere in the room.

Clearing my throat, I spoke softly, my voice fighting for air space above the constant drone of the machine as it picked up speed. 'I honestly don't know what else to say. I really don't.'

They both nodded in unison, their faces riddled with concern, echoing my own sentiments. I wondered if they had already knocked at Gavin's door, whether they had been pointed in that particular direction by embittered locals who wanted him caught: people who would have him publicly flogged and lynched if they thought it was at all possible to do so. They hated him with a passion. But then what did I know? Maybe he was as bad as they all believed him to be. Maybe Gavin Yuill had it coming to him.

'If you remember anything Mr...?'

'Ray,' I said quickly. 'Just call me Ray.'

Redmayne held his pencil over his notebook. His hand hovered there, heavily, deliberately, waiting for me to speak.

'Surname please,' Trewitt said briskly. 'This is a serious investigation we're conducting here, Ray. A man is in hospital suffering from major injuries after being badly beaten with what we believe could have been a large, heavy implement. So, if you don't mind, we'd like to know your last name.' His voice had changed. It was clinical, ice-cold. Sharp and demanding.

I met his steely gaze and saw he wasn't in the mood for any games or evasive techniques. Delores had my number but she didn't have my address. I doubted PC Redmayne and DC Trewitt were about to track her down and hand over my personal details. They had more pressing matters to be getting on with – crimes to solve, potential murderers to catch. I took a long, trembling breath and banished all thoughts of Delores and Samantha from my mind. Delores didn't know where I was and, if I had a say in it, would never find me.

'Smith,' I said at last, a thick, hammering pulse starting up in my neck. 'My name is Ray Smith.'

26

ME

They happened frequently, the exorcisms. I have no idea of their regularity, no concrete timeline in my head to give you an idea of whether they occurred weekly or monthly or indeed daily. I think I possibly blanked it out of my mind, surrounded myself with a protective layer that allowed me to become marginally desensitised to them. Not that they no longer affected me. That would never happen. I was a pariah, and each and every ritual had made me feel less than human.

In all honesty, I think my parents were the ones who became desensitised to their bizarre rituals, thinking it was normal to punish a child in that way, to pin me down and use such draconian measures whenever I misbehaved. They showed no remorse for their actions, no shock or pity at my reactions whenever they subjected me to it. All they had was a clawing need to rid their family of the demons that they felt certain dwelled in my soul.

After my sister was born, there was a small hiatus, a lull that allowed a tiny crevice of light to creep into my life. I honestly thought it had all ground to a halt, their hatred and abuse, that it was all behind us and we would gel as a family. How wrong I was.

My younger sister was, without any shadow of a doubt, a beautiful child. Everything a baby should be: soft, loving, easy to feed, always happy. She was everything I wasn't. My mother told me often how angelic and easy she was compared to me, how I was the complete opposite, refusing the breast and sleeping little, making her miserable from the day I was born.

'Such a difficult, angry baby,' she would say when talking to others about my early infantile years. 'Quick to anger, slow to please,' were her words when referring to me.

As I grew older and began to comprehend what it was she was saying, I used to smile and gloss over her phrases, pretending I wasn't bothered by her words, but of course I was. I was very bothered. They hurt. Because they weren't used in the context of entertaining people, regaling them with tales of my cute naughtiness and her lack of peace and quiet as mothers often do; they were said with real malice behind them. They were intended to cut, to make me bleed. I knew then that the damage was done. Not only had my father subjected me to years of abuse, but he had also managed to convince my mother, who had previously sometimes showed me signs of brief affection, that I was a terrible child. The worst. Not worthy of love or attention. Not worthy of anything.

Day by day, I died inside, tiny fragments of me turning to ash, blackened and charred by the events of my short life, until I no longer cared about anything or anybody. I was a lone wolf in the wilderness, desperate and frightened, filled with a seething anger that fought to be free. I hated them all: my family, friends, teachers, neighbours. By that point, I saw them as my enemies, people who meant me harm and had forgotten how to protect me. Wolves have survival techniques, methods honed by years of evolution to make sure they survive. Attack others before they attack you. That was me. An aggressor, ready to fight, but slowly learning that I had to wear a mask of normality in order to conform, to mix with others and not be seen as the obvious perpetrator when all the while, I was wreaking as much havoc as possible, doing as much harm as I could within the confines and limitations of my daily life.

So I learned how to be pleasant, how to act accordingly and follow the rules. And it served me well. My robotic, soulless existence began to pay off. I did well at school, got half-decent reports, even made friends who weren't put off by my bizarre reactions and anger issues. Because by that point, I had learned how to control that aspect of my personality, to keep it all under wraps. They didn't know me, not the real me. They couldn't see the thoughts that randomly exploded in my head, or see the irreparable damage caused by years of abuse. Just as well really. Who would want to spend time with such a person? Who would want to be around an individual who wished them harm?

By the time I started secondary school, I was a ticking time bomb. The exorcisms had stopped. I was too big by then for them to pin me down – too strong for them to even risk it – but their hatred towards me continued unabated. Our house was a cold one, full of hostility and arguments and simmering anger. I tried to be civil but they had cut me too deeply for me to ever forgive them. And as for their feelings towards me? I think they had kept me at arm's length for so long, convinced themselves I was an evil being and beyond redemption for so many years, that they had forgotten how to love me, how to even attempt a reconciliation of sorts. We were separate entities living under the same roof, disparate beings unable to bond again or forge any kind of spiritual or physical connection. We simply co-existed under the same roof. It was too late. Everything was in pieces, ripped apart. Never to be repaired. Everything was too far gone. We were a broken family. They hated me and I hated them right back. So what point was there in even attempting to heal?

27

Jim had been out in his garden with his telescope when the attack took place, according to police reports. Mary, accustomed to his ventures out there, had thought nothing of it when he didn't come back in after an hour or so. She had gone to bed, fully expecting him to follow her up later, and then fallen asleep. Only when she woke up at 5 a.m. to find he still wasn't in bed did she panic. She had pulled on her dressing gown and raced downstairs. The house was still lit up, the television on – just as she had left it hours earlier – because Jim hadn't come back in from the garden and switched everything off. He had been attacked from behind as he leaned down and peered into his telescope, hoping to catch a glimpse of the Perseid meteor shower. Somebody had clambered over the fence carrying a heavy implement – possibly a piece of wood – and struck him hard, knocking him to the ground. No sound. Nothing. Nobody had heard a thing according to police reports. An intruder, a violent attacker who operated with stealth and precision, had struck an old man, beating him to within an inch of his life. While Jim was on the floor, probably unconscious, the attacker had hit him repeatedly, bringing the weapon down on his body and face again and again and again.

Alice told me this as we stood on the village green, talking despondently about what had occurred. There were tears, near hysteria, accusations and incredulity at the whole situation as everybody gathered around and tried to console one another. I recognised some faces but not all. Diane was there, no Terence. No Dominic either. Nobody from the pub. Just the older villagers or people who knew Jim well.

'I hope they lock him up and throw away the bloody key!' Alice shouted, just loud enough for everybody to hear.

Nobody asked who she was referring to. They didn't need to. We all knew.

Emily stepped forward and raised her hand authoritatively. 'Stop that sort of talk please, Alice. We both know that Gavin wasn't even here last night.'

A silence descended; the atmosphere was charged, a haze of invisible static hanging over everybody, swirling ominously, ready to ignite.

'He wasn't here?' a voice said from the back of the crowd.

'No,' Emily reiterated firmly. 'He wasn't here. The police have already confirmed that he was in Oxford visiting friends, so can everybody please stop with this silly talk and the false allegations? It's serves no purpose and is of no help to anybody.'

'He could have got somebody to do it for him!' Alice cried. I watched her mouth wobble and her body practically vibrate as her temper took hold and she refused to accept Emily's words. 'For all we know, he could have sent one of his burly, thuggish friends here to do it. Probably somebody he was in prison with. I have no idea why you're being so lenient with him, Emily! I'm convinced he went away as a ruse to cover his tracks, then he sent one of his henchmen here to almost kill Jim.'

She collapsed into a state of frenzy, tears bursting out of her eyes, her body almost bent double as she wept hysterically. Nobody made any attempt to console her. She stood alone, weeping and wailing and showing no signs of letting up. I was half tempted to move closer, to reach out and let her know I was there for her, but somebody spoke, stopping me in my tracks.

'Who says it was a man who did it?' I recognised the voice immediately. I turned around to see Lily striding over to us. Her white hair was piled on top of her head and a stripe of bright-red lipstick stained her full mouth. She wore a scarlet, off-the-shoulder sweater and tight skirt that nipped her waist in, accentuating her slim figure and long legs. My skin warmed at the sight of her and a slight ripple of excitement slithered inside me, coiling itself around my bones and nestling into my veins.

Nobody answered her loaded question as she sidled up next to the crowd of mainly elderly residents. Lily positively shone, making Diane and her expensive clothes look shabby and unkempt. She flashed us a wide smile and nodded at me, her gaze resting on me for longer than was necessary. A slight tingling sensation crept over my flesh as I watched her blink, lick her lips, then look away.

Lily stayed for a short while, chatting to people, looking suitably concerned as they spoke and told her what the latest updates were, then I watched, fascinated and slightly aroused, as she left the murmuring crowd and made her way over to the pub. Nobody took her remark seriously, or reacted to it in any way, shape or form. That was Lily all over. I knew her well enough by now to know that, despite her genuine concern and caring nature, she also liked a bit of friction – to throw an unexpected comment out there as bait, just to see who would bite.

Nobody did. Not that time anyway.

I listened to the array of voices and the unfounded accusations being thrown around as I left the group and started to make my way back home. I could hear Emily's slightly nasally voice as it whistled around the throng, telling everyone to calm down and be rational. Every now and again, Alice would let out a howl of anguish and take centre stage with her sobbing and bawling. Dominic must have joined the group after I left as I'm almost certain I heard him speak. I could have sworn I heard his calm, measured tone as I reached my front step and slid my key in the lock, his soothing, pleading words the voice of reason amid a sea of utter despair.

I stepped inside and closed the door with a small *click*, shutting out the misery and worry. They could all remain out there if they wished, clutching at straws as to who did it, shouting and yelling and turning against each other. I had better things to do than be caught up in divisive dialog that would solve nothing.

I dropped into a chair in the living room, glad to be away from the melee, and turned on my laptop, keen to catch up with the latest headlines and make contact with the rest of the world outside of Whitchurch.

My stomach tightened as I read the news and caught up with what was taking place back in Birmingham: drugs raids, the jailing of a paedophile, a missing woman. I scanned the page and quickly closed it. No good news to be had there.

I placed my head back on the cushion and closed my eyes, a sudden wave of fatigue swamping me. Swirling shadows flitted about behind my eyelids until I felt a welcome darkness begin to descend and gladly went with it, allowing myself to be shrouded in its warmth, where I was free from any harm.

* * *

Insistent knocking filtered into my dreams. I was running, galloping along at an immense pace, too afraid to turn and see who it was that was chasing me, when I fell. I hit the ground with a crack, my heart thrashing around my chest, adrenaline whistling around my system as I waited for my enemy to pounce. Summoning up all my strength, I turned, squinting to see who it was that was behind me, who the person was that seemed hell-bent on catching me and hurting me. There was nobody there. My body froze as, in the distance, I heard a rattling sound, a metallic clanging that terrified me. I knew something dreadful was going to happen. I could sense it. I waited. The noise grew closer, the sound of terror creeping up on me. I looked again and then I saw it. A shadow, holding something; clinging onto a large object. It was too dark to see properly. I dragged myself up off the floor, limping away. My vision cleared and I listened again as the portentous-looking figure took a long piece of wood and dragged it across a set of metal railings. *Clank, clank, clank.*

They took a step closer to me, then closer still. My blood ran like sand; oxygen built up in my lungs, unable to escape as I held my breath and watched in horror.

And then I saw it. My eyes widened.

It was me.

The figure behind me in my dream, swinging a piece of wood, was me. I stared into my own face, a mirror image of my own features, and listened to the clanking sound again as the wood was dragged over the metal, hitting each and every railing slowly, deliberately, forcefully. The figure smiled, a reflection of my expression staring back at me as it let out a hollow laugh and dragged the wood over the metal once more, the sound bouncing around my head, torturing me, terrifying me.

I awoke with a start, sweat coursing down my back, my head pounding as a loud banging came from the hallway. The front door. Somebody was knocking at the front door.

Disorientated, I raced out of the room, a pain shooting up the back of my skull as I forced myself forward.

My eyes felt heavy, my vision blurry as I struggled to focus properly. My palms were sweaty and the key slipped in my fingers as I turned it and pulled at the handle. Every part of me wanted to ignore the knocking, to head back into the living room, slump onto the sofa and curl up in a ball.

The walls closed in; the floor tilted and shifted under my feet. I just wanted that godawful noise to stop. Whoever was on the other side would get short shrift. I was drowsy and bleary-eyed, in no fit state to converse with anybody. If it was religious zealots wanting me to find God and repent, they could piss off. If it was neighbours wanting to talk about the attack on Jim, well they could piss off as well. I was beyond tired. I felt utterly exhausted.

The door swung open and it took a couple of seconds for it to register, for me to see her face clearly and realise who it was. I was worn out, still groggy and in no mood for visitors. She stared at me, saying nothing. I stared back, desperately trying to get my brain to function properly. Her eyes bored into me, her pupils black and precise as she stood there unmoving. Watching me closely as if I were bacteria under a microscope.

'Mary?' I said, hoping she would snap out of her trance-like state.

But rather than answer me, she simply took a step closer, lifted her face up to mine and nodded. Her lips formed a tight, accusatory grimace. Lines formed from years of disapproval and discontent splayed out from the edges of her mouth. I took a step back and shook my head at her, bewildered. Then, without a single word, she turned and walked away.

Feeling angry at being disturbed for no good reason, and putting Mary's strange behaviour down to the shock of discovering her husband bleeding and half-dead on the back lawn, I slammed the door shut and locked it. My hands were shaking. Why were my hands shaking? I had no reason to feel alarmed. I'd been disturbed, that's all it was. I was confused, trying to fling off the heavy shroud of sleep that was still wrapped tightly around me. I just needed a few minutes to bring myself to.

I leaned back against the door, the cool surface a welcoming sensation on my burning skin, and closed my eyes.

28

Sleep that night didn't come easily. I couldn't settle and was on edge, listening out for sounds that weren't there and jumping at shadows that didn't exist. It wasn't like me, not like me at all. By the time dawn broke, I was both exhausted and deeply uncomfortable, my legs restless, my entire body itching to get moving, yearning to do something productive. Anything to rid myself of the desolate feelings that had settled in my soul, the feelings of desperation that had set up camp and were refusing to leave.

Jumping out of bed, I showered and dressed and headed downstairs. The police were still hanging around the village. I stood and watched them for a while, then moved away from the window, a cup of coffee in hand, and slumped at the table. I didn't want to be around Whitchurch today. I decided I would finish my caffeine hit and head further afield, avoid the people and the endless speculations and accusations and remove myself from the tittle-tattle that would undoubtedly be in full flow by now.

I took one last sip of my coffee, slipped on my boots and set off out of the village, a location already in mind. It didn't take me long to decide where to go.

Heading past St Oswald's, taking a route over the fields, I took a walk to Whitchurch Farm, hoping to catch Terence or Diane in. I had no idea what I would say, how I would explain my unexpected appearance at their house. I couldn't tell them I was just passing. I had to cross a stream, two bridges and walk a good half mile down a country lane that led to their home and nowhere else just to get there. Such a venture could hardly be explained away as stumbling across their house while going on a ramble. I'd been invited over twice now, though, hadn't I?

A myriad of reasons for my visit ran through my head as I walked the last few yards to their grand but fashionably shabby-looking abode. It was everything I had expected it to be: a large, rambling old house with arched, Gothic-style windows, three large chimneys, a sweeping gravel drive and a couple of old dogs barking furiously in a nearby barn. I heard their chains rattle ominously as I neared the front porch, and felt my skin stiffen and grow cold as their howling reached a frenzied fever pitch. A streak of deep anxiety nipped at me. One angry dog I could possibly handle. Two was an unfeasibly difficult number to fend off. I prayed those chains were strong and the dogs were well fenced in. I liked animals as much as the next person but they never truly warmed to me. It was as if they could sense my mild fear and thinly disguised tolerance and treated me like they would a naughty puppy, always watchful and ready to jump in and take charge should the need arise.

I stopped and stared up at the stone arch above the doorway. The property may well have been called a farmhouse, but I doubted its owners had ever had to toil and put in hours of backbreaking work in the nearby fields. I felt sure the barns were more likely used to store a range of expensive classic cars rather than tractors and cumbersome farm machinery. I couldn't be certain but I got the distinct feeling that Terence and Diane were landed gentry and had never ploughed a field or got up at the crack of dawn to harvest crops in their lives. I wondered if they knew how fortunate they were, how being born into money had allowed them to lead a sheltered existence, free from the worry or burgeoning debts, free from the exhaustion of holding down a full-time manual job just to pay the bills and eat.

The brass knocker clanged loudly as I leaned forward and rapped it against the solid oak door. I was making assumptions about these people, stereotyping them and making rash judgements before I really knew anything about them. I was here as a visitor and reminded myself to keep my manners in check.

Behind me, the barking increased. Metal clanked and rattled as an unknown number of dogs yanked at their chains, desperate to break free and reach me. I swallowed down my fears and knocked again.

'Jasper! Casey!' The voice behind me caught me by surprise. I felt my legs weaken slightly and grabbed at the door frame to steady myself. The dogs didn't respond. Their howls grew ever louder. I visualised a pack of hungry, rabid dogs pelting towards me at any moment, their teeth bared in anger, drool dripping as they bounded forward, my outline fixed firmly in their sights, their noses finely attuned to my scent.

'Sorry,' the voice said brusquely. 'Damn mutts. They bark at any bloody thing. More sense in that tree trunk than in those two put together.'

I turned to see Terence emerge through an arch of

foliage next to the house. He looked as if he were appearing from another garden that sat behind the stretch of hedge. He stopped when he saw me, undoubtedly trying to work out where he knew me from.

'Hi, we met the other evening?' I said a little too enthusiastically. 'You were at the end of Church Lane taking photographs.'

The bemused expression disappeared from his face and, much to my relief, was replaced by a genuine, welcoming smile. 'Ah, yes. Of course!' he half shouted, stepping forward with his hand outstretched.

A woman's voice pierced the air, her sibilant tone and perfect English accent so clear and commanding, it almost made me stand to attention. 'Terence! Can you shut those bloody dogs up? What is their fucking problem?'

Terence looked at me, hitched his eyebrows up and smiled as we shook hands. 'Sorry, old chap. She'll have a hissy fit and be embarrassed to death when she sails around the corner and sees we have a visitor. I keep telling her about her potty mouth but it doesn't seem to stop her.'

I laughed and assured him it was fine. 'I'm partial

to a bit of swearing and cursing myself,' I said. 'It's not a problem at all.'

And then she appeared in all her glory. Diane strode towards us, her cream, skin-tight jodhpurs giving her the appearance of being completely naked. I blinked and cleared my throat, a small pulse tapping away at my temple as I watched her. Her fair hair was tied back in a tight ponytail and her skin was free of any make-up. Even without her expensive aids and accoutrements, her appearance was still immaculate and screamed wealth and status.

A wide smile appeared as she saw me, which filled me with relief. I would have expected a momentary scowl, the sort of expression that conveyed disappointment at being disturbed by an unannounced visitor. Her gait and general countenance didn't display any of those features and neither did Terence's. They seemed genuinely pleased to see me.

'Ray! So good to see you. We're delighted you decided to visit us at last, aren't we Terence?'

I was whisked away before Terence had a chance to respond. Without any pretentiousness or any of the airs or graces I half expected her to adopt, Diane slipped her arm through mine and guided me to the house. She heaved the old oak door open and we stepped into a large vestibule where she leaned down and practically ripped her boots from her feet, throwing the brown, muddied footwear to one side in an untidy heap.

I leaned down to remove my shoes and was stopped as she shook her head and took my hand, pulling me into the large hallway. 'It's fine. I only took mine off because I've been mucking the horses out. Poor Tilda, our cleaning lady, has to clean up all the shit I drag in if I don't take them off.'

I nodded and followed her, my heels making a rhythmic tapping sound on the parquet flooring as we walked across the huge hallway. Terence was behind us. He too took off his wellies and padded through in socks that were practically threadbare. Such an odd couple, and yet I found that I was quickly warming to them. Their eccentricities made them human, made me forget about the vast difference in our social standing. We weren't equals – probably never would be – but I felt comfortable being around these two with their unpredictable ways and endearing eccentricities.

'Coffee?' Terence said as he stepped forward and led us into a large room which I assumed was a library or a study.

Rows and rows of books lined the walls, many of them old and decaying and probably worth a fortune.

I wondered how many first editions were slotted in there and slowly scanned the shelves with a keen eye. As a younger man, I had once made an attempt to collect first-edition books and still had a few even now, although I doubted they were anything as important or substantial as the books that were contained within this room.

'Or would you prefer something a little stronger?' Terence moved over to a bureau at the far end of the room where a tray of amber liquid sat in a crystal decanter. He held up a couple of squat glass tumblers and shook one of them at me, a mischievous twinkle in his eye.

'Terence!' Diane cried as she slumped onto a nearby sofa and indicated for me to do the same with a sharp nod of her head. 'For God's sake, man. It's not even lunchtime yet. Poor Ray here will think us a pair of old alcoholics. A coffee will be fine. Has Hubert already left?'

'He has left, but no matter, I'll make it,' Terence replied brightly, showing no signs of annoyance after being publicly humiliated by his wife. There was no doubt where the balance of power lay in this relationship. Terence was a quiet, biddable character and Diane, by comparison, was confident and driven. Perhaps they preferred it that way. Perhaps Terence enjoyed being bossed around by a strong character like Diane. Some men thrived on being ground down by powerful women. I was glad I wasn't one of them.

He bustled away, whistling as he left until Diane and I were left alone in the large-panelled room, surrounded by hundreds if not thousands of books. A small silence took hold before Diane's voice echoed around the place.

'So, Ray. How are things in Whitchurch today? Poor old Jim, eh? What a terrible carry-on,' she said, her voice softer now. Her legs were swept up under her bottom and she had pulled her hair free of the ponytail. Great locks of dark-blonde tresses framed her face, making her look petite and vulnerable. Which of course, she wasn't. I was certain Diane was many things, but vulnerable didn't strike me as being one of her foremost or outstanding traits.

'Yes, completely terrible,' I replied, echoing her sentiments. 'I think it's frightened a lot of people. Everyone is wondering what's next. And it was totally unexpected too.'

'Oh, I don't know,' Diane murmured as she leaned back and flicked her long, slender fingers through her silky hair, teasing out the golden strands with her fingernails. 'Jim has always been a pretty controversial figure in the village. Not quite as meek and mild as he would have you believe.'

I took a deep breath, crossed my legs tightly, then leaned forward, my body angled towards Diane as I studied her expression closely. 'Really? How so?'

'He used to be a local councillor. Pissed quite a few people off,' Diane replied breezily, as if it were the norm to discuss such matters given the fact that Jim was currently laid up in a hospital bed, connected to a drip, with half a dozen police officers trying to work out who it was that had put him there.

'Including us,' Terence said as he came back in the room carrying a tray of cups. He set it down on a nearby coffee table that wobbled about precariously on the old wooden floor. My eyes were drawn to the dusty, cracked floorboards that had seen better days. They looked original to the house, which I assumed was built many centuries ago. I was willing to bet it took a small fortune just to maintain this house, let alone update and modernise it.

'If you must know, I can't stand the man,' Terence barked, his face suddenly full of thunder.

I almost laughed. Did either of them have any idea how they sounded, how their words could be construed as having 'just cause' for attacking a seriously wounded man? I remained silent. The look on

Terence's face was enough. His eyes creased at the corners as he set about handing out the cups of steaming coffee, his lips white and thin, set in a determined line.

I took my drink and sipped at the hot coffee, wincing as it burnt my gullet. A protracted silence took hold. It didn't last long. Terence sat down beside Diane, their eyes locking briefly before he took a deep breath and began to speak.

29

'We had a major fall out with him,' Terence said quietly. His eyes were dipped to the floor as he spoke. He looked up and over to Diane before continuing. 'We applied for planning permission quite a few years back to extend the farmhouse and turn the barns into an annexe. We planned to use them as a B&B. Jim was dead against the idea and blocked us time and time again.'

'Not only that,' Diane added. 'He got others on board with his negative vibes and ideas about how it would drag the area down, bringing in hordes of tourists who would litter the place and clog the roads up. He was a fairly influential councillor and made sure that we'd never be able to go ahead with our plans. He also spread rumours that we had tried to bribe him, which was utter nonsense, but unfortunately people believed him. He was a churchgoer and a man of influence. Everyone went along with his stupid claims whether they believed him or not. They were all too scared to speak up.'

I continued to sip at my coffee, thinking how best to reply. 'You said he pissed a few people off and yet all the villagers took his side?'

Terence sighed and ran his fingers through his hair wearily. 'Like Diane just said, Jim was a man of influence, a person in authority. I think they felt pressured by him, too afraid to go against anything he said. But then things changed. A few years before Jim retired and a few years after he blocked us, Jack Radcliffe over at Winston Farm applied to do the same thing. He had inherited the place from his parents along with a shedload of mounting debts. He figured he would turn the place into a guest house and try to make it pay. Once again, Jim Speight took it upon himself to block Jack's application, claiming tourists would spoil the surrounding countryside and citing lack of proper access as another reason.'

'And this Jack Radcliffe never managed to overturn Jim's decision?' I finished my coffee and placed it down with a dull thud. I stared at the cup. It was chipped and had seen better days. Maybe I had got it all wrong about these people. Maybe their finances weren't as healthy as I had initially thought. Or maybe they simply had better things to spend their money on. Like this house, for instance. They needed money for this place and had thought a B&B would be the answer to their prayers, only for it to be knocked back by Jim. A house of this size and age must eat cash. I imagined even the wealthiest of folk still needed extraordinarily deep pockets to keep a place of this size in a half decent state.

'He tried but couldn't afford to keep putting in appeal after appeal. He had bills to pay. The bailiffs were regular visitors at Jack's house.' Diane's voice had lost its authoritative air. There was no strength to it, just a streak of sadness as she said his name.

'So, what happened?' I asked, almost certain this story had no happy ending.

'He shot himself,' Terence cut in, his voice thick with unreserved resentment and anger. 'Twenty-five years old, just a few years out of university, and he took one of his father's guns, put it in his mouth and blew his brains out. It was a debt collector who saw his body through the window and called the police. Fucking awful. Absolutely fucking awful. So, when you talk about Jim bloody Speight being beaten up, believe me when I say, there are plenty of people out there who have every reason to hate the old bastard. I don't care how injured he is or how much pain he might be in, he'll get no sympathy from me.'

I could hear Terence's breathing from where I was sitting, rasping and laboured. I had stirred up a hornets' nest coming here. There were, it would appear, plenty of people who had reasons to hate poor old Jim.

'Jack was a popular lad.' Diane spoke slowly; her face was fixed on Terence's as he stared at the floor. 'He'd grown up here. He lost both his parents in quick succession to cancer and tried to make a go of the farm but to no avail. It was heartbreaking to everyone who knew him. A terrible, terrible tragedy.'

Stillness gripped us. Anything I said would have been deemed insulting to the lad's memory. I couldn't make any of it any better so I sat for a short while and thought about what Terence and Diane had just told me. So many people who disliked Jim. He didn't come across as a particularly wicked man, but then you never can tell, can you? People have hidden depths, facets of their personality they keep concealed away from the watching world. We all want be perceived as friendly, affable. Delve inside our heads and you may well find another person lurking, somebody entirely different to the mask we wear on a daily basis.

At last, I broke the silence. 'I guess the police will know all of this? The bit about him refusing planning permission, I mean.'

Both Terence and Diane shrugged listlessly as I spoke.

'Possibly,' Diane said.

'Shouldn't they be told?' My voice was a like a whip cracking between us, bouncing off every surface, every syllable sharp and accentuated. I had phrased it badly, making it sound like an accusation. I hadn't mean it to come out that way but the words were out there now. I couldn't take them back.

Terence's head shot up. He glared at me and scowled. 'And put ourselves forward as possible suspects? What do you think we are – completely insane?'

'No, sorry, I didn't mean that. I just think—'

'It wasn't either of us who attacked Jim, if that's what you're thinking,' Diane interjected. Her voice was calm, measured. 'We're not violent people. We don't even go hunting, for God's sake. What we're saying is, if the police want to find whoever it was that tried to bash Jim's brains out, then they'll have a hefty list to go through. Like we already told you, he wasn't

– and as far as I'm concerned, still isn't – a popular man.'

I nodded, keen to convince them that I wasn't here to cause trouble or point the finger. 'You said he was a churchgoer?'

'Used to be. I don't attend so couldn't tell you if he still goes there every week. I pray God forgives him for what he did to that boy. Because I most certainly don't.'

I couldn't help but admire Diane's dogmatic view of Jim. Many would have yielded to pressure, said the right thing, tried to show compassion when all the time they felt none for the man who had wronged them and many others. At least I knew where I stood with these people. They were truthful, tenacious. A far cry from the weeping and wailing of Alice and some of the other locals who obviously saw Jim as a pillar of the community, a man who knew right from wrong, somebody whose word should be taken as gospel. And if he was still a strong churchgoer, that would explain Alice and Emily's obvious distress, especially Alice. She was a devout Christian. The church was her life, or at least that was how it came across. Myself, I had little or no time for the church. If that was how some people chose to spend their days, then that was down to them, but it most certainly wasn't for me.

A thought occurred to me just as I was about to announce that I should be leaving. I placed my hands on my knees and leaned forward, towards Terence, wanting to bring him back into the conversation. He was still scowling and it seemed as if his mood had soured. I didn't want our possible friendship tainted by what I had said. 'Lily's dad?' I uttered softly. 'Apparently he used to be the rector at St Oswald's?'

'He did. What of it?' Terence bristled as he spoke. I wasn't yet forgiven then.

'No reason really. Somebody mentioned it recently. I was wondering if he is friendly with Jim. I'd heard—'

'That he's another shit of a man?' Terence replied, the beginnings of a sardonic smile showing on his face.

'Well,' I said tentatively, 'I'm not really placed to say too much, having just moved here, but yes, somebody happened to mention it and I bumped into Lily the other day. She was really upset after an argument with him.' I stopped suddenly, no idea of where my probing was actually leading us. 'Anyway,' I added, 'it doesn't really matter. It's not relevant to anything.'

'Dominic is the best rector Whitchurch has had for years,' Diane said brightly, her voice like a sudden shining light in a dimly lit room. 'He's human. He cares. As I said, it's not that I'm a churchgoer. But I do know that before Dominic, we had Alan Hambling, Lily's dad. He and Jim were good buddies for years and years, right up until Alan's retirement. Jim's been friends with every vicar we've ever had. Of course, it doesn't matter that he and Dominic aren't best mates. Not that they don't get on, you understand, but there's no real incentive for Jim to be really close to Dominic. Vicars have no real power any more, do they? Not like the good old days when their word carried a fair amount of weight. Dominic is a new breed of vicar and exactly how a reverend should be: compassionate, kind, always thinking of others.'

I understood. I understood completely.

'It's all new to me. I guess I'm just trying to find my feet and work out what is going on in Whitchurch at the minute.' I stood up and exhaled loudly. 'I'd best be off anyway. Thanks for the coffee. And it's a lovely house you have here.' I almost added that it would have been a perfect location for a B&B but thought better of it. I'd already put my foot in it and upset Terence. Best to leave things as they were.

They both stood up, the mood between us lighter as I made my way out into their grand hallway with its sweeping staircase and the prerequisite chandelier and large ceiling rose. I liked these people, I really did. Despite our obvious differences, they were truthful and I respected them for that.

Being frank was a trait I liked in people. Hidden agendas and lying, I deplored. I'd grown up around untrustworthy, controlling people and I'd had a gutful of it. Samantha had been controlling. She'd done her best to steer me in the direction she wanted me to go, to alter the natural trajectory of my life. I'd resisted. We'd fought. And now it was over.

'Call around again, Ray. Anytime at all. I love Whitchurch, I really do,' Diane said chirpily, 'but it can be quite claustrophobic at times. Everybody living so close to each other, knowing one another's business...' Her voice trailed off. We couldn't all live in such grandiose surroundings and she knew that. I didn't doubt for one minute that it would be lovely to have so much space, to be surrounded by rolling fields and splendid views of the hills, but we didn't all have Terence and Diane's advantages in life, their breeding or obvious birthright. I didn't hold her comments against them. I had my own life, a nice place to live, my own plans. I didn't envy them one little bit.

'I'll see you around,' I said cheerfully as they walked me to the door. I stepped over the threshold and out into the scorching heat. I shielded my eyes against the glare of the sun and gave them a curt wave. They responded accordingly, waving back and smiling before turning to look at one another, then moving back into the shadows of their enormous hallway and closing the door with a resounding bang.

30

ME

The friends I had soon disappeared off my radar and I became quite the loner. It was easier that way. I developed an edge and learned how to keep people away. While other teenagers partied and mingled, had sex and got drunk, I stayed at home, feeding my fury with books. I read them all: fiction, non-fiction, love stories and crime thrillers, but I focused heavily on psychology texts that explored the links between religious mania and mental illness. I knew my father was psychotic, had known it for many years, but felt a deep desire to see it in print, to confirm my own suppositions and theories. Seeing it written down made me feel slightly less lonely. Those words were my friends. They cemented my suspicions, allowed me to explore the idea that none of what had happened was my fault. My father was obviously unbalanced, his thinking skewed and unfathomable, his actions most definitely vile and unforgiveable.

And as for me? I knew even at that early juncture of my life that I was damaged, my own thinking and logic too dented and misaligned to ever be put right. It was all too late. My life was on a downward spiral, with no way back up. My family life had turned to dust; friends were few and far between. It was at that point, I disappeared inside my own head, to never truly re-emerge as the person I was.

I suffered terribly with nightmares, lost weight and oftentimes wished I was dead. But then I figured, why should I continue to suffer? I'd undergone enough hardship, endured enough pain for a hundred people. It was time I lived a little. Time I started to be me, the real me, no matter how badly spoiled and damaged I was, I needed to do something, to find an outlet for my slowly festering anger. So, I honed my social skills, modelled myself on other people, learned how to act like everybody else while harbouring the darkest of thoughts. It became my little secret. Nobody knew, least of all my parents. They thought I'd finally grown out of my awkward teenage phase and developed into a smart, pleasant young adult.

How little they knew.

They thought they had the measure of me when in truth, they didn't understand me and had never really known me at all. I was their enigmatic child, the one they fought hard to control, and at long last, I had started to advance my own thoughts and feelings which were in direct contrast to the ones they tried to instil in me.

So, here we are again – back to the original debate about which is the greater driving force, nature or nurture? Was I really born bad or did they make me that way? While trying to drive the demons out of me, did they pave the way for more to sneak in?

Talk to any of the villagers and they will tell you what a lovely person I am, how helpful and polite I am. I chat, mingle, smile. I go through the motions of being a compassionate, thoughtful person but deep down, I am nothing like them. I am under no illusions that they actually do care about their fellow humans, whereas I only pretend to. I am an outstanding performer when it comes to emulating others. The best there is.

Don't get me wrong, there are some of them that I quite like. Perhaps that's too strong a word; I admire some of their personality traits. I tolerate them. At least, I don't spend my every waking moment fantasising about hurting them. Then there are others that I could easily kill with my bare hands. But not just yet. All in good time.

I've enjoyed teasing them with my little misdemeanours, whipping them into a frenzy over threatening letters and dog shit and a bit of graffiti. It's been hilarious to see how small their lives are and how fast they implode over the tiniest of inconveniences, because let's be honest here, that's all those happenings were. Just minor occurrences in the lives of a pack of nobodies. The same nobodies who knew of the abuse meted out to me and did nothing. So they deserve all they get. And there's more to come.

Catching Jim unawares as he leaned over his telescope was a stroke of luck. I had seen him from my bedroom window and on impulse decided to creep around his back garden. Silly move on his part, not replacing the broken padlock on the side gate that led around the back of his house. The village was in silence but I wore a dark, hooded top anyway. Whitchurch doesn't have any CCTV. There's no need. Or at least there wasn't then. Maybe now some overzealous neighbour will install a camera of their own with which to catch their homegrown terrorist.

I'm not even sure they suspect a local. Unless the name of the local person is Gavin Yuill. Did you know that wood barely makes any sound when it hits solid bone? So little noise, but the thrill of seeing all that blood spurt form the back of Jim's head was practically orgasmic.

After dragging his body into the darkness behind the huge old shed, I hit him again and again. I had no idea whether or not I wanted him dead. I just needed to vent my anger, to rid myself of the mounting feelings of resentment and hate that had been building for weeks and weeks. And it worked. Afterwards I felt pure, my body and mind as clear as spring water. It was like a purge, freeing myself of the terrible memories and hatred. Afterwards, I went home, showered, cleaned up and slept the sleep of the dead.

The furore next morning was exhilarating. The crowds of onlookers, the wringing of hands, the sobbing and crying. I almost laughed.

It's so humorous and entertaining, keeping them all guessing, seeing the torment on their faces, the bewilderment in their eyes as yet another crime is committed. They honestly have no idea what to expect next. Every time something happens, they are blindsided, such is their ignorance. And that's the fun part. They don't know why any of this is taking place. They are all too stupid, too wrapped up in their own selfish little worlds to begin to comprehend why they are being punished, why their quiet little village is slowly being torn apart piece by pathetic little piece.

But they will. Soon, they will all know. Jim isn't the only one who is going to suffer. My next victim's injuries may not be of the calibre inflicted upon that sad little man, but they will know when I strike. Nobody is going to forget me when I'm done with them. I'll make my mark. I'll dent their memories, make them suffer, just like I suffered while they all stood by and did nothing.

By the time I'm done, Whitchurch will bitterly regret their lack of assistance; they will wish they had done the right thing and intervened. I'll make sure of it. Because it wasn't only my parents who made me the monster that I am today; they all played a part. Their obliviousness, turning a blind eye to it all – every little act of indifference helped to shape me. How does the old saying go? *All that is necessary for evil to triumph is that good men do nothing.* And they all did just that – nothing. Not a damn thing. They all played a part in making sure my soul rotted at the hands of my father.

And now they are being punished.

31

The police continued hanging around the village over the next few days, making door to door enquiries until everybody had been interviewed, every avenue of possibility explored. And they didn't appear to be any closer to finding out who had beaten Jim to within an inch of his life. No evidence, no witnesses, and despite what Terence and Diane had said earlier in the week, no motive.

Jim remained in hospital. His recovery was a slow but steady one, his age a determining factor in how long it would take for him to recuperate fully. In spite of the battering he'd received, his injuries weren't as severe as first feared. He suffered a fractured cheekbone, two broken fingers from his attempts to protect his face and two fractured ribs. His bruises, according to locals who had visited him in hospital, were pretty traumatic and the psychological impact would probably stay with him for quite some time.

Whitchurch was eerily quiet, even more so than usual. I would have liked to say that with the passing of time – almost a week since Jim's attack – people were feeling better, but that would have been a lie. Everybody was on edge. It was like treading on eggshells. Village folk too afraid to stop and speak to each other, everyone watching from behind their curtains, jumping at unexplained noises and lurking shadows as the sun made its sleepy descent every evening. The atmosphere was charged with real fear, a sense of dread so thick and impermeable, you could practically touch it. Chatting to the locals, I could almost taste their terror and see the film of fear that covered them, worming its way under their skin and burying itself deep in their emotions. Nothing anybody said or did would alleviate the deep unease that had settled on the place. We were shrouded in fear, waiting, wondering what or who would be next.

We didn't have to wait too long to find out.

Exactly a week after Jim was attacked, the residents of Whitchurch were woken in the early hours by screaming and the incessant high-pitched howl of a smoke alarm that tore at our eardrums and forced us out of our beds and into the road to see what was happening.

I pulled at my joggers, stepping into them roughly, and ran barefoot across to the green where a small crowd of people were staring up at a house. Emily's house. A ball of orange was visible through the living room window and black smoke billowed out of the open front door, great plumes of it trailing down the path like huge, elongated arms of death, beckoning the stupid and the fearless inside.

Somebody punched at their phone with trembling fingers, their eyes wide and dewy under the ochre glow of a nearby streetlight.

'We've called. It's okay, the fire brigade is on its way!' a voice cried out.

'Emily? Where the hell is Emily?' a female voice shouted. 'We opened the front door but couldn't get past the smoke. Jesus Christ, she's still in there!'

'Emily! Emily!' A cacophony of voices screamed her name, the sound escaping into the darkness, swallowed up by the crackling of the fire. A sudden burst of flames licked at the window, shattering the glass with an ear-splitting boom.

People screamed and scurried around me like ants, moving, turning, bumping into each other. Confusion reigned; sorrow and terror gripped everyone. Voices yelled out, and sobbing came from behind me, muffled by the sound of breaking glass and howling flames.

Time seemed to slow down; everything became a blur. Then, to the screams of everybody standing close by, two figures appeared from behind the burning building. We all watched as a couple of hunched shadows emerged from the narrow opening that led down to the back garden of Emily's house.

'Oh my God, she's here! She's alive!'

The shrieking, terrified crowd threw themselves towards the silhouetted pair, arms and voices raised, chaos and disorder slowly turning into suspicion and anger as they tore the elderly lady away from her rescuer and rounded on the man, who was bent double, coughing and gagging, saliva hanging from his lower lip as he gasped for breath in the warm night air.

'You! Why the hell are you here? And how did you find Emily?' a voice roared in the darkness as Gavin Yuill caught his breath and stood up to face the angry throng.

His skin was blackened by smoke. He staggered back and forth, disorientated and confused, before collapsing where he stood, hitting the ground with a heavy thud.

The whine of sirens infiltrated the screaming, angry voices. Two fire engines rumbled to a halt in front of Emily's house and a team of firefighters spilled out and parted the crowd, taking control of the situation.

I stepped over to where Gavin lay, accompanied by a concerned firefighter who called for an ambulance and then rolled him onto one side and placed Gavin's blackened body in the recovery position.

Two police cars arrived and in a matter of seconds, I was relieved to find that I was gently pushed back while they dealt with the situation and took charge.

Moving away, I stood on the periphery of the huddle of people, listening to their wild accusations and unfounded suspicions about Gavin and his involvement with the fire and Emily's subsequent rescue.

Two villagers tried talking to the police, shouting their theories at them, but were pushed back and told to wait until the fire had died down and Gavin was dealt with and given proper medical assistance before they made any assumptions about the source of the blaze. This response seemed to rile them all the more. Their voices hit a pitch so high, I had to cover my ears and take a step back. They screamed that they wanted him arrested, taken in for questioning. Gavin Yuill was given a public trial on the village green of Whitchurch and found very much guilty of arson and the attempted murder of Emily Dawson, the retired schoolteacher. The residents of Whitchurch were baying for his blood.

As discreetly as I could, I disappeared from the screaming gang, slipped into the shadows and hid behind the large trunk of a nearby conifer. We would all be interviewed again in the morning. The police would undoubtedly work their way through everybody in the vicinity, asking us where we were in the early hours, and I'd be willing to bet that our answers would be almost identical – in bed, sleeping. Unless the fire service and police found some sort of incriminating evidence, this fire could either be put down to an accidental occurrence, or it could be added to Whitchurch's ever-growing list of recent atrocities that remained unsolved. Such a small village and yet so many crimes and heartache. Perhaps, given recent events, the investigating officers would decide to put more effort into this particular incident, have more people working on the case to find out who was behind it all. Because the villagers did actually have every right to be angry, to feel incensed. The last two incidents were attempted murder. In the last week, the person behind these crimes had definitely upped their game.

* * *

My body felt like a lead weight as I slid between the bed sheets and closed my eyes. I caught sight of the clock. It was 3 a.m., the green glow of the numbers on my bedside clock projecting a thin beam of light onto the adjacent wall.

I sighed softly, expecting to lie awake for the rest of the morning, ruminating over what had just happened, my mind mulling over everything that had gone on since my arrival in Whitchurch. Instead, I fell into a deep and pleasant slumber and awoke later in the morning to the sound of birdsong from the blackbird that sat in the tree at the bottom of my garden.

Stretching gratefully, I threw the covers back and sat up. Today, I would keep myself to myself. I would let the locals do their thing, let them continue to throw their collective weight around, accusing Yuill and pointing the finger at him despite not having a shred of evidence. Their minds were already made up. Gavin was their man. They were all so sure of it. Nothing I said or did would change that. The fact he lived next door to Emily and had probably been able to access her house from the back and climb in to rescue her didn't occur to any of them. It also never dawned on them that he could have actually saved her life. Were it not for his actions, she could still be there now, gasping for breath, close to death in her burning home. Their view of him was so deeply distorted that cold, hard facts no longer mattered. I smiled sadly at poor Gavin's predicament, knowing it was what it was and nothing anybody said or did would change their minds.

Today I would stay home, read the paper, watch TV. I fully expected a knock on the door from the police asking me where I had been when the fire started. That didn't disturb me. It was routine, part of their investigative work.

I showered, the hot water burning my skin as I stood, letting it pummel my body. The smell of smoke had clung to my clothes and hair and the noxious stench was making me feel rather nauseous. I scrubbed at my flesh until it was raw, and washed my hair twice until it squeaked. I just wanted to feel clean, to rid myself of the overpowering odour of burning that seemed to permeate everywhere.

I dressed, stripped the bed sheets off, gathered them up along with my clothes from last night and jumbled them all into a big pile ready to be washed.

But first I would eat breakfast, read the news once more on my laptop, find out whether or not anything had changed out in the big wide world, see if any murders had been solved or missing people been found.

32

It was a terrible mistake, catching up on what was happening elsewhere in the country. I slammed the laptop shut. More depressing news from down in Birmingham. I didn't live there any more so had no idea why I'd even decided to read it. The pictures had jumped out at me, making me feel sick as I scanned the local news. The photographs, large and lifelike and staring out at me from the computer screen, had caught me unawares. I just needed a few seconds to gather my thoughts and do my best to shut those images out of my head. I took a few deep breaths and stared out of the window.

Birmingham was a big city, with lots going on; many crimes would be forgotten within a few days, only to be replaced by more current ones. I had no need to fret, no need at all. Today's news was tomorrow's history.

Outside, the sun climbed in the sky. Inside, the heat grew. My skin was clammy. My stomach let out a howl of protestation at being deprived of food, yet I didn't feel hungry. What I actually felt was quite sick.

Standing up, I paced around the kitchen. I had to snap out of this. It was ridiculous. I was getting myself involved in matters that were no longer of any concern of mine. Birmingham was my other life. I needed to focus on the here and now. Whitchurch and its residents were my life. And I liked living here, I really did. It was quirky and mundane and hilarious and depressing all at the same time. There was nowhere else like it.

I sat down again and ran my fingers through my hair, feeling weary and exasperated. Food. I needed some sustenance, whether I felt the pangs of real hunger or not. If anything, it would help pass the time.

I rummaged through the cupboards, ate a bowl of cereal and made myself a cup of coffee. The cereal was tasteless and the coffee weak, but bit by bit, the sense of dread that had clawed its way inside me and settled heavily began to lift.

I vowed to steer clear of reading anything else to do with my old home town. It was all too disheartening. Everything about it reminded me of Samantha and I really, really didn't want to give any thought to her. She simply wasn't worth it. I wasn't normally the sort of person given to such sentiments. Misery, worry, regret – they all washed over me. I had no time for them in my life. Our time here on earth is too short to spend it worrying over things that have gone before, things we can't change.

And yet there was no escaping that story, those photographs. So clear, so striking.

Putting my pots in the ancient dishwasher, I dispensed with the idea of staying in. Disappearing inside my own head and getting lost in unwelcome thoughts wouldn't be good for me today. What I needed to do was get out, clear out the cobwebs, take a walk, go to the pub, do whatever was required to get myself back in top form. The notion of sitting with the usual crew in The Pot and Glass lifted my spirits almost immediately. Seeing Lily would cheer me up even more.

I laughed quietly. I liked being me; I loved the fact it didn't take me long to crawl out of the deep hole of despondency and despair that sometimes appeared in my life unbidden. I would go to the pub, chat, mingle, probably talk, mainly about the fire, and listen to everybody put their views forward as to what was going on in Whitchurch, who it was that had spread the dogshit, spray-painted the gravestones, attacked Jim and then tried to burn poor old Emily's house down. I would drink, listen and return home to my little house, happy in the knowledge that my life was back on track. Samantha and Delores were far behind me. I'd left no forwarding address. I'd blocked Delores from my phone and changed my email address. Any further missives she may have sent were currently bouncing around the ether, looking for a recipient that would never be found.

I tried with those two women, I really did, but there comes a point in everybody's life when enough is simply enough. They were draining the lifeblood out of me with their incessant nagging and controlling behaviour, so I left. They gave me no other options. It was all their fault. And yet in a way, they did me a huge favour, allowing me to find a new life for myself, to throw off the shackles of a toxic relationship and start again anew. I had everything I wanted right here.

It was fortuitous, this house being available at exactly the right time. Like fate giving me a helping hand, pushing me on, giving me its blessing.

I decided to go into town, do some shopping. I was low on food and needed a change of scenery and it was too early to go to the pub. I had to do something to pass the time. If the police called, they would have to come back later. I wasn't about to sit around waiting for them to come to me. I had a life to live.

* * *

The town was relatively quiet considering it was still the school holidays. A handful of sweaty-looking toddlers clung onto their mothers' hands. Everybody appeared miserable. The heat was too much. After a freezing winter, we had all cried out for the warmth a decent summer would bring and now it had arrived in all its blazing glory, we didn't want it. It was extreme and we weren't equipped to deal with it. All we wanted was the rain.

Shops had bottles of water stacked in doorways, pharmacies were offering two for one on purchases of sun lotion and crates of beer and lager were strategically placed near the entrances of supermarkets, alongside barbecue equipment with signs that screamed at customers to *buy, buy, buy*.

I browsed the aisles, untouched by the madness of it all, and bought what I needed before returning home to the relative quiet of Whitchurch. Even after the attack and the fire, and everything else that had gone on, compared to the mayhem of Durham, the village seemed unnervingly quiet, as if everybody had decided to hibernate and shut themselves away from the most recent tragedy.

The pungent smell of smoke still hung in the air. People in official-looking uniforms stood outside Emily's house, holding clipboards, surveying the damage with serious expressions on their faces.

I pulled up outside the front of my house and yanked the handbrake on. Further along the road, two police cars pulled up, their wheels crunching on loose stones as they parked up at the kerbside. I watched as four uniformed officers got out and stood on the pavement near Emily's house, their eyes drawn to the blackened windows and charred brickwork. I had hoped I'd missed them and their questions while I was out in town. Three interviews in a matter of weeks was more than I could stomach.

A younger officer turned and looked at me, his eyes locking with mine then travelling over the length of my car as his gaze moved away from me. His steely glare made me apprehensive. On impulse, I decided to park my car in the alleyway behind the house. It made sense. I had bags of shopping to unload and access was easier.

Turning the key in the ignition, I rotated the steering wheel and reversed the car into a layby before spinning it around and heading up towards the back of the house. I glanced in the rear-view mirror to see the watching officer turn away from me and focus his attention on his colleagues, who were making their way towards Emily's property. I drove on and puffed out my cheeks. As it should be. That was where the incident had taken place, not in my car or near my house. He would probably be knocking on my door at some point, needing my help, asking me what I knew about the fire, so he had better improve his scowl and stop looking at every neighbour as if they were a possible suspect.

By the time I had parked up, hauled the groceries out of the car and emptied all the bags, I was feeling hot and bad-tempered. I didn't like being scrutinised by somebody young and inexperienced who, at some point in the next day or so, may need my assistance. I hoped, if he did come calling, asking for information, that his manner was more refined than his countenance and body language, which lacked finesse and a certain amount of discretion.

I didn't have to wait long for the call. I had just finished making a cup of tea when I heard the rap at the door. I knew immediately it would be them. After the previous visits, I recognised their style – the sustained and rhythmic fashion they applied when knocking on people's doors. It reverberated throughout the house, making my skin prickle. I'd had enough of police interviews but knew there would be no escaping it. It was just a formality, something everybody would be having to go through until the investigation was complete.

I drained the last of my tea, shuffled through the hallway and opened to the door to two burly policemen. The younger officer was missing, probably interviewing other villagers. A wave of relief swept through me. I had no reason to feel that way, apart from the fact I had taken an instant dislike to him. He'd had a knowing look about him, the sort that a young buck who always goes the extra mile to prove his worth has, and I wasn't in the mood for that sort of questioning, for any tricks from a smart-arsed young kid barely out of nappies who thought he could solve a crime just by turning up.

I nodded at the pair standing on my front step, listened to their spiel – the formalities informing me who they were and why they were here – then stepped aside and let them inside my home.

33

It didn't take long. They had a lot of people to speak to, they told me, many houses to visit. I debated whether or not I should inform them of Gavin's sneaky exit from the graveyard. Would it be worth backtracking to such a minor incident? My promises to meet up with Gavin to socialise and have a pint hadn't materialised and, given recent events, it looked unlikely it would ever happen. I had nothing to lose by telling them about it. If Gavin Yuill was innocent then it was down to these people to prove just that. Not telling them would be withholding evidence.

'I realise this isn't directly relevant to what happened at poor Emily's house,' I said after I had told them that I was in bed when I heard the smoke alarm go off and that no, I hadn't seen anybody hanging around and no, I hadn't noticed any unusual activity the day of the fire. 'But a few weeks back, some of the gravestones at St Oswald's were desecrated. The headstones were covered with spray paint, flowers were tipped over and vases smashed.'

The two men nodded and waited for me to continue. I had half expected it to be the same officers who had called last week – Trewitt and Redmayne – when I got the knock at the door, but instead I'd had to be introduced to two different people. More relationships to build, more trust to attempt to gain.

'Well, I was going to speak to the two officers about it last week, but I wasn't sure if it was relevant or not. However, given recent events, I think every piece of information is useful, isn't it?' I looked at them for affirmation before continuing. The older of the two at least had the good grace to nod at me and smile.

'Anyway,' I murmured, feeling slightly less enthusiastic about imparting this new piece of information now I had started to open up, 'I was out walking. Since moving here, I've been taking daily walks around the local area to familiarise myself with the place, and on my way back, I bumped into Gavin Yuill on his way out of the churchyard. That was the night before the vandalism was discovered. Now, I'm not saying he did it or anything like that,' I said firmly, 'but I wouldn't feel good about myself if I didn't tell you. Especially with the most recent spate of crimes that have happened.'

The two officers glanced at each other, then back at me. I got the distinct feeling I had said something that didn't ring true with them, something that was starting to make me feel uncomfortable.

The older guy, who introduced himself as DC Bradbury, clasped his hands together and smiled at me. He had a look on his face I didn't care for. 'Right,' he said lightly, as if I were a naughty schoolchild telling tales to teacher, 'we'll certainly look into that. Of course, Mr Yuill isn't considered a suspect at the moment but any information is always welcome.'

I suddenly remembered Emily's statement about Yuill being in Oxford when Jim was attacked and winced. It looked like I was trying to frame the guy. I should have remembered that vital fact. It would make me look stupid if I started throwing accusations around without any hard evidence to back it up. They would think me an idiot.

A hot flush crawled up my spine and planted itself in the back of my skull. I was ready for them to leave now. I'd had enough of police interviews and probing questions. I needed a break from it. More than that, I needed a drink. I visualised an ice-cold pint served up by Lily. I could almost see her soft hands caressing the glass, the way she ran her pink tongue over her perfect teeth as she handed it over to me.

'Right, sorry,' I said quietly, furious with myself for speaking before I'd thought it through properly. 'Silly of me to even mention it, but as I said, I'd feel permanently guilty if I didn't and it turned out to be important afterwards.'

There was a short silence and I wondered if they had something else they wanted to say. It only lasted a matter of seconds but felt much longer. Eventually, Bradbury stood up and his colleague followed his lead, striding towards the hallway ducking to get through the doorframe.

'Thanks for your help, Mr Smith. We'll be in touch if we need anything else. Or if you remember anything that you think might be important, contact us on this number.' Bradbury handed over a small card. I took it without looking at it. I was pretty sure I had nothing else to say to them, no nuggets of information hiding away in the deepest recesses of my brain that would help with this case. They were the detectives. It was up to them to solve this crime.

I said goodbye and closed the door, assuring them

I'd be in touch if anything leapt into my mind that I thought may be important.

Breathing a heavy sigh of relief, I dashed upstairs. Perspiration coated my skin. I ripped off my clothes and stepped into the shower, letting the cool water trickle over my aching body. I closed my eyes and almost immediately, images swamped my brain, making me dizzy. I brushed them away, furious with myself for allowing them to take up space. I figured the intensity of the last few weeks was finally getting to me, taking a toll on my thinking. I couldn't allow that to happen. A relationship ending, moving halfway across the country, two major crimes within the space of a week; it was bound to have an effect, but what I couldn't do was let it take over completely and define me. I had moved here to escape that sort of pressure. There was no way I could allow myself to be sucked back into it. I needed to take a more linear approach to how I dealt with things and not get dragged into the minutiae, the whys and wherefores, to follow the events down a different path when all I wanted to do was live an easy life and enjoy what I had here in Whitchurch.

I finished showering and dressed in clean clothes. I didn't care if the police were still wandering around the village. I didn't care if they were propping up the bar when I got to the pub; I was determined to have a pint. I'd earned it and I would savour every drop.

The sky had darkened somewhat as I stepped outside and locked up. Forecasters had mentioned the possibility of rain overnight but nobody dared hope. So many promises had turned out to be empty ones. Like the clouds above, they simply didn't deliver. Farmers had already begun to harvest months earlier than usual, their fields of crops dying in drought conditions.

In the distance, the deep drone of combine harvesters filled the air. The farmers would work through the night, clearing their yields before the crops became too desiccated, salvaging what they could of one of the cruellest summers we had seen for decades. I thought about my conversation with Terence and Diane about poor Jack Radcliffe and his inability to make a profit from his farm, and what it had done to him. It was a tough existence in conditions like this – relying on the weather, wishing there was an easier way, then discovering one and being blocked by councillors who had gold-plated pensions and didn't understand true hardship.

I shook my head and headed towards the pub. I needed to clear my thoughts, relax a little and enjoy myself. It had been tough lately. Delores and her earlier threats hadn't helped. It was nothing to do with me if her daughter hadn't been in touch with her. Why was she making it my problem? Samantha was probably away at some business convention, or off on one of her expensive jaunts with her many friends who were as superficial as she was. They were possibly even at some expensive spa or a country house somewhere, swigging down overpriced champagne and getting massages and facials that would make no difference to their sagging bodies and permanently scowling expressions. I had told Delores as much, but this had simply fuelled her rage and sent her into a meltdown. Of course, I had known that that would be her reaction and rather enjoyed the subsequent wrath that followed.

By the time I reached The Pot and Glass, the clouds had bubbled up into an angry mass overhead, casting an oppressive spread of darkness over the village and the sprawling hills beyond. It felt good to have a change, to see something other than bright, burning sunshine and not much else. I had forgotten how much I enjoyed the change in seasons, the different moods brought on by a slight transformation in the weather, the feelings of optimism a peak in pressure could bring as well as the deepening feelings of despair I sometimes felt when a storm was on its way.

I missed the inky blackness of a winter sky that twinkled with distant stars. We all need to experience those sorts of changes in our temperament to remind us that we are still very much alive.

I felt the first drops of rain as I opened the door to the pub and stamped my feet on the mat. Already, this place was beginning to feel like an old friend, somewhere I could turn to when I was feeling down, somewhere I could disappear into when everything became too much for me to bear. After the frostiness I encountered on my first visit, I had grown rather attached to The Pot and Glass. It wasn't such a bad place after all.

The sound of the chatter and clinking of glasses inside was music to my ears. In the corner sat the usual crew and behind the bar stood Lily. Everything I needed was right here. In this place, everything was exactly how I wanted it to be.

34

ME

It's all coming together nicely. Everything is how I have always wanted it to be. Jim and Emily aren't dead but that is no bad thing. They suffered. That was always part of my plan. I wanted them to feel pain, both physically and emotionally. I wanted to see the look of horror on their faces and watch as they squirmed in pain. I was desperate for them to exhibit the same feelings of terror that I endured as a child, for everyone to witness their downfall and wonder who was behind these heinous, heartless acts. I doubt anybody has had the wisdom or prudence to join up the dots, to begin to link things together. They're all too selfish, too immersed in their own little worlds where they're safe and comfortable. It would take effort and a huge amount of insight and raking over the past do that. Nobody thought to look too deeply at the headstones of the desecrated graves. They assumed they were randomly chosen, just a case of thoughtless vandalism and sheer bad luck. If they had taken the time to look closely, they may have questioned why those particular graves were covered with those dreadful emotive words. But they didn't. They were all desperate to put things back how they were, to focus on the perpetrator and catch them so they could rest easy in their beds at night instead of questioning the motives and putting some thought into what was going on inside the head of the culprit.

At one point, I thought the game was up, but so far nobody has said anything. It will be over soon though. I can sense closure coming. It's not far away: a dull featureless point in the distance, tugging at me, insisting I bring an end to this particular chapter of my life. It's not so far away. Not far at all.

Sometimes, I think I've done enough and then other days, I feel as if I haven't even begun my retribution plan. I am one person, however, and my capabilities are limited. I'm a mortal after all, not the Devil, not a demon, just a complicated individual who doesn't think like you do; I am quite simply somebody who has just lost their way.

I'm sure you have already realised that a lot of my memories are simply too clear, too precise for me to have remembered them that way. What child has that level of clarity at such a young age? I do have many memories but they're not quite as detailed as I've described, so I've taken the liberty of adding bits in, filling in the blanks. This was not for added dramatic effect, but simply to give you an idea of how bad it was, how bad I was and how difficult my life has been. How terrible my upbringing was. Otherwise, you would think me a monster without reason. And I do have a reason. A very good one.

Believe it or not, I never wanted it to be like this, but I can't see any other option. It's part of who I am, hardwired into my brain. I have read up on how these things work. Genes are self-organising, shaped by their environment, moulded by nature, ruined by poor nurturing. That's why it has to end soon otherwise this rot will continue to self-perpetuate. I have enough insight to know when the end is near, and it is definitely close by. I've enjoyed it while it lasted but like all good things, it must come to an end.

I don't have a definite plan for my grand finale, more of a hazy outline. I don't fear it. It was always going to happen. That's how I live my life, or at least that's how I've always thought my life would pan out.

Anyway, I'm rambling, going off on a tangent when what I need to do is stay on track, stay focused and see this thing through to the very end. So, I will leave you now, but only for a short while because I will be back. And when that happens, you will all know about it. I'm hoping for a grand climax, a show-stopper that nobody will forget in a hurry.

35

There was a definite buzz about the place. The fire in Emily's house was being talked about in every corner of the pub – people shaking their heads, tutting loudly, saying how sorry they were for the retired schoolteacher whose house had been ravaged by a ferocious blaze. According to the local gossips, which included Davey and Simon, Emily had spent the night in hospital being treated for smoke inhalation and, upon being discharged the following day, had travelled up to Newcastle to stay with her sister.

'The investigation team think it was definitely deliberate. Nothing's been officially released as yet but I was chatting to one of their guys and reading between the lines. That's what they're thinking.'

Coming from anybody else, I would have put this statement down to salacious gossip peddled by locals who knew no better, but the fact that Davey had said it gave more credence to the idea that somebody had in fact tried to kill Emily.

I took a long gulp of beer and shook my head despondently. 'Why? And have they made any links to the fire and Jim's attack?'

Davey sighed and lowered his gaze. He looked like a man beaten by life, somebody who wanted to remove himself from all of this heartache and damage and hide away somewhere until it was all over. 'No idea. Got be the same person though hasn't it? Too much of a coincidence. Jesus,' he whispered into his beer, 'anybody would think we lived in the middle of a big city with all that's gone on, not a tiny little village in the middle of the countryside. It's bloody crazy.'

I pulled my stool closer and lowered my voice. Simon was spouting off about who he thought the obvious suspects were and I didn't want to become embroiled in any of his nonsense. 'Do you think the body found last year is connected to any of this?'

Once more, Davey shook his head and when he looked up at me, I saw real sadness in his eyes. 'Again, I've no idea. I've lived here for over twenty years. Moved here when I was a teenager and up until last year, it was a really quiet place to live. A sleepy English village. And now look at it. It's a fucking disgrace, what's gone on. A complete fucking mess.'

A voice behind me caused me to turn around. They weren't speaking directly to me but the timbre and pitch of the voice caught my attention. It was instantly recognisable. A whiff of expensive cologne drifted my way as Terence and Diane made their way to the bar. I gave them a smile as Terence spotted me and waved. He nudged Diane, who glanced my way and grinned.

'Mind if we sit with you?' Diane shouted over.

I looked at Davey, who shrugged nonchalantly, not seeming to care either way, and nodded his head. He didn't look like he had the energy to put up any sort of resistance even if he didn't want them with us.

I stood up and dragged two more chairs over from a nearby table, pulling them close to my stool before sitting down again.

Within a couple of minutes, Diane and Terence came wandering over, wine glasses in hand, and sat next to us. The mood wasn't exactly sombre, but an unexpected hush descended upon their arrival, everyone seemingly too afraid of saying the wrong thing.

'Another terrible state of affairs, eh?' Diane said

after taking a long slug of her wine. 'When's it all going to end?'

'When they bang the offender up, and we all know who that is, don't we?' Simon's words boomed over the distant clatter of crockery and low drone of nearby conversations. He had the sort of pitch to his voice that could shatter crystal. His anger was undoubtedly fuelled by beer. I stared at his crumpled clothes – the business suit that, upon closer inspection, was cheap and shiny, a thin fabric with a limited life. I looked at the many glasses stacked up next to him on the table, and was under no illusions as to how long he had been in the pub or how many drinks he had guzzled back while he had been here.

Nobody replied or became embroiled in his rhetoric. Instead, people chatted and were sympathetic rather than angry, frightened yet stoic at the same time. Just a group of villagers trying to cope with a series of terrible events that had befallen their little community.

I considered bringing Jim's name into the conversation to see what sort of reaction it would provoke – just a quick mention of his recovery – but thought that perhaps Terence and Diane would see it as some sort of insult. After our recent conversation, I was extremely aware of their feelings towards the man. I just wondered if others felt the same way. I was curious to see whether or not their faces would pucker up into an angry frown at the sound of his name, if they would grimace and stare into their drinks, too angry or afraid to say how they really felt about a frail retiree who was still in hospital after having the shit beaten out of him. I erred on the side of caution and remained silent, sipping at my beer dolefully.

Over at the bar, Lily bustled about purposefully, her hair pinned into place with an array of slides and colourful ribbons. Once again, she looked immaculate. I admired her sense of style: a look that was all her own. The fact she didn't feel the need to adhere to any particular fashion or fad said all that needed to be said about her character, about how strong and resilient she was despite the adverse circumstances of her upbringing. She had regularly endured more than most and complained little, doing her crying in private, keeping her emotions hidden from the rest of the world and always putting a brave face on.

I longed for her to glance my way, to smile and reveal those perfect teeth, for her eyes to light up and crease at the corners as she mouthed a quick hello to me. But the bar was busy. A sea of people, waves and waves of them, thirsty and demanding, pushed their way forward, heads bobbing about as they tried to catch her eye and order their drinks.

Sighing wistfully, I looked away and finished the remainder of my beer, the heavy brown ale settling nicely in my belly. Soon I would go home and revel in the solitude. I didn't want to have too many beers. Drunks are unattractive people. Real drunks are anyway: those who consume vast amounts every single day and let it impair their judgement and outlook. I am not one of those people and never will be.

I stared over at Simon, glassy-eyed, rosy-cheeked and still lecturing anybody who was mad enough to listen on the perils of living near an ex-offender and not taking the law into your own hands. I didn't want to be like him. Simon wore his heart on his sleeve, whereas I was fairly reserved, more able to keep my deepest emotions in check in the company of others. I watched him while Davey chatted to Terence and Diane, their voices a quiet murmur as they pondered over the latest occurrence.

'I can't for the life of me work it out.' Davey's voice was tinged with more than a touch of melancholy as he placed his pint down and rubbed at his face wearily. 'I mean, if it was deliberate, why Emily? She's a harmless old lady. She doesn't have an ounce of malice in her.'

'Maybe,' Terence volunteered, 'none of these incidents are related? We're all assuming they are but are we just putting two and two together and coming up with five?'

Diane shrugged and took another long sip of her wine, almost draining the glass. 'All I can say is, if each and every crime is unconnected, then it's the biggest coincidence of the decade. Especially in a village this small.'

'I suppose,' I said quietly as I finished the last of my drink, 'the police will look into it in greater detail now. An isolated crime is one thing but a string of them will set alarm bells ringing.'

'Let's bloody well hope so!' Simon roared.

I took a deep breath. I'd hoped I'd kept my voice low and that he had been unable to hear me. Obviously not.

'The police are barking up the wrong tree if you ask me. They need to pull their finger out and make an arrest. Just 'cos they're in a village, they think they can be on a go-slow and take their time. That stout fella thinks he's Hercule fucking Poirot. Have you seen him? The way he saunters around as if he hasn't got a care in the frigging world.' Simon stopped, waiting for somebody to reply, to say something in return.

A hush descended, everybody faintly embarrassed by his outburst.

'Well,' I said as I drained the reminder of my beer, 'all I can say is, whoever is behind all of this should be ashamed of themselves. Jim and Emily are elderly people, frail and unable to defend themselves. Emily managed to escape but poor old Jim is still in hospital. Fractured ribs at his age could easily turn into pneumonia. He's not out of the woods just yet.'

I couldn't swear to it, but I thought I saw Terence stiffen, his body locking into position beside me as I spoke. I sneaked a glance at Diane. Her face was flushed. Whether it was from the wine or something else entirely was anybody's guess. I was certain they had nothing to hide. Everybody was on edge, feeling more than a little frightened at being thought of as a possible suspect or perhaps even wondering if they would be the next victim.

Standing up, I said goodbye to everybody, an idea already formulated in my brain as to where I was going. Chances were the place would be closed, but it was worth a try. I'd promised myself a visit since moving here and had never got around to it. Tonight felt right for some unfathomable reason, whether it was just good timing after the slightly depressed atmosphere in the pub, or whether it was the mood I was in. I smiled. Maybe it was the stars aligning or some other unexplainable ethereal reason, but whatever it was, I felt drawn to it, pulled there by invisible strings that tugged at me as I headed towards the door.

'See you soon,' Terence called after me as I walked. His voice was strained and slightly muffled by the din as a group of people entered and made a surge towards the bar.

I waved and gave everybody what I hoped was a genuine smile. Things in Whitchurch would pick up soon enough. I could sense a change coming, something cataclysmic that would bring an end to their misery.

36

As expected, St Oswald's was closed. The churchyard, however, was very much open. The ground was wet from the rain that had fallen in the past hour or so. It was getting heavier, the sky continuing to darken, the pressure plummeting second by second.

The moss underfoot was oily and slippery, my feet squelching over it as I made my way through the lych-gate and towards the gravestones that stood like squat soldiers, rows and rows of them lined up, some leaning and crumbling with age and neglect, others shiny and new looking, the bodies buried beneath only recently deceased.

I picked my way through each one until I reached

the spot. The two headstones were still smeared with traces of red paint, the words legible even after all of poor Dominic's scrubbing. I ran my hand over the rough surface, the gritty sensation slightly repulsive under my fingers. I knelt down and rearranged the flowers, steadying the overturned vase and putting everything back in place. The rain gained momentum. It fell on my shoulders and ran down my back, the pitter-patter echoing around me as it hit the trees and bounced off leaves overhead.

Two headstones, two people buried decades apart. The dates were clear enough to read, the words poignant. My eyes scanned them both before I stood up and turned to look at the church. It would have been nice to go inside, to sit for a while and gather my thoughts.

I had promised I would visit this place and look inside the actual building yet somehow had never got around to it. It had been on the edge of my thoughts since moving here and tonight, something had stirred within me, beckoning me here. It was as if the time were suddenly right. And yet it wasn't. The door was definitely locked. I tried it several times and padded around the back for another way in to no avail. There was only one other small back door and that too was locked. Hardly surprising after recent events.

A shiver ran through me. Although it wasn't cold, the temperature was dropping rapidly. Soon summer would leave us and autumn would step into its place. Russet leaves would flutter down from high branches to the rapidly cooling earth beneath our feet. The nights would draw in; the darkness would come.

I swallowed and stepped away, my feet following a track trodden through the rows of stones. The ground was beginning to feel like mulch. It squelched and shifted as I walked towards the lychgate. Droplets of rain landed on my head and ran down my forehead, dripping onto my eyelashes. I ran a hand over my face and blinked the water away. The smell of petrichor clung to my clothes, seeping through the fabric and soaking into my skin. Nature was rewarding us at long last. We had had a punishing summer – crops dying, grass bleached to straw – but it was finally coming to an end.

I closed the gate behind me and craned my neck to take in the magnificence of the towering spire. There was no denying that St Oswald's was a truly radiant piece of architecture. I wondered if its almighty presence and overpowering atmosphere had had a detrimental effect on Lily's father. Had it driven a wedge between him and his family? Perhaps his calling was so strong, it obliterated everything else, leaving little room in his heart for his nearest and dearest.

I sighed heavily and stepped out onto the pavement. Perhaps he was just a horrible shit of a man. Even in retirement, he was still causing trouble, reducing his daughter to tears.

People are what they are. Growing old obviously hadn't changed him, turned him into a more caring being, somebody who put others before himself. Then again, the compassionate and unselfish end up in the same size grave as the cruel and thoughtless. They all lie beside one another, the decent people buried alongside the ones who acted selfishly in life, and perhaps even wronged them, so what is the point of being selfless? Being the better person gets you nowhere.

The rain came down in sheets as I rounded the corner and made my way home. A mass of bodies tumbled out of the pub as I passed, their voices raised in surprise as they held their hands up to the sky and stopped to look heavenwards, their mouths open and eyes wide as they welcomed the overdue downpour.

A lone figure behind them stared at me, his arm raised as he hollered at me to wait and gave me a wave. Before I could say or do anything, Simon ran over the road and caught up to me, his head dipped against the driving rain.

'Ray! How about a nightcap?' His voice sounded slightly distorted against the crack of the deluge as it increased in intensity and hit the trees and the tinder-dry grass. The leaves rustled wildly above our heads.

I shook my head and smiled at him, keen to get home and dry off. My clothes were saturated and I was beginning to feel a chill creeping in. 'I'm heading home, Simon. I'm soaked. Maybe another time?' I shouted through the roar of the thunderous volley of water that cascaded down on us.

'I'll come with you!' he said chirpily, like an outrageously jolly schoolboy who was too dim to comprehend the well-intentioned meaning of weary friends who had had enough of him.

Before I could protest any further, he was alongside me, mirroring my footsteps as we ran along the path next to the village green. For the first time since moving here, I wished Samantha were living with me, or somebody like her. Anybody to save me from Simon's relentless chatter. A person waiting inside who would give Simon and his unexpected appearance short shrift. Somebody who would shoo him away and shut the door in his face.

'We'll have a Whisky Mac. You a whisky man, Ray?' His nasally voice and overly cheerful demeanour irritated me. I wanted to brush him off but he didn't seem to take the hint. Even my silence didn't put a stop to his endless questions and ridiculous, childish statements. 'Red wine makes me aggressive,' he exclaimed with a hooting cackle. 'Once had a punch-up with an old guy in a pub after I downed two bottles of Merlot. Woke up in hospital. What a laugh we had that night. I was out in Durham with the lads I used to work with – me, Robbo, Sticky, Fat Baz and Tony.'

On and on he went, his voice ringing in my ears until we reached my front door. I slid the key in, doing my utmost to wish him away, to give off vibes that would make him realise he wasn't wanted.

'Make yourself at home,' I said listlessly as I took the stairs two at a time. Even my socks were wet. Every part of me was slick with rain and perspiration. I was tired, pissed off and looking forward to spending the rest of the evening on my own and now here I was, stuck with Simon and his stupid fucking stories.

I stalked into the bedroom, slammed the door behind me and flopped heavily onto the bed, hoping against hope he would be gone by the time I eventually got downstairs, although my gut told me he would still be there regardless of how long I kept him waiting. Whether I liked it or not, Simon, it would appear, was here for the night.

37

Simon had already helped himself to a glass of my best Talisker single malt by the time I had dried myself off and headed back downstairs. He was busy in the freezer as I entered the kitchen, his hand curled menacingly in the top tray as he scooped up a palm full of ice cubes and clutched them tightly. His fingers resembled bony red claws, his long fingernails like the talons of a huge predatory bird.

I watched, my fury slowly building as he dropped the frozen cubes into his drink with a deep clunk. I eyed up the tumbler, almost half full of amber liquid, and had to stop myself from rushing over, snatching the drink out of his hand and throwing it in his face.

'Now then, big guy. Hope you don't mind?' he said

a little too casually, lifting the crystal glass up and waving it at me amiably. 'Yours is in the living room. I put ice in it. No ginger wine to make the Whisky Mac I'm afraid. Well, not that I could see anyhow. Not unless you've got it stashed away somewhere?'

I shook my head, too irritated to speak. I couldn't trust myself with what might come out of my mouth, so I said nothing instead, but somehow managed a weak smile.

The chair scraped over the floor behind me. I listened to the faint rustle of Simon's clothing as he sat down at my table and made himself at home. 'Get your drink and we'll put the world to rights, big fella.'

His voice trailed in my wake while I went to get my drink. I wondered how he would react if I took my whisky and went straight up to bed, leaving him to sit downstairs on his own. Would he finish it and leave? Or was he so incomprehensively stupid and so deeply insensitive that he would actually follow me up and continue talking to me, boring me with long-winded immature tales of his drunken antics and who he thought should be hung, drawn and quartered for the crimes committed in Whitchurch? I managed a wry smile at the thought of it and took a glug of my drink, enjoying the dry burn on my gullet and the acrid taste that the single malt left on my tongue.

Clasping my whisky tightly, I walked back through to the kitchen and sat down next to Simon, whose eyes were beginning to glaze over. God knows how much he'd had to drink. He had probably been in the pub since lunchtime, steadily knocking back the beers, and now here he was, topping up the alcohol level in his bloodstream with whisky. My whisky.

I saw him watching me as I took a sip of my drink. He was being cautious. Had he detected my irritation at his presence here? Or was he, as I suspected, simply trying to work out what his opening gambit would be as he tried to initiate conversation with me?

I was correct with the latter assumption. Simon leaned forward, his elbows resting on the table, his breath hot and sour as it wafted over to me, hot pockets of pungent air that hung in the atmosphere, causing me to turn away slightly. 'So, Ray, my friend, let's talk possible culprits, shall we?'

I suppressed an eye roll. I'd had enough of hearing about his thoughts on this matter, his endless postulating and senseless inane comments, how he was prepared to have it out with Gavin Yuill if the police didn't make an arrest in the next few days. I didn't think I could take much more of it. I took another long slug of my drink, the sound of ice clinking against the heavy crystal glass ringing in my ears as I swallowed and took another gulp of whisky. I figured I was going to need it if this is how our night was going to be. Any more talk of Gavin Yuill would very probably be enough to tip me over the edge.

Simon pulled at his collar, dragging it from side to side in a drunken bid to loosen it. The skin on his neck was a deep shade of pink as he drunkenly groped at the fabric of his shirt. A few curls of dark hair sprouted up from his chest as a button popped in protest under his tight grasp. He let out a deep sigh as more skin on his chest was revealed. He leaned back and smiled at me, then let out a small burp or satisfaction.

'I honestly don't think any of this was Gavin Yuill,' I said suddenly, knowing my remark would rile him. 'I met Gavin recently. He seemed okay actually. We even arranged to go out for a drink.'

Sweat bloomed on Simon's face and the colour of his skin deepened, turning from dark pink to near crimson. He leaned forward and stared at me, fire in his eyes. 'You're frigging kidding me, surely?' he shouted.

The glass in his hand tipped slightly. He straightened it, ice knocking against the tumbler with a clear chime. The honey-coloured liquid sloshed over the sides as he finally put the squat tumbler down on the table. I watched two perfectly formed tear-shaped drops land on the teak surface and soak into the wood, the smooth lines turning into ragged edges as they melted into the table top, disappearing into the dark, mud-coloured grain.

'No, I'm not kidding, Simon. And I know for sure that it wasn't him. Gavin Yuill is not responsible for any of the things that have happened in Whitchurch.' I didn't say anything else. My words were lodged between us like a cloud of poisonous gas. I observed Simon as a scientist would study a wild animal in captivity, watching and waiting for his primal tendencies to emerge. Suddenly, his stupidity had begun to fascinate me. He was even more foolish than I'd initially thought. His lack of insight was astounding. Alice had been right. This man knew nothing about nothing. He was the lowest of the low.

I waited for his response, watched the shock slowly take hold of his features. I could almost hear the cogs whirring in his brain, dulled by an inordinate amount of alcohol and years of ignoring cold hard facts.

He swiftly sprang to life, a look on his face that stilled my blood. 'How do you know it wasn't him, Ray? You keep saying it wasn't Gavin but how the fuck do you know that for sure?' Simon's face loomed close to mine, his flesh bright red with frustration and undisguised rage.

'Because I just know,' I answered quietly, leaning back in my chair away from him until the edge of it touched the kitchen counter. The foul odour of Simon's fetid breath hung in the air. The stink of him seemed to fill the entire room.

'How do you know? Is it because you're suddenly his best buddy and drinking mate?' Simon's chest rose and fell as he spoke; his voice echoed across the kitchen, bouncing off the tiles, sarcasm and disbelief dripping from every syllable.

'No, not because I'm his best buddy or, as you so crudely put it, his "drinking mate",' I said, a small pulse beginning to build on my temple. I closed my eyes for a second to control my temper and took a deep shuddering breath.

'Then how the *fuck* do you know Gavin Yuill isn't responsible for all the things that have happened around here?' Simon glared at me. His nostrils flared, two enormous black holes of fury as he waited for my reply. His eyes were dark, pitted with unadulterated anger. He looked ready to turn on me at any moment, to take hold of me and give me a sound beating.

'I know he didn't do it because,' I said, reaching

around behind me and catching sight of a length of glinting metal lying on the kitchen top, 'it was me.'

Before Simon could utter a sound, I grabbed at the long, jagged blade, swung it around and lunged it hard into his gut, pushing at it, driving it home through his ribs and deep into the major organs behind his belly. I made sure it went far enough in to cause maximum damage. I wanted him dead, not injured like Jim and Emily. With any luck, I had pierced his liver and he would bleed to death in no time at all.

I had had enough of his relentless chatter and pointless accusations. He was an irritant, like a fly in its death throes, constantly swarming around and around, unsure of any direction but continuing regardless because they don't what else to do when their life is drawing to a close. He had gone on and on about Gavin and I had grown tired of it.

It was fun at first, seeing Gavin take all the blame and be the fall guy, watching him be held culpable for everything that had happened in Whitchurch, but then the novelty began to wear off and I started to feel more than a little pissed off about it. I had put a lot of thought and effort into those little games, those upsets that had had the locals wringing their hands and gnashing their teeth. I had laughed heartily at it all when I was alone in my bed at night, had enjoyed the meticulous planning, even making myself part of the community and forging friendships with people I hated – people like Simon here – and now fucking Gavin Yuill was getting all the credit.

I leaned further forward and looked deep into Simon's eyes, letting out a sigh of satisfaction as I gazed at his face.

His pupils were dilated, his eyes bulging and flickering for a couple of seconds before stopping. No more movement. Smooth and unseeing, they shone like marbles, an accusatory darkness to them as I moved even farther in, pushing the knife in some more for good measure, before giving it a quick twist then tugging at it to remove it from his abdomen. The blade was sharper and longer than I had realised. Pity. I would have liked to see him suffer, hear him beg, just so I could refuse and then twist the knife a little bit more and see him gasp his last.

I gave a small moan of displeasure. Warm, sticky blood pumped out of his stomach. I pulled away in disgust and moved over to the sink where I turned on the hot tap and rinsed my hands thoroughly.

Why do people have to bleed so much when they're cut open? It's filthy and inconvenient. And it's not even the actual blood that repulses me; it's the warmth of it, the heat that emanates from another person's innards. The heat of their bleeding body and the fact I have to clean up after them. Even in death, people are thoughtless and selfish.

I cleaned my hands thoroughly and wiped the kitchen down, then turned to face Simon. He was slumped in the chair at an angle, his body twisted slightly, his head tipped back. His eyes were wide open and staring at the ceiling. The top half of his body was soaked with blood, some of it dripping down onto the floor. I would have to mop it all thoroughly. Soon it would stop flowing. Soon it would dry up and rigor mortis would set in. I needed to act before that happened. I had to get moving. I had a brief window of opportunity in which to execute the next part of my plan. Time was of the essence.

38

Outside, the rain continued to pummel at the windows. At long last. We had waited for what felt like an age for the weather to break, for the rain to come, and now it had arrived with a flourish and I prayed it wouldn't stop. It lashed at the glass and pounded on the roof like stampeding cattle. I closed my eyes and listened to it, relishing the sound it made as it battered against the patio doors. It was therapeutic, like a form of healing. It relaxed me, cleansed my soul and made me pure. That's all I had ever wanted: to get revenge and allow myself to be purged of my demons.

I exhaled and opened my eyes, hot breath rising up over my face, then looked around the room as if for the first time. I knew then where I would go to, what my next move would be. It was all coming together. Maybe God existed after all. After years of not believing, maybe I was wrong and there was a God looking down on me. Tonight, he had sent the rain and then he had sent Simon. Stupid, banal, loudmouthed Simon. It was definitely a sign.

I pulled the curtains apart slightly and peered through the crack out into the back garden. The strength of the downpour increased once more, filling the garden with a pool of water that gathered on the lawn. It was dark out there, the clouds dimming the summer light with their heavy bellies full of rain. Months and months of it stored up, bursting out, providing us with a fierce growing storm, the likes of which we had never seen before.

I could do it while nobody was around: drag Simon out there and dispose of his body. Anybody going out in this weather would need a good reason. And I had a good reason. The best of reasons.

I pulled my coat on and went about my task. Simon was heavier than he looked. I had forgotten that, how cumbersome and weighty people became when they died.

The myth that people become lighter in death as their soul leaves them and ascends to a higher plane is exactly that – a myth. Cadavers are heavy, weighty and unwieldly; they are difficult to transport and even the most dextrous of people would have the Devil's own job shifting them on their own. Disposing of a body is harder than most people realise. And I should know.

My father was a big man and even after cancer had ravaged his body, he remained larger than most. He was a striking individual in life and his long road to death didn't dilute his formidable presence. I imagine he would have been immensely heavy if I'd had to move him. Fortunately, I hadn't.

Smothering him while he slept was too easy for him. He had been on his deathbed, ill and alone, his body quickly succumbing to disease after my mother's unexpected heart attack, so nobody suspected foul play. And no-one had any idea that the mystery person who paid him a visit that day would be the one to end his life. But that was because they hadn't known me and they definitely hadn't realised our history – the chequered and painful past that bonded us. They had thought of him as a weak, helpless old man. They hadn't known him as I had. They hadn't had the hurt and hatred buried deep inside them that I had lurking there. And they also hadn't known that it was my father who had put it there, securing it in place with his cruelty and bizarre behaviour.

I attended my mother's funeral a few months earlier in Sacriston, a town slightly north of Durham, the place my parents had moved to after we left Whitchurch all those years ago, but contact with my father over the years had been erratic. Just as I have done with the residents of Whitchurch, I had watched his life from afar, monitored his movements from a safe distance and then done what was required when the time was right.

I left the hospital that night telling not a soul that he had taken his last breath. Some unsuspecting nurse would have discovered him on their rounds later that evening. They would have slipped into his side room and spoken softly to the man they all believed to be some sort of saint, looking into his eyes and then shaking their head sadly at his demise.

I was long since gone, on my way back down south, excitement fizzing through my veins, hoping the man who ruined me was rotting in hell.

Samantha, a slight woman in life, took on gargantuan proportions when dead. I didn't want to do it, to actually kill her, but she left me with no other option. Our relationship had gone stale and she was had started to hem me in with her endless questions and threats. She had found my journal, you see. My private journal where I had written in delicious detail all about killing my father, about how he had fought against his inevitable death, his frail body bucking beneath my strong arms as I held the pillow down over his face and smiled as he fought to breathe.

She initially thought it was a work of fiction, an idea for a novel I had spoken about writing, but then she began to probe and I began to open up about my past and she started to piece it all together in her feeble little mind. She didn't want to believe it, that her partner of two years could be capable of such a thing. But I was, and slowly she knew it to be true. So she had to go. It was her own fault. She had nobody to blame but herself. She shouldn't have looked at my personal effects. She had always accused me of being too private, incapable of divulging my innermost thoughts and so in desperation, thinking I was having an affair, she had riffled through my things and stumbled upon my secret. That was the beginning of her end.

Cassandra, my sister, always told me that Samantha was the wrong woman for me. Or she would have done if she had lived long enough to meet her. The last time I saw Cassandra, she was face down in the pond in our garden. I was eleven years old and she was just five. It was an accident. Or at least that's what I've told myself over the years. I had been given the task of caring for her while my mother and father tended to the needs of their parishioners. What those needs were, I will never know, and how they were greater than the needs of their own children will always remain a mystery to me.

I had always resented Cassandra. She had been everything I wasn't: the perfect child my parents had hoped I would be. She'd been kind and compassionate, obedient and kind. She'd also had the hearts of my parents – something I had never had. And I'd hated her for it.

It was only a little push. She fell so easily, her slight body yielding to the pressure I exerted on the back of her neck, her tiny frame struggling for air as I held her down under the water. I was helping her. What if one day, our parents decided to punish her as they had done me? I couldn't allow that to happen so I saved her from it all, from a fate worse than her untimely death.

People believed me when I said she tripped and fell. They actually believed me. For the first time in my blighted little life, they all sat up and took notice of what I had to say. I spun a good tale, a sorry tale that made everyone cry. I had them eating out of the palm of my hand and it felt glorious. Even then I was quite the proficient liar.

I stared over at the picture on the wall, the one I put up last week. It's a photograph of me and a friend's sister. I smiled wistfully. I see Cassandra everywhere I go, her face appearing unbidden, implanting itself in the features of other people around me – childhood friends, colleagues, Lily...

I also hear her voice wherever I go, whispering to me, guiding me, helping me to navigate my way through this difficult journey we call life. She has been good to me over the years and has forgiven me for all my wrongdoings. Like I said earlier, she always was compassionate: the eternal good girl. She was the one who talked me into ending it with Samantha. I used to wake on a morning with Cassandra's voice in my head, urging me to do it, to put an end to all the arguments and rages and misery.

After my father, Samantha was easy prey, putting up barely any fight, although as I said earlier, she appeared to gain an extra ten pounds when dead. I got so much satisfaction from seeing the life drain out of her, from feeling the soft skin of her throat pucker in resistance and then go slack under my fingers as I held her tight. By then I was getting a real taste for it. There is no sensation like it: that rush of excitement, the feeling of exhilaration and power that surges through you when you take somebody's life. I felt like God the day I killed Samantha. I still do. I have no regrets, no wish to turn back the clock and do things differently. What's done is done and cannot be undone.

Getting rid of the body wasn't as easy as I imagined. She was hidden in the apartment for two days while I got myself organised and packed up my belongings. She was trussed up in the spare room, her body bound by thick fabric and tape. She spent two days and two nights in there – the place we used to use as a dumping ground. The place where we put all our unwanted goods that we had no room for. Good enough for her.

Once I was ready, I prepared to put her in the boot of the car. I threw stones at the CCTV camera that sat in the corner of the underground car park to break it, smashed a few lights then dragged her body across the concrete at midnight when nobody was around.

I dumped her body in a forest near Sheffield on the way to Whitchurch. I had to take a detour off the M1 on my way here, find a deserted wooded area and make sure she was completely covered with leaves and branches. I dug a deep enough grave and put her in it, dragging the leaves and woodland detritus across to make sure she was well hidden. I'm hoping wild animals find her before any unsuspecting hikers or dog walkers do. Is it any wonder I was worn out when I arrived here? I had taken a life and was about to embark on a new one.

The whole thing was both cathartic and exhausting. But it was worth it. I was free. Free of Samantha's constant whining and moaning and free to live in Whitchurch, the place I had watched from a distance, the place I had travelled through many times and kept a check on. The place I now called home.

But things changed. After reading the news earlier, I could see it all coming to an end. I knew then that my time was up. Opening my laptop and seeing the story of Samantha being reported as missing had thrown me off-kilter. I had hoped it would take a little longer for the police to get involved and story to hit the headlines. I guess Samantha's employers had verified she hadn't been into work and that she wasn't away on a business venture. I had to give Delores some credit. She had certainly done her homework and got the ball rolling a lot faster than I had expected her to. And of course, my name was in the article as somebody police were trying to trace. A person of interest. I knew then it was time to speed up my plans or my game would be up.

39

Deciding I needed to get rid of Simon's body as quickly as possible, I went upstairs, found a large blanket and carried it down to the kitchen. I covered the carcass up as best I could, pushing his flesh inside the fabric. I was dismayed to see that his body was still bleeding. Streams of scarlet continued to seep through the blanket, infuriating me and causing me to swear out loud. I had hoped that by now, the flow would have ceased, his body fluids slowly coagulating within him, but it continued to seep out, warm and sticky to the touch. I spat on his face and turned away. Simon was as awkward and defiant when dead as he had been when he was alive.

I ran upstairs and found another thick blanket to

stuff over his stomach, hoping it would stem the disgusting tide of crimson globules that oozed out of his belly – thick clots of slowly congealing blood that turned my stomach.

I stopped in the bathroom and washed my hands again. Other people disgusted me, especially Simon. I hated the fact he was still warm and despised his bodily functions, the smell that emanated out of him and the blood that simply wouldn't stop leaking out of his dead body. I gritted my teeth and found myself loathing him even more.

Striding back into the kitchen, I grabbed a roll of duct tape from under the sink, threw the heavy sheet over him and bound him tightly. Once he was completely covered, I could go about cleaning up the mess he had made on the kitchen floor. Disgusting. He was a filthy creature and all I could think about was getting rid of him. I wanted him gone.

My knuckles and fingers felt raw by the time I had finished with the duct tape, wrapping it around him over and over, feeling the coldness of his limbs against mine as his body temperature gradually dropped.

I checked the fabric covering his midriff and was relieved to see that it was stain free. The bleeding had finally stopped. At long last, Simon was giving in to death.

I had to get this done quickly; time was against me. Soon nature would take its ugly course, locking his limbs into place, making him impossible to manoeuvre into the car.

I stood up straight, braced myself for what I was about to do, took a deep breath and set about my task.

40

ME

So, did you ever think it was me who was behind all of this? I'm willing to bet that you knew all along. Please don't judge me. I've spent my whole life being judged. That's why I am the way I am. You may be wondering why I chose Whitchurch, why such a small, close-knit village deserved to be subjected to such misery. I could say, *Why not?* But that's not what you want to hear, is it? You need a reason. We all need reasons. And here they are.

I grew up in Whitchurch, spent my formative years there. My father was the rector at St Oswald's over thirty years ago. We moved away after Cassandra left us. I say left us, but she never ever left me. She has always been there in my head, helping me, telling me what to do next. Lovely helpful Cassandra, with me every step of the way.

And as for my father, his heart always remained here, in the village where his daughter was born. That's why he is buried here, alongside her. My mother's ashes were scattered to the four winds high on a clifftop next to the North Sea, but my father had always insisted he wanted to be back here, next to Cassandra. I didn't attend his funeral. Standing there, watching all the mourners weeping and wailing, would have made me a hypocrite so I lied, told people I was ill abroad and unable to make it back in time. After that night in the hospital, I disappeared off the radar, took a few days away on my own. It was for the best. My father still had many friends. They were able to organise his funeral. Everybody knew my father and I were estranged and had been for a long time.

And I guess you've already worked out whose graves were vandalised? Of course you have. You'll be putting all the pieces together now. It's easy when you know, isn't it?

I thought I had been rumbled when I first bumped into Jim and Mary in the pub. It was the way she looked at me, her eyes full of knowing. I felt sure she recognised me even though I hadn't seen her since I was a child. And then she turned up on my doorstep and simply stared at me. I'm pretty sure she was starting to piece it all together at that point. Along with the news naming me, and Mary's possible recognition, I knew my time in Whitchurch was coming to a close. It had been brief, but fulfilling.

I've done my utmost to be a confident adult, different from the clumsy, awkward kid I used to be, the badly-behaved, gibbering wreck who spent his life stumbling from one catastrophe to another. I also worked really hard at being accepted as one of the locals, becoming one of them, thinking like they did and eventually being thought of as a close friend. And of course, if I sent threatening letters to myself and smeared my own car with dog shit then they were hardly likely to suspect me of any wrongdoing, were they?

Perhaps Mary always knew, deep down, from the very first time she met me. She and Jim were close to me as a child, friends of my parents. And they were culpable. I hope she realised that her past had finally caught up with her. They aided my parents, you see, helped them to inflict cruelty on me of the highest order. Avid churchgoers, they fully believed in my father's actions, backing him up, helping him to hold me down while he carried out his highly unorthodox practices on me. Is it any wonder I wanted to see them suffer? I hadn't seen them since we left Whitchurch shortly after Cassandra's death but had monitored them closely. It also came as no surprise to me to hear that many people hated Jim. A man with so many enemies. And to think he believed me to be the evil one.

Battering Jim was so fucking easy. I saw him from my window, so frail looking and unsuspecting, fully immersed in his hobby, his back arched as he gazed into his beloved telescope. He quite literally didn't know what had hit him.

I found the piece of wood in my garden, lovely and dry and solid after standing in the hot sun. Just a pity there weren't any nails sticking out of it.

And Emily: cool, reserved, sensible Emily. Always the voice of reason. She wasn't so reasonable when she was my teacher and made the proposal that I see a behavioural psychologist. She hadn't forced the issue but it was exactly what my parents had wanted to hear. It reinforced their belief that I was damaged, somebody who needed to be mended. They upped their game after Emily's unwanted intervention and recommendations.

I never did get to see a psychologist but I was subjected to more punitive punishments because of her. Did it never occur to her that my behaviour was driven by something else? That my behaviour was a manifestation of what my parents were actually doing to me? No, I don't suppose she ever thought of that. People rarely do. Few of them see beyond the end of their own noses. They want immediacy, quick solutions in a fast-moving, difficult world. She had a boy she couldn't control and needed a solution when all the time, it was me who needed her help.

There should have been others I hit back at, but as is usually the way, many of them had moved away from Whitchurch or died. I suppose that worked in my favour. Less is more. And I was running out of time. Simon was just an added bonus. I'd had no truck with him apart from the fact that he was an idiot who had tried to steal my thunder, dragging Gavin's name into it time and time again.

Changing my name helped my anonymity. As a child I was Charles Raymond Smith. As an adult, I became Ray. Having one of the most common surnames in England was fortuitous. I turned from Charlie Smith the scoundrel and often uncontrollable child, to Ray Smith the psychopath.

And I'm not a teacher. Not any more anyway. I left that thankless profession years ago. Funny, isn't it? The government think they've got it sorted with their DBS checks whenever anybody enters the job but of course that particular system only checks for people who have criminal records. What about those of us who've never been caught?

After leaving teaching, I spent my days doing something many people only ever dream of doing – absolutely nothing. It was Samantha who had the high-flying career as a sales director for a well-known pharmaceutical company. I had a bit of money saved up and after moving in with her into her large apartment, we pooled our resources, which came to a pretty hefty sum, leaving me sitting pretty. But then the nagging started. On and on she went, asking when I was going to start looking for a new job, telling me she didn't feel comfortable with the fact that I was sitting at home all day while she worked her arse off. There was no end to it. Day after day after day she went on, her voice droning on in the background about how unfair it was that she was keeping me, that she was tired, that I was making the place look untidy. She became such a mean bitch. The happy-go-lucky woman I'd met the previous year had turned into a complete harridan and I became tired of it.

It was an added bonus that she travelled as part of her job. It made it easy for me to dispose of her. I planned on putting her disappearance down to her work. Of course, I knew that story would only hold for so long. And that's when Delores started to hound me with her relentless messages and emails. I kind of knew after getting rid of Samantha that the game would be up. Moving to Whitchurch to get my revenge on the people who helped to make me into the man I am today was my swansong. They are the ones who should be held responsible for Samantha's death; they made me do it. They helped form me, manipulate me, assisted my slow but sure transition into the psychopath that I surely am.

But what about the other things that happened in Whitchurch last year, I hear you ask? Just a stroke of luck for me. The gods were smiling down on me when that body turned up. I did a bit of research and as far as I can gather, the woman whose body was found in the woods just beyond the village green had previously been subjected to domestic abuse. Her husband, a man from a village in North Yorkshire, had an alibi for the night she died and as much as the police tried, they couldn't get enough evidence to charge him. The case was closed and police issued a statement saying they weren't looking for anybody else in connection with the crime.

That body and an unsolved case put everybody in Whitchurch on red alert, set their minds off looking for things that ordinarily would have gone unnoticed or been put down as isolated incidents. But under such circumstances, people get whipped into a frenzy, their imaginations pushed into overdrive as they convince themselves and others that something is amiss, that their usually quiet village is practically under siege.

The girls who saw somebody hanging around the youth club? Probably no more than a passer-by, an innocent man who just happened to be in the wrong place at the wrong time. And the person in the car outside the school? Again, the police came up with nothing. All it takes in such situations is for one person to see something innocuous, put a suspicious slant on it, and suddenly every parent is convinced somebody is out to kidnap their child. The local gossips fan the flames of the fire and before you know it, the whole place is ablaze with unfounded theories and unlikely scenarios.

But what about the child who disappeared into the woods? I did some digging into that particular story as well and, as is usually the case, all was not what it first appeared to be with that tale. The boy had been in trouble at school and was worried about his parents' reactions. My guess is he went into hiding, hoping their distress and ensuing sympathy at him going missing would outweigh their anger at him for being in trouble at school, and that when he finally emerged a few hours later, everything would be forgiven and forgotten.

As for Mrs Batton's feline friend? Well, cats roam the streets eating everything and anything. The likelihood is it swallowed something it shouldn't have and paid the ultimate price.

Put all these things together along with a healthy dose of fear and people start believing that they are all linked. Folk are actually really easy to work out if you're prepared to take the time to study them, to watch their reactions, to get inside their heads and think like they do. Some, like me, are quite unique but in the main people are all the same. They follow each other like sheep and are so easily prone to panic when tragedy strikes. They rarely use logic to solve crimes or unpalatable occurrences, relying instead on their hearts. This is their downfall. For them, anyway. For people like me, it's an opportunity. I was able to step in and add to their misery, to watch their dramatic downfall in all its glory, knowing worse was yet to come.

My daily walks allowed me plenty of time to do things like send threatening letters, smear dog shit and spray paint on my sister and father's headstones. Seeing Gavin Yuill sneak out of the graveyard was just a bizarre coincidence. I spoke to Dominic and found out that Gavin had been visiting him regularly, helping out with bits of DIY in the crumbling interior. Dominic needed a helper and Gavin was bored and ostracised. What better place to hide than in church when services weren't taking place?

Setting fire to Emily's house proved to be relatively easy too. Whitchurch is mainly full of retirees who close their curtains and go to bed early. Creeping along in the early hours, dressed all in black, was one of the easiest things I've ever done. Nobody saw a thing. The whole thing was so easy it was pitiful. A piece of lit paper wrapped around a few pieces of dried wood did the trick. I shoved them through her letterbox knowing they would go up a treat.

I didn't hang around to watch. Instead, I went back home and slipped back into bed, falling quickly into a deep sleep. So it was true that the smoke alarm did actually wake me up. That part wasn't a lie.

For years, I have dreamed about returning to Whitchurch. My parents and I moved away when I was eleven years old but I always knew I'd be back at some point. Wanting to leave Samantha coincided with a vacant house being available in the village. It didn't take me long to set my plan in motion. Samantha had become a source of real irritation. It was time for her to go. I emptied our bank account before I left, and I knew then that my actions would be deemed suspicious. At that point, I knew my time to get even was limited. And that was when it all began.

My only regret is not getting to know Lily a little better. We had so much in common. Both of our fathers were evil bastards. Both were also men of the cloth in positions of trust that they abused. I did ponder over such a coincidence and wondered if it was a prerequisite that all religious leaders had to possess a certain amount of malevolence in order to fulfil their duties. But then, Dominic skews that particular theory, doesn't he? Such a quiet, kind soul. I don't mind admitting that I kind of envy his morality and integrity, something I don't possess. I'm glad he's the rector of St Oswald's. The place needs a sprinkling of goodness. Whitchurch also deserves to be blessed by somebody who actually cares, and is compassionate and generous of nature after years of being led by holy people who were actually the Devil in disguise.

And now here I am, with a corpse in the back of my car, the body of a local man I actually murdered, and I find myself thinking of Dominic and his parishioners and wondering – when they hear of this terrible deed, will they pray for my soul?

41

The rain was a force to be reckoned with as I made my way to the place I needed to be. The place that had called to me as I hauled Simon's body across the garden in the darkness and into the boot of my car. A vision of its heart-pounding, gut-wrenching beauty had filled my mind. I remembered the first time I had seen the location. I was completely mesmerised by it, held captive by its sheer magnificence and the way it commanded respect and attention just by being there. Its very existence was enough to strike wonder into the hearts of the hardest of individuals.

Simon seemed to have gained another half a stone as I lifted him into my vehicle, his limbs stiff and inflexible as nature took hold of his body and began its ugly course. Cleaning up had taken longer than I had expected, after which I'd needed a shower. Time had run away with me. By the time I got the body to the car, rigor mortis had begun to set in, making the process so much more difficult than it should have been.

Only when I turned onto the main road out of Whitchurch did I begin to relax. The rain continued to lash down, the windscreen wipers dragging back and forth at high speed, making me slightly dizzy. Having a corpse in the car with me didn't faze me in the slightest. I'd done it before.

The dead can't harm us. It's the living we should fear. I'm proof of that.

I tore down the country lanes at speed, enjoying the rush of adrenaline that surged through my system as I pushed my foot further to the floor. The movement and rhythm of the wipers as they cleared the windscreen of the deluge that slammed against it with force helped to focus my mind, to streamline my thoughts and shut out all the peripheral things that no longer meant anything to me. Delores, Samantha, Whitchurch – they were all behind me now. Cassandra's voice soothed me, her whispers urging me on, telling me I was doing the right thing.

As assured and confident as I am, it's been a relief

having her beside me. She is my voice of reason, my purpose for doing what I do. Everything that has led me to this point has all been driven by her. She was the starting point of my actions and will be waiting for me at the finish line. Gentle, compassionate Cassandra, the one who got to leave this cruel world while I was left to live it, to endure all that life had to throw at me.

The route there took longer than I expected, the adverse weather conditions hindering my progress. The country lanes were flooded, large muddy puddles almost taking the steering wheel out of my hands as I manoeuvred my way around the sharp bends and tight corners. The hedgerows and nearby towering foliage were a smear of dark green as I hurtled down each winding narrow lane, refusing to slow down. I had to get there. I suddenly felt a clawing need to reach my special location. I just knew that I would feel at peace once I got there. Even the downpour couldn't dampen my spirits. I felt as though I was already elevating to a higher plane. My soul literally sang at the thought of what I would do next.

I pulled out of the tiny lane and onto the main road that would lead me to my place, to where it would all happen. My stomach tightened at the thought of it and a pleasant buzzing sensation took hold in my head.

A sudden piercing sound behind me cut into my thoughts, slicing through the sense of calm and solitude that had settled upon me, killing the moment. I looked into the rear-view mirror and saw the flash of a blue light as it hurtled closer and closer, the fluorescent hue causing me to squint against its glare. I blinked and swallowed hard. The sound of the siren in the distance stirred a furnace of fear that had begun to build in my abdomen. I screwed up my eyes and concentrated as the noise grew in crescendo. I exhaled and tried to steady my breathing, small staccato gasps coming out of my chest in fluttery bursts. This wasn't how I had planned it. I had a scenario in my head – a clear picture of how things would work out – and speaking to the police didn't figure in it. I'd done my bit in assisting them already. Three times I had spoken to them in as many weeks. Enough was enough. I deserved to be left alone to get on with the next part of my plan.

My fingers tapped heavily at the steering wheel, my knuckles white and jammed into position. They felt like blocks of wood as I braced myself for being pulled over and speaking to a couple of stern-faced officers who would probe and ask questions, perhaps even requesting that I step out of the car while they search mine. I had no idea what my next move would be, what I would say. I had never been backed into a corner before. It wasn't a sensation I was familiar with and one I didn't care for. I'm used to being in control, being the cool, calm and collected one.

Fear coursed through my veins as I tried to think rationally. Had somebody seen me load Simon's body into the car? Had somebody discovered Samantha's decomposed corpse, informed the police and they were now onto me, tracking my movements? Both ideas were unlikely and improbable, but not impossible. At some point, some poor, unwary dog walker would possibly stumble upon Samantha's dead body, but not just yet. I hoped I'd made her final resting place so hard to find that locating her would take years rather than months, especially with the density of the foliage in the forest. It would take more than any normal family pet to sniff her out. Even a cadaver dog would struggle to find her body under all the leaves and soil and logs that I had piled on top of her. Though if I do say so myself, I did a fine job of disguising her body. Still, nobody disappears forever. I had a mental picture of some cute, unsuspecting Labrador stumbling upon her stinking flesh, or running back to its owner with one of her fingers lodged between its teeth. A pulse began to tap at my temple as I put my foot down and increased my speed.

I didn't have enough time to go through any more possible situations in my head as the blue light disappeared from my rear-view mirror and flew past me. Rain from its wheels sloshed up against the side of my car, obscuring my view as the passing police vehicle tore up the road, spraying dirty water far and wide. I watched, a pocket of air held in my chest, as the police car continued its journey and disappeared into the distance. I let out a trembling sigh. Not for me. It wasn't coming for me. I slapped my hands on the steering wheel and let out a loud roar: a combination of happiness and relief at being passed by. They weren't after me. I knew that deep down. What would they want with somebody like me? As far as everybody who knows me is concerned, I'm a decent, law-abiding guy. I have no criminal record and wasn't even over the speed limit. They were probably on their way to some accident caused by idiot drivers who couldn't handle their vehicles in wet weather. The important thing was they weren't coming for me. I could go ahead with my plan, see it through to the very end.

Fire raged within me. Relief ballooned in my chest. I was free to continue. Had I been pulled over, that would have been it. Game over. I couldn't have explained away a dead body in my car. And prison isn't an option for me, never has been. I'm not cut out for that sort of environment: a secure building full of alpha males, people who use their fists to exercise power instead of using their brains. I'm better than that.

I spent the remainder of the journey humming along to tunes on the radio and listening to presenters who spoke plenty but said nothing. Their talk was empty, devoid of any meaning, just a string of words designed to fill the silence between songs. It didn't bother me too much. My mind was on other things, matters of great importance. I was about to undertake something different, something that six months ago, I never thought would ever come about. I'd come so far in my life, making some gargantuan leaps and advances in the last few months alone. Gone was the sad, rejected little boy that misbehaved and lashed out because he knew no other way.

I took a corner too quickly and felt the weight in the rear shift and roll to one side. I heard the body as it slammed into the sides of the interior of the boot with a thump and winced, thinking of any fluids that may not have yet coagulated. I imagined skin splitting and fluids leaking out of Simon's slowly rotting corpse, dripping out of the thick fabric I had wrapped him in and spilling into my car. The thought didn't sicken me but it didn't fill me with a great deal of pleasure either. I wanted a nice clean ending to this; no stinking flesh and body fluids ruining the moment.

I slowed down slightly and steadied my breathing. I had to stay in control. Losing it at this point would do no good. I'd come this far. All I had to do was be my usual self. No need for panic. The police were gone. Everything was back to how it always was. I was in control of this situation. I could do it.

The road to my destination took longer than I expected. Getting to it on foot had been so much easier. The footpath leading there ran as the crow flies, whereas the road ran in a sweeping arc, and I ended up doubling back on myself. The weather also hindered me, slowing me down due to poor visibility. The rain continued to splatter against the windscreen and the wind had increased in strength. The car rocked as the sudden squall hit me side on, the gust taking me by surprise. I gripped the steering wheel tighter and smiled. Soon I would be there and then everything would be just perfect.

I almost lost control of the car again as another gust of wind hit me head on. I swerved into a deep puddle and heard the tyres screech as I fought to drive out of it and back onto the road. My heart thumped in my chest and I castigated myself for letting my guard down. I was better than that; superior, more intelligent than your average individual. I had always had clarity of thought and took command with ease. The cream always rises to the top. I just needed to have a little more faith in my own abilities.

Cassandra's beautiful face filled my mind. She would help me get through this. I could sense it. She had always been there for me in the past and I just knew she wouldn't let me down when I needed her the most. Cassandra was my reason for living and she was my reason for what I was about to do next.

42

I eventually reached the quarry and ground to a halt next to a thicket that shook in the breeze, its leaves rattling and rustling as the wind hit it, and rain pelted down with no let-up in sight. There was nothing up here to shield the foliage, nothing to shield me. The wind howled, reaching a crescendo as the storm took hold, commanding the sky and the earth and everything in it.

I yanked the handbrake on, relieved to have finally arrived. As expected, it was pitch black. This was both a blessing and a curse. It was doubtful that anybody else would be around but I couldn't take any chances. I rested my head back against the seat and tried to clear my thoughts. My eyes felt gritty and my neck was tight with tension. I rotated my shoulders and listened to the click of bone against bone as my spine gradually freed itself.

Nearby, an owl let out a powerful hoot that echoed around the open land, accentuating the isolated setting. I was truly alone. I wondered who would want to visit such a place? Especially on a night like tonight where the elements wreaked havoc, the wind sounding like a beast unleashing a long-concealed anger. Everybody was at home, watching the storm unfold, grateful for the security of their four walls.

I smiled. The owl let out another long, drawn-out hoot that sounded like a child's cry. I shivered and closed my eyes for a second before opening them and grabbing the door handle. No more prevaricating. It was time.

The wind hit me full in the face as I stepped out of the car and stood up. I was drenched in seconds. Sharp wet pellets bashed me, liquid razors hitting my exposed skin, causing my flesh to sting and making me shiver. I wasn't about to let the weather stop me. Not now. What sort of man would it have made me if I let a little storm get in the way of what I was about to do? I'd weathered far worse. My tenacity and resilience are the only things I have to thank my father for. Had it not been for the beatings and manic religious practices that he heaped upon me, I doubt I would be half the man I am today.

I opened the back door of the car and grabbed the torch I had placed in there before setting off. It was a necessity. As expected, the darkness was impenetrable – no light pollution, nothing to guide the way. I flicked on the torch and held it in front of me. A beam of yellow light spread out ahead, pooling at my feet and illuminating the nearby area. I would have to be careful here. Even with the small arc of light, I knew there were plenty of potholes and loose stones underfoot. And of course, the immense drop down to the quarry. A bolt of excitement travelled through me at the thought of it. It was almost sexual, the thought of being so close to it, and the threat it posed. I swallowed and took a sharp breath.

The rain gained momentum. That was good. Everything was as it should be. The more rain, the better.

I stepped around to the back of the vehicle, leaned down and opened the boot. Holding the torch over Simon's body, I trailed the light up and down the length of his frame. Everything was as I had left it when I set off. The bumping around hadn't appeared to have caused any damage. No ruptures, no more blood loss. I let out a short, barking laugh. Not that any damage to his corpse would make any difference. It was just that I liked things to be orderly and tidy, to be exactly as they were when I left them. Cleanliness is next to Godliness, isn't it?

I almost laughed. My father would have been proud.

Slamming the boot lid shut, I turned and pointed the beam of light towards the small copse of trees. I was almost certain the quarry was just beyond that point. I considered driving closer to save time but was concerned with how close to the edge I would be. Going on foot seemed like the best option. If I needed more light, I could always turn on the headlights, although that in itself seemed to be pointless. The torch would be enough light for what I was about to do. I would make sure it was enough.

Moving through the trees, the rustle of each leaf and the snapping and cracking of every twig and small branch underfoot was accentuated in the darkness and surrounding silence. My steps were slow and deliberate. I had to be careful. There were things I needed to be clear on before I put everything into action. I stopped and leaned against the trunk of a small tree, running my hand through my wet hair to shake off the excess water. Fat raindrops found their way in between the foliage above me and hit me square in the face. I blinked and shook them off. It would take more than a bit of water to stop me. Everything was too far gone to go back. It had all been set in motion.

I moved the torch from side to side to illuminate the way ahead, the yellow light allowing me to see a few feet in front of me. It was enough. I stepped carefully as I emerged out of the trees. The edge was close by. The feel of the ground underfoot had changed, the topography and consistency of the surface markedly different. Fewer twigs, more stones and rubble. I was definitely getting closer.

Dropping to my hands and knees, I held the torch aloft and crawled along, patting at the floor with my free hand. Gravel and pebbles dug at my knees and at one point, I cried out when a sharp stone stuck in my kneecap. I didn't stop. No time for self-pity. I had to keep going and despite the searing pain I felt in my knee, it was still the best way to do it, to put my body close to the earth and let my senses do the rest. The edge was close by and I needed to look over it to the bottom of the quarry before I made my next move.

It seemed to take an age before the light finally stopped revealing rocky ground beneath me and finally showed nothing but blackness.

I was there.

At long last, I'd reached the perimeter of the quarry. I pushed myself forward, my stomach now flat against the rough ground. Using my hands, I slowly inched towards the rim of the opening until at last, I felt the sudden slap of cold air as it surged upwards from the cavernous drop below and hit my face. The rain continued to batter my unprotected body, my flimsy summer jacket a weak barrier between my skin and the unforgiving elements.

I shone the torch down towards the huge opening beneath me and let out a small gasp, smiling as my eyes swept over the endless pit of nothingness beneath me. It was deeper than I'd remembered, and as far as I could see, the quarry had water in it. Not that it mattered, but there had been enough rain to fill that gaping hole in the earth. Right on cue, the downpour suddenly grew heavier, becoming a torrent as it fell from the dark sky above me. I didn't move. I didn't scramble away from the edge or try to find shelter. Instead, I lay down on the floor and welcomed it, closing my eyes and relishing the sensation as the heavy drops pounded my skin like small bullets hitting their target. This was all so fitting, so right. Everything was perfect. The darkness, the rain, the quarry. Everything I would ever need was right in front of me.

I was as still as death itself, savouring the moment,

feeling the thrill of being unprotected, so close to the edge in the dark and out in a storm. Nobody knew I was here. Simon was dead. Samantha was dead and I had caused it. It was me who brought their short lives to a close.

I did that.

I thought of their still, cold bodies, of Samantha's rotting carcass and of Simon wrapped and bound in the back of my car, and the sensation that pulsed through me was almost orgasmic. I wanted to roar out to the world that I was the most powerful person on earth. I could do anything. Anything at all.

I had no idea how long I was there for, lying flat on the cold, wet earth. It could have been minutes, it could have been hours. Time lost all meaning out there. It became unimportant, a distraction on the margins of a more pressing, more important task.

Dragging myself up to a sitting position, I swept the torch around the nearby tract of land and nodded. Just as I thought: heaps and heaps of rubble. Everything I needed was close by. I cast another glance down to the bottom of the quarry. The water looked even deeper than it had just a few minutes ago. Nature was doing its damnedest to help me tonight. Maybe there was a God after all.

Like a cat on the prowl, I crawled along the floor,

collecting as many stones and pebbles I as I could, dragging them towards me with the crook of my arm. I swept them all into one big mound and shone a light on them. The pile I had was big but not nearly enough to weigh a body down and drag it to the bottom. I needed a mountain of them just to be certain. There was no room for error. I had to get it right.

I continued scouring and gathering stones like a primeval hunter until I was sure I had enough, that the collective weight was sufficient to sink a body and make absolutely certain it wouldn't resurface.

My breath came out in short, disconnected bursts as I sat trying to gather my thoughts. I silently thanked Cassandra for her help and direction and for always being there for me. She understood. She knew this was all for the best, that I had no other option. Sometimes life pushes you down a certain path and no matter how hard you try to deviate from it, there is no turning back. The trajectory of my life began all those years ago when my father raised his fists to me and my mother did nothing to stop him. From thereon in I was doomed. The damage was irreversible.

Standing up, I turned and looked behind me towards the car. I had come a long way. My vehicle was a mere speck in the distance, a small, indistinguishable object far beyond the copse of trees.

The rain continued, bouncing off the ground, spreading in large puddles at my feet. I looked up to the inky starless sky and rubbed at my wet face with weary fists. I was unexpectedly overcome with tiredness, an aching lethargy that bled deep into my bones. I had to shake it off. There was no way I could allow it to stop me or slow me down. Fatigue was for lesser mortals. I was stronger than that, able to rise above such weaknesses. I needed to finish this task, not make a half-hearted attempt and appear like a weakling, somebody who lacked enough courage to see this thing through to the bitter end. I was better than that, too good for this world. Soon they would realise this. Soon, the waiting world would see exactly what I was capable of.

43

I concentrated on my breathing, keeping it regular as I lifted my arms up to the sky and stretched, the receptors in my joints flexing and bending in preparation. I would need all my strength for my next task. The stones were substantial. It was still pouring down and the darkness seemed to have increased in strength, wrapping itself around me like an impermeable shroud.

I was struggling to see. Even with the light of the torch to guide me, I strained to see anything at all. This was all so much harder than I could ever have anticipated.

I stopped, feeling myself falling into an unwanted slump. My limbs unexpectedly seemed heavy, lead appendages, cumbersome and lacking in any co-ordination. It was as if they were working against me, stopping me from doing what I wanted to do. I was wading in treacle, every movement a gargantuan effort, every ragged breath clunky and painful as air exited my body in repeated, arrhythmic gasps. No matter how hard I tried to concentrate, to keep my breathing steady and consistent, I felt as if I were about to collapse. Loath though I was to admit it, fear had crawled into my psyche and was doing its damnedest to put a stop to what I was about to do next.

I closed my eyes, suddenly furious with myself. Rain cascaded over my lashes, running down my face in cold, wet streaks. What had I turned into? I was better than this, wasn't I? An educated individual, erudite and logical, and although I could hardly be categorised as well-balanced or even well meaning, I knew without doubt that I possessed a greater intelligence than anybody else who had ever crossed my path. My actions showed as much. I was a stronger person than Simon, who had succumbed so easily to death. A better person than Samantha, who had courted an early demise with her constant whining and neediness. I was superior to them. Surely I had the ability to rise above fear and lassitude, to break free of the torpor that had me in its grip?

I let out an involuntary roar and with a burst of energy, I began gathering the stones up and shoving them deep into my pockets. This was more like it. This was what I had to do. It was right and fitting. The heaviness of them was cathartic, adding to my bodyweight, making me feel a hundred feet tall. My chest swelled with excitement and anticipation, expectancy blooming within me like a young bird about to take flight for the first time.

My hands stung. Sharp edges of stone cut into the soft flesh of my palms. Blood mingled with rain as I grabbed at more pebbles and handfuls of shingle and stuffed them into every pocket I had. I even scooped up the smaller pebbles as well as fistfuls of gravel, and rammed them down my socks. I stood up straight and stared out into the blackness. It felt remarkable. I had no fear. That momentary flutter of panic had dissipated. All that stood between me and eternity was the next few minutes, perhaps even seconds.

I had entertained the idea of using the car to do this but the thought of being in such close proximity to Simon sickened me. I didn't want to be anywhere near him. He could stay where has was, shut in and closed off from the rest of the world until the police eventually located his body, by which time he would have hopefully rotted to nothing. I was thrilled at the prospect of being alone, so close to nature, at becoming part of the earth. It was where I belonged. People with their strange unpredictable and cruel ways had never been my thing.

I crawled to the edge of the quarry and leaned over, staring down to the bottom. I wondered how long it would take the police to find my car. I pictured their faces when they opened the boot of my vehicle and saw a body lying in there. How long would it take them to work out my story? Would they ever be able to piece together the jagged parts of my life that made no sense to anybody but me? I somehow doubted it. Even in death, I would be on a higher plane, my story too complex, too difficult for anybody to fathom. Life may have dealt me a poor hand but death would be the making of me.

I angled my body closer to the watery grave that lay in wait for me many feet below. I longed for it, dreamed of that final fall into oblivion where eternity beckoned. Already, I felt death wrapping its cold arms around me, its fingers reaching deep into my flesh and stealing my soul.

The rain continued to lash at my face. The wind howled over me, coursing over my limbs, fluid and relentless. I was part of it. It was part of me. Ashes to ashes, dust to dust.

Staring up at the sky, I said a few last words of thanks to Cassandra for being the only stable force in my life. She was there above me, watching over me, her face warm and tender. I didn't deserve her. She was the compassion and empathy I lacked. She everything I wasn't. I turned away, shame fuelling my need to escape this life.

With one last surge of energy, I thrust my entire body forward and felt the solidity beneath me vanish. In a cold rush, I became swallowed up by the darkness. Hard, icy air pushed up under my belly, pressing at my guts, while the strong hand of gravity forced me down. On and on I travelled, cocooned in a pocket of nothingness that would eventually be the undoing of me.

There was no fear, no wishing to go back. Just a feeling of sheer exhilaration, of being stripped of all my sins. The water below would be my final forgiveness, absolving me of everything I had ever done. It would cleanse and purify me. God is, after all, merciful and lenient, isn't He? Even with the most heinous of sinners. And I am a bad sinner. One of the worst. Or one of the finest, depending on your perspective and whose side you are on.

I took a deep breath as the water closed in on me. I could feel its coldness, visualise its icy depths as gravity took its inevitable course and plunged me earthwards. I closed my eyes for one final time as I hit the shallow lake of rainwater at speed, its clean lines and firmness taking every last breath out of my body. And the last thought that crossed my mind as I sank under it was, *Forgive me, oh Lord, for everything I have done.*

44

SIX WEEKS LATER

Emily leafed through the album, her eyes scanning an array of old photographs. Photographs of many of the classes she had taught over the years. The box of pictures had been stacked in the loft and thankfully the fire hadn't reached that far. Her house repairs had only been completed last week. The insurance company had been uncharacteristically swift, meaning her stay in Newcastle at her sister's house hadn't lasted as long as she had initially anticipated. She let out a trembling sigh and managed a weak smile. Despite everything that had happened, it felt good to be home.

She had got the photographs down and begun scrutinising them when the identity of the bodies found at the quarry made the news. It didn't come to her immediately who it was, this man who had moved into their village and duped them, making everybody think he was a decent sort of chap when all the while, he was wreaking as much havoc as possible, injuring people, attempting to murder them while they slept in their beds.

While *she* slept in *her* bed.

She had taught thousands of children in her time and not all of them lodged in her brain. Those that left her thoughts, never to return, usually went on to live happy, successful lives, to become parents themselves and be productive members of society with much to offer. And those that stayed in her head, often causing her to lose sleep, didn't. They made more of an impact. Negative memories of children always made a greater dent than positive ones.

Charlie Smith was one of those children. For years after he and his parents left Whitchurch, she had thought about him. A troubled, unhappy boy, he had been a disaster waiting to happen. What she hadn't expected was for him to come back, for him to unleash disaster right here in her home.

She remembered Charlie Smith well enough. What she hadn't done was link him to Ray Smith, the grown man. Ray had wormed his way into their lives and had done his best to burrow deep into their hearts. Alice had talked about him plenty before his dirty secret was exposed, and Dominic had told others what a wonderful man he was: warm, kind, thoughtful. Just goes to show. You couldn't trust anybody.

Emily's eyes unexpectedly filled up. She blinked and closed them for a few seconds before opening them again and staring over to the other side of the room at nothing in particular. No more. She refused to weep. She was beyond crying now. So many tears shed in the last few weeks, so much heartache. She promised herself there would be no more and leaned back in the chair, her fingers tracing the outline of one particular old picture.

This was the photograph she had been looking for. This was the one.

Placing it on her knee, she stared hard at it. That was him. Her finger rested on his face, following the grainy shape of his features in the faded image.

Peering closer, she squinted to get a good look at the dark-haired boy in the back row, the one with sorrow in his eyes that, over time, had turned into hatred and malevolence. Could she have stopped it? She cast her mind back, thinking about those times in the classroom, the fights and incidents that had followed him wherever he went. She remembered one time, trying to intervene, speaking to his parents about his behaviour, suggesting some sort of assistance or therapy to help him work through his anger. They had been more than a little reticent. Emily's lip trembled. She had no idea if they had taken her up on her suggestion. She should have tried harder, got the educational psychologist involved herself, but recalled the parents baulking at the idea. They had been private people, austere and all too aware of their standing within the local community. They would have taken any further interventions as an insult and eventually, after many lengthy meetings, they'd insisted they would provide their own therapy for their son. She had no idea what form that had taken, if indeed it had actually materialised.

It had worried her. The things he did – it wasn't simply a case of boys being boys. There was more to it than that. He had seemed to enjoy hurting people, watching them suffer. More than that – he had relished it. It was the only time he was truly happy. Like the day he pulled another child under the water at the swimming baths. It took two members of staff to get him to let go and resurface. And he hadn't even tried to defend his behaviour, to put it down to horseplay or just a bit of fun, as other boys would have done. When questioned as to why he did it, he had simply replied that he wanted to see the other child cry.

Emily felt sure that that incident could have resulted in something far worse if the screams of the other children hadn't alerted the staff.

Afterwards, Charlie had showed no regret and had refused to apologise. She'd known then that something was terribly wrong. All kids showed remorse when taken to task over their wrongdoings. But not him. Not Charlie Smith. He'd had an inner core of iron, unlike anything she had ever seen before or since.

And then there was his father. He had been the pastor at St Oswald's for many years. As a non-believer, she hadn't known the man that well apart from seeing him around the village to say hello and his occasional visits into school, but he had seemed like a good person, a respectable sort of chap with strong family values. He had been a tad overpowering, however. She had sometimes wondered if the child was scared of him. There had never been any bruises or visible signs of abuse on Charlie's body. That much she did remember. What more could she have done?

She thought of the little girl that they had lost and wondered if that had had a profound effect on the whole family. Had it affected Charlie more deeply than anybody knew? She seemed to remember that the boy's problems had started well before that tragic incident but time often played tricks on her. So many children over the years. Her memory wasn't always as accurate as she would have liked it to be.

Standing up, Emily walked to the window and stared out over the village green. Everything looked quiet out there: not exactly relaxed, but neither was it the tense atmosphere they had encountered of late, where people were on edge, wondering what or who was going to be next. There had been a palpable sense of mild relief when they'd realised it was all over, mixed with deep sorrow at losing Simon in such dreadful circumstances.

After the police had found both bodies, it took some time for the truth to emerge. The newspapers had a field day, picking through it, dissecting every little detail until they got to the bones of it, the real story. They'd wanted the dirt and hadn't stopped until they'd found it.

Emily finally let the tears fall. She stood staring out of the window at everything and nothing as they rolled down her cheeks and dripped onto the back of her hand. She wiped them away and sat back down. She didn't suppose anybody knew the real facts. How could they? Nobody had walked in Ray's shoes, seen things as he saw them. How could they ever climb inside the mind of a psychopath and understand his motives? He had taken his secrets with him to his cold, watery grave.

She rubbed a damp hand over her face. Apparently, the police had found a journal in his house that led them to believe there were other murders. There was also a woman in Birmingham that they were still trying to trace, a woman who, up until recently, he had been in a relationship with. It seemed that the new, reserved, friendly man in their village had left a trail of destruction behind him and a deeply complex case for the police to unpick. They weren't stopping there either. A previous girlfriend had yet to be traced, as had one of his childhood friends. Both were registered as missing persons. The police now had a link, something to go on. Prior to recent events, neither of them had seemed to have any connection to each other. Now they had Ray, the lynchpin, the man who held all the answers. Emily just hoped he had left enough behind to allow everyone to find answers.

And of course, the village gossips were having a fine old time. Despite the sombre faces and acts of quiet dignity at Simon's funeral, they clacked their tongues relentlessly, some even taking offers of payment from national newspapers to tell their story. Blood money, that's all it was. It disgusted Emily that Simon's friends and neighbours would stoop so low as to do such a thing. It seemed to her that moral fibre was sadly lacking in her hometown. She had taught a lot of them, tried to instil morals and values in them, and then they had let her down, selling their souls for cold, hard cash. She had expected better.

Her eyes grew heavy as she leaned her head back and pondered over it all. The whole thing was a mess, a terrible tragic tangle of events that had taken over their lives, turned them inside out until they hadn't known which way was up. They had to move on from this, each and every resident, and not let it define them. But it was hard, so bloody hard. Already the papers were referring to Whitchurch as the *Village of the Damned*. If they'd thought they'd had it bad with reporters roving around the place last year after the discovery of the mystery woman's body, it was nothing compared to the amount that they had had turning up on their doorsteps in the past few weeks, microphones in hands, bulky cameras hanging around their necks, ready to photograph anybody or anything once the story began to unfold and gain traction. People loved murders. They enjoyed reading about them, following the lives of those involved. It sickened

Emily, made her lose sleep and despair for what the world was coming to.

A rambler had alerted the authorities to Ray's car. It had taken them a little longer to locate his body. The poor weather had hindered any searches and rather than dredge the quarry, the police had decided to search the nearby woods. It had seemed the obvious place to look. Only when the rains stopped and the water began to evaporate had it become apparent what he had done.

Jim had recovered and kept a low profile since returning home. He refused to speak about the whole incident, even claiming he couldn't remember Charlie Smith. Emily knew this was a lie. Jim had been close to the family when they lived here, that much she did know. She had no idea why he was lying but put it down to shock and distress and decided it was probably for the best anyhow. Who would want to rake over such times after what he had been through? The whole thing was best put to bed.

The police had rearrested the husband of the lady whose body had been found last year. His alibi had recently been blown wide open and they were hoping to unearth new evidence after a recent search in the woods nearby.

Emily sighed. She was getting too old for this: all

this misery and worry. The world moved too fast for her. She struggled to keep up. And somehow, deep down, she felt responsible for everything that had happened. If she had taken the time, spent more time with the boy, then maybe all of this could have been avoided. Or maybe not. Perhaps people were what they were. Ray was clearly a psychopath and Emily had no idea if such people were born that way or forced into it by various means.

Closing her eyes, she wished it all away. She wanted to wake up in world less violent, one sprinkled with kindness and varnished with love. That was definitely what she wanted. It was all she had ever wanted.

45

Lily pulled her hair back, clipped it into place and rummaged in her bag for a lipstick. Running it over her lips, she smacked them together, glancing in the mirror as she gave a small pout. Her mouth was a slash of scarlet, shimmering as she puckered her lips and scrutinised her flawless skin and immaculate application of make-up. She smiled and winked at her reflection then laughed and turned away.

A line appeared between her perfectly shaped eyebrows as a lock of white hair sprung free and hung listlessly over her right eye. She flicked it away only for it to bounce back almost immediately. She tugged at it, strategically angling it and twirling it with her thumb and forefinger to curl it into place, then grinned. People often told her she had the look of a post-war film star. Names like Lana Turner and Jayne Mansfield were often bandied about when her dress sense and unique style was mentioned. She liked it when they said such things. It gave her a lift, made her feel like she could do anything, go anywhere, be anybody she wanted to be. It was part of her job to look good and be easy on the eye. She didn't want the customers thinking she hadn't made an effort. She always liked to look good for the punters. She was the one they saw first as they entered the pub. The better she looked, the more they drank. And the more they drank, the more she earned with extra hours worked and tips given. It was simple mathematics.

The house was quiet as she slipped out of the front door and locked it behind her. Her parents had been arguing again last night. Today, her dad wouldn't wake up until well after lunchtime. He was sleeping off the bottle of gin he had drunk before going to bed last night. Her mum was probably in the spare room still seething and wishing she'd divorced him years ago. Lily no longer cared about either of them. Soon she would be back at university, away from this house and far away from their constant arguing. It wasn't the best option, leaving Ciara here with the warring couple, but what choice did she have? If Lily had the means, she would take Ciara with her, away from Whitchurch, away from their useless mother and bullying brute of a father, and let her sister shack up with her in the tiny rundown flat in Leeds that passed as her university accommodation. But she didn't have the means. She could barely afford to keep herself, let alone a younger sibling. She had some money set aside right now but it wouldn't last forever. That was the only upside of her father's drunken state. He didn't notice cash going missing from his wallet when she was home during the holidays. It wasn't a lot, just £20 here and £10 there, sometimes more. It all depended how big the wad was he had stashed away and how drunk he was when she did it. And of course, she had her wages from her shifts working in The Pot and Glass – again, not a huge amount but since her parents gave her next to nothing to help out and her student loan barely covered the rent, it provided her with a tiny bit of spare cash with which to live on. Without it, she would be practically destitute.

She set off walking, enjoying the slight dip in temperature that had happened over the past few weeks. She had already made some plans for her younger sister. She would leave some money under Ciara's pillow when she left to go back to university. And anyway, she didn't have to worry too much about her. If she was being perfectly honest, her parents had always favoured her over Lily anyway. Ciara would be just fine. She would have to be.

A light breeze tickled her skin as she threaded her way through the line of parked cars and over the road towards the village green. A chorus of mellifluous birdsong chattered above her, a variety of soothing, honeyed calls that mellowed her mood and lifted her spirits, giving her goose bumps as she lifted her face up to the warm sun and listened to their stream of chatter.

It felt good to be back in a routine again. After recent events, Whitchurch had begun to feel like a chaotic place to live – everyone anxious and rigid, people walking around in a fog of confusion, incredulous at what had gone on in their tiny little village, their minds working overtime, trying to fathom what had happened and how they could have stopped it. They couldn't. It was what it was and none of them could have predicted it or pre-empted it. Constantly raking over it again and again solved nothing.

A reporter had promised her money if she would

tell her story. He had seemed like a nice sort of guy. She'd said she would get back to him. Which she would. Once she was back at university, she would give him a call, tell him everything she knew. She needed the money. Not that she knew that much anyway, but she had little snippets stored in her head, things she and Ray had spoken about, the sort of things that people liked to hear, like how flirtatious he was and what a charmer he could be. And the stuff she didn't know, she was quite prepared to make up. The odd lie wouldn't matter too much, would it? It was, after all, what people wanted to hear. They all loved it, sucking up every bit of dirt. The seedy stuff, the gory bits, the completely outlandish bits. The sort of ridiculous rubbish that sold papers. She would say exactly what they wanted to hear. Scruples meant nothing when pitted against a promised payment that would feed and clothe her for an entire year.

She would write it all down once she was settled back in her flat. Then the money would come rolling in. She didn't want to speak to anybody while she was here. Small villages had big ears and even larger mouths. She knew that some people had already sold their stories but she had more integrity than that. Or enough common sense to hide what she was really doing. Nobody would ever guess that she would be the type of person to do such a thing: to spread malicious gossip and lies and speak ill of the dead. That was because they didn't really know her. They thought they did. They couldn't have been more wrong.

Lily let out a wild laugh as she turned onto Church Lane and ambled along in the shadow in the dancing trees, their branches creaking and groaning above her as a gust of wind caught them and rattled at their leaves. It was like nature had suddenly become angry, furious at everybody and everything. Hardly surprising. Most of the time, people were shit. They were all so naïve. They thought they had her sussed; they were convinced they knew her and thought of her as one of their own. Yes, her father was a useless bastard, but she had learned how to survive it all, grown a second skin and developed into a tenacious character with traits that would serve her well in life. She wasn't the helpless victim they all wanted her to be. Victims got nowhere in life. They got trodden underfoot, left to rot with the weak the lame and lazy. That wasn't her. She was better than that.

Everybody had cried when they found out what Ray had done. Lily hadn't cried. If anything, it had given her a bit of a kick hearing about his crimes and, if she was going to be brutally truthful, she admired him. He'd done what he'd had to do, hadn't let anybody stand in his way and had just got on with it. And the letters and dog shit were a stroke of genius. A complete hoot. Lily only wished she had thought of it first.

She lengthened her stride and turned out of Church Lane onto the main road through the village. At least Ray had had the balls to do what he'd done. Lily only wished she had enough courage to do the same. She did manage to work her anger and frustrations out a few times, but nothing on the scale that Ray had managed. He had been the master at it. Pity he'd died. She could have learned from him. He would have made a good mentor. They would have made a good couple. They'd had chemistry, their lives running almost in parallel with similarities too striking to ignore. He might have been a bit older than her but kindred souls locked together by misery and madness surpassed any age restrictions placed upon them by everyday conventions.

Still, at least she'd got to kill Mrs Batton's cat. And she had enjoyed it too. Old woman Batton was a horrible old bitch and had always shouted at Lily and her friends when they were kids, chasing them away from playing outside her house. She deserved everything she got. Her cat had been ancient anyway, on its last legs and practically at death's door long before Lily had stepped in and done her bit. If anything, she had done them both a favour. After an argument with her dad, Lily had needed to take her temper out on something or somebody and the cat had been there at her feet, meowing and angling for food. A weed killer pellet wrapped in a bit of ham was all it had taken. It had all been easy. So fucking easy. Like taking candy from a baby.

Buoyed up by the memory of it, Lily couldn't help but smile. It gave her a real buzz, tricking people, making them think they knew her when they actually didn't really know her at all. It was the only bit of power she had, the only thing that stopped her from screaming out into the empty sky above at the injustice of it all, the unfairness of being born into a dysfunctional family where love was absent and beatings were the norm.

Killing that cat had helped restore some equilibrium of power, reset the scales that for so long had been tipped out of balance, leaving her feeling empty and useless. Perhaps one day she would strike again when the time was right. Not just now though. Too much attention focused on them all. Their every move was being closely monitored by teams of journalists and reporters hoping to dig up more dirt. They waited around every corner, cameras at the ready, itching to get it all into print and make a fast buck.

Maybe she would never feel the need to do it ever again. Or maybe she would. It all depended on what life decided to throw at her. Sometimes she did and said things just for kicks. Just because she could.

Soon she would be away from here, far away from the village full of secrets where abuse and murder were commonplace and recognition for sins wasn't mandatory. She would continue with her studies and work hard, try to forget about her shitty father and the beatings he had inflicted upon her as a child.

She wondered if Ray had also had a diabolical childhood and if that was why he had done what he'd done. Or had he just been born that way? They would never really know. A few of the older people remembered him from when he lived in Whitchurch, but everyone was still at a loss as to why he had carried out such acts of monstrosity. Had he just been mad or had there been some sort of reason for his actions?

Lily heaved a sigh as she pushed at the door of the pub and quietly slid inside. Thinking about it all made her head ache. Sometimes people did things just because they could. Like killing the cat. It was right at the time. Gave her such a kick, put her on a high and helped her to calm her anger. She only wished she'd done it to her dad many years ago.

She smiled as she sauntered into room behind the bar and pulled on her apron. Killing her own dad, getting rid of that monster and setting the rest of her family free from his tyranny. Now there was a thought that made her soul sing...

ACKNOWLEDGMENTS

First and foremost, I would like to thank Boldwood Books for taking on this book when I had lost all hope of it ever reappearing again. The team have been nothing short of brilliant in their efforts to rebrand and republish my back catalogue.

The Stranger first appeared on the shelves as *The Cleansing* and after a brief flash into the Top 100 on Amazon, it disappeared out of view. I'm delighted to see it once again, being bought and read by people who were attracted to its new cover and blurb. I sincerely hope you enjoyed reading it.

A huge thank you to my friends and family who have supported my writing career every single step of the way. There have been many high points and many low ones too. I hope the low days are behind me and I can continue writing and producing many more books.

Thanks again to a small clutch of authors who

keep me going. Anita Waller, Valerie Keogh and Diana Wilkinson, you ladies are brilliant!

Thanks also to the many book clubs who have helped my career over the years. The clubs are run by volunteers and having been a member of the admin team for an online club for a few years, I know how time consuming and difficult job it is, so thanks to each and every one of you for giving up your time and supporting authors, especially Susan Hunter, Anita Waller, Tara Lyons and Mark Fearn. You guys are amazing.

I'd like to thank my ARC readers for their loyalty and timely reviews and to Dee Groocock for her eagle eye! I'd be lost without you all.

I'm certain to have missed somebody out and if I have, I apologise, but know that if you have helped and supported me in any way, I'm eternally grateful to you.

Please feel free to contact/follow me on social media. I love to chat and always in need of a distraction from my writing! An author can only use so many methods of procrastination before running out of ideas...

ABOUT THE AUTHOR

J. A. Baker is a successful writer of numerous psychological thrillers. Born and brought up in Middlesbrough, she still lives in the North East, which inspires the settings for her books.

Sign up to J. A. Baker's mailing list here for news, competitions and updates on future books.

Follow J. A. Baker on social media:

facebook.com/thewriterjude

twitter.com/thewriterjude

instagram.com/jabakerauthor

tiktok.com/@jabaker41

ALSO BY J A BAKER

Local Girl Missing

The Last Wife

The Woman at Number 19

The Other Mother

The Toxic Friend

The Retreat

The Woman in the Woods

The Stranger

The Intruder

THE *Murder* LIST

THE MURDER LIST IS A NEWSLETTER DEDICATED TO ALL THINGS CRIME AND THRILLER FICTION!

SIGN UP TO MAKE SURE YOU'RE ON OUR HIT LIST FOR GRIPPING PAGE-TURNERS AND HEARTSTOPPING READS.

SIGN UP TO OUR NEWSLETTER

BIT.LY/THEMURDERLISTNEWS

Boldwood

Boldwood Books is an award-winning fiction publishing company seeking out the best stories from around the world.

Find out more at www.boldwoodbooks.com

Join our reader community for brilliant books, competitions and offers!

Follow us
@BoldwoodBooks
@TheBoldBookClub

Sign up to our weekly deals newsletter

https://bit.ly/BoldwoodBNewsletter

Milton Keynes UK
Ingram Content Group UK Ltd.
UKHW041328060923
428160UK00003B/42

9 781805 492115